P9-BBP-202

Praise for *The Gardens of Kyoto*

"Like the gardens of its title, this debut novel is an exquisite conundrum, replete with ghosts and hiding places. . . . In precise, delicate prose, the author renders with equal power the quiet desperation of a girl growing up in 1950s America, and the ethereal."

—*The New Yorker*

"[A] . . . haunting, accomplished first novel . . . the writing . . . is lightened by flashes of humor and redeemed by moments of great tenderness and beauty."

—Elizabeth Ward, *The Washington Post*

"Walbert's true gift is her ability to create passages and phrases of beauty, colorful prose. . . . Readers in love with language will adore this book."

—Carol Memmott, *USA Today*

"Walbert writes delicately on weighty themes, making a lyrical examination of unrequited love. This is a haunting, thoughtful work that, without lapsing into cliché, depicts the sad realities of love and war."

—*Publishers Weekly*

"[With] understated intensity . . . Kate Walbert's luminous debut novel . . . is a pattern, as delicate and elliptical as an Asian ink-brush painting, of lost loves, sacrifice, mistaken identities, tragic misunderstandings, and buried secrets."

—Francine Prose, *Elle*

"This resonant, moving story is ambitious and complex . . . [a] painstakingly wrought novel of sorrow and secrets."

—Heller McAlpin, *Newsday*

"Walbert seamlessly weaves fragments to make this story, each piece of memory connecting to another in a nearly organic way. The result is a breathtakingly complete picture of grief and devotion, a life turned over in the mind."

—Ashley Warlick, *The Hartford Courant*

"Kate Walbert's fine, delicate prose captures voices that we don't hear much anymore, and she guides us from past to present, and from death to life, with affectionate detail and deep understanding. *The Gardens* of *Kyoto* is a ghost story, a mystery, a love story, and an intentionally modest chronicle of the middle part of this past century."

—Amy Bloom, author of *Love Invents Us*

"Kate Walbert has crafted the kind of old-fashioned novel that is increasingly hard to come by: beautifully written, painstakingly structured, and seemingly effortless in its evocation of place and character."

—Lisa Darrell, *The Guardian*

"There are so many nice things to be said about this novel. The story lingers in your mind long after you've closed the book. It is stylishly written and wistful and will touch your heart. . . . There is a wonderful lushness in this novel. The characters are so gracefully and elegantly created that they spring from the page."

—William Gray, *The Tampa Tribune*

"An artful, fluid first novel . . . Walbert . . . constructs her novel as carefully as Kyoto's fabled gardens."

—Nancy Pate, *The Orlando Sentinel*

"Like the gardens for which it is named, this hypnotic, elegant book will leave a lasting impression."

—Ann Hood, *Providence Journal-Bulletin*

"A beautifully written debut novel."

—*Booklist*

"She is a powerful storyteller who delivers the unexpected with great gentleness. Highly recommended."

—*Library Journal*

"This moving story, set in the land of memory and broken destinies, is simply magnificent."

—Jacques Baudou, *Le Monde*

"Walbert writes beautiful, lyrical, endlessly detailed sentences; they are as multilayered as her plot. They can be mesmerizing, alternately captivating, and lulling, and always maintain a mysterious, steadily probing air."

—Suzy Harsen, *Salon.com*

ALSO BY KATE WALBERT

Where She Went
Our Kind
A Short History of Women
The Sunken Cathedral

The Gardens of Kyoto

A NOVEL

Kate Walbert

SCRIBNER

New York   London   Toronto   Sydney   New Delhi

For my father, J. T. Walbert
And in memory of Charles Webster, 1926–1945

SCRIBNER
An Imprint of Simon & Schuster, Inc.
1230 Avenue of the Americas
New York, NY 10020

This book is a work of fiction. Names, characters, places, and incidents
either are products of the author's imagination or are used fictitiously.
Any resemblance to actual events or locales or persons,
living or dead, is entirely coincidental.

Copyright © 2001 by Kate Walbert

All rights reserved, including the right to reproduce this book or portions thereof
in any form whatsoever. For information address Scribner Subsidiary Rights
Department, 1230 Avenue of the Americas, New York, NY 10020.

First Scribner trade paperback edition 2003

SCRIBNER and design are registered trademarks of
The Gale Group, Inc., used under license by
Simon & Schuster, Inc., the publisher of this work.

For information about special discounts for bulk purchases,
please contact Simon & Schuster Special Sales at 1-866-506-1949
or business@simonandschuster.com

The Simon & Schuster Speakers Bureau can bring authors to your live event. For
more information or to book an event contact the Simon & Schuster Speakers
Bureau at 1-866-248-3049 or visit our website at www.simonspeakers.com.

Designed by Kyoko Watanabe
Set in Trump

Manufactured in the United States of America

11 13 15 17 19 20 18 16 14 12

The Library of Congress has cataloged the Scribner edition as follows:
Walbert, Kate.
The gardens of Kyoto : a novel / Kate Walbert.
p.   cm.
1. World War, 1939–1945—Fiction. 2. Mothers and daughters—Fiction.
3. Kyoto (Japan)—Fiction. I. Title.

PS3573.A42113 G37 2001
813'.54—dc21   2001018876

ISBN 978-0-684-86948-3
ISBN 978-0-684-86949-0 (Pbk)

Chapter one, book one, originally appeared in *DoubleTake* magazine, and was
reissued in *The Pushcart Prize 2000* and *O. Henry Prize Stories 2000*.

It is not the materials in isolation that
form a garden, but the fragments in
relation . . .

—*A Guide to the Gardens of Kyoto*

· Book One ·

1

I had a cousin, Randall, killed on Iwo Jima. Have I told you? The last man killed on the island, they said; killed after the fighting had ceased and the rest of the soldiers had already been transported away to hospitals or to bodybags. Killed mopping up. That's what they called it. A mopping-up operation.

I remember Mother sat down at the kitchen table when she read the news. It came in the form of a letter from Randall's father, Great-Uncle Sterling, written in hard dark ink, the letters slanted and angry as if they were aware of the meaning of the words they formed. I was in the kitchen when Mother opened it and I took the letter and read it myself. It said that Randall was presumed dead, though they had no information of the whereabouts of his body; that he had reported to whomever he was intended to report to after the surrender of the Japanese, that he had, from all accounts, disappeared.

*　　*　　*

I didn't know him too well but had visited him as a young girl. They lived across the bay from Baltimore, outside Sudlersville. No town, really, just a crossroad and a post office and farms hemmed in by cornfields. Theirs was a large brick house set far back from the road, entirely wrong for that landscape, like it had been hauled up from Savannah or Louisville to prove a point. It stood in constant shadow at the end of an oak-lined drive and I remember our first visit, how we drove through that tunnel of oak slowly, the day blustery, cool. Sterling was not what we in those days called jovial. His wife had died years before, leaving him, old enough to be a grandfather, alone to care for his only child. He had long rebuked Mother's invitations but for some reason had scrawled a note in his Christmas card that year—this was before the war, '39 or '40—asking us to join them for Easter dinner.

Mother wore the same Easter hat and spring coat she kept in tissue in the back of the hallway linen closest, but she had sewed each of us a new Easter dress and insisted Daddy wear a clean shirt and tie. For him this was nothing short of sacrifice. Rita said he acted like those clothes might shatter if he breathed.

Daddy turned off the engine and we all sat, listening to the motor ticking. If Mother had lost her determination and suggested we back out then and there, we would have agreed. "Well," she said, smoothing out the lap of her dress. It was what she did to buy time. We girls weren't moving anyway. We were tired enough; it was a long drive from Pennsylvania.

"Wake me up when it's over," Rita said. She always had a line like that. She curled up and thrust her long legs across Betty and me, picking a fight. Betty grabbed her foot and twisted it until Rita shrieked *For the love of Pete!* Mother ignored them, reapplying the lipstick she kept tucked up the sleeve of her spring coat. I looked out the window. I'm not sure about Daddy. No one wanted to make the first move, Betty twisting Rita's foot harder and Rita shrieking *For the love of Pete, get your gosh darn hands off me!* and Mother jerking around and telling Rita to stop using that language and to act her age.

The last reprimand struck Rita to the core. She sat up quickly and yanked the door open.

Did I say oak? It might have been walnut. I believe at that point, standing outside the car, we heard the comforting thwack of a walnut on a tin roof, the sound popping the balloon Rita had inflated, releasing us to walk, like a family, to the front door, where Randall already stood, waiting.

He had some sort of sweet-smelling water brushed into his hair. This I remember. It was the first thing you would have noticed. He also had red hair, red as mine, and freckles over most of his face. He stood there, swallowed by the doorway, his hand out in greeting. His were the most delicate fingers I had ever seen on a boy, though he was nearly a teenager by then. I have wondered since whether he polished his nails, since they were shiny, almost wet. Remember he was a son without a mother, which is a terrible thing to be, and that Great-Uncle Sterling was as hard as his name.

Anyway, Rita and Betty paid him little mind. They followed Mother and Daddy in to find Sterling and we were left, quite suddenly, alone. Randall shrugged as if I had proposed a game of cards and asked if I wanted to see his room. No one seemed much concerned about us, so I said sure. We went down a water-stained hallway he called the Gallery of Maps, after some hallway he had read about in the Vatican lined with frescoes of maps from before the world was round. Anyway, he stood there showing me the various countries, pointing out what he called troublespots.

I can still picture those fingers, tapering some, and the palest white at the tips, as if he had spent too long in the bath.

We continued, passing one of those old-fashioned intercom contraptions they used to have to ring servants. Randall worked a few of the mysterious oiled levers and then spoke, gravely, into the mouthpiece. "I have nothing to offer but blood, toil, tears, and sweat," he said. Churchill, of course, though at the time I had no idea. I simply stood there waiting, watching as Randall hung up the mouthpiece, shrugged again, and opened a door to a back staircase so narrow we had to turn sideways to make the corner.

"They were smaller in the old days," Randall said, and then, perhaps because I didn't respond, he stopped and turned toward me.

"Who?" I said.

"People," he said.

"Oh," I said, waiting. I had never been in the dark with a boy his age.

"Carry on," he said.

We reached a narrow door and pushed out, onto another landing, continuing down a second, longer hallway. The house seemed comprised of a hundred little boxes, each with tiny doors and passages, eaves to duck under, one-flight stairways to climb. Gloomy, all of it, though Randall didn't appear to notice. He talked all the while of how slaves had traveled through here on the underground railway from Louisiana, and how one family had lived in this house behind a false wall he was still trying to find. He said he knew this not from words but from knowing. He said he saw their ghosts sometimes—there were five of them—a mother and a father and three children, he couldn't tell what. But he'd find their hiding place, he said. He had the instinct.

I'm not sure whether I was more interested in hearing about slaves in secret rooms or hearing about their ghosts. This was Maryland, remember, the east side. At that time, if you took the ferry to Annapolis, the colored sat starboard, the whites port, and docking felt like the flow of two rivers, neither feeding the other. In Pennsylvania colored people were colored people, and one of your grandfather's best friends was a colored doctor named Tate Williams, who everybody called Tate Billy, which always made me laugh, since I'd never heard of a nickname for a surname.

Anyway, Randall finally pushed on what looked like just another of the doors leading to the next stairway and there we were: his room, a big square box filled with books on shelves and stacked high on the floor. Beyond this a line of dormer windows looked out to the oaks, or walnuts. I could hear my sisters' muffled shouts below and went to see, but we were too high up and the windows were filthy, besides. Words were written in the grime. *Copacetic,* I still recall. *Epistemological, belie.*

"What are these?" I said.

"Words to learn," Randall said. He stood behind me.

"Oh," I said. This wasn't at all what I expected. It felt as if I had climbed a mountain only to reach a summit enshrouded in fog. Randall seemed oblivious; he began digging through his stacks of books. I watched him for a while, then spelled out *HELP* on the glass. I asked Randall what he was doing, and he told me to be patient. He was looking for the exact right passage, he said. He planned to teach me the art of "dramatic presentation."

Isn't it funny? I have no recollection of what he finally found. And though I can still hear him telling me they were smaller then, ask me what we recited in the hours before we were called to the table, legs up, in his window seat, our dusty view that of the old trees, their leaves a fuzzy new green of spring, of Easter, and I will say I have no idea. I know I must have read my lines with the teacher's sternness I have never been able to keep from my voice; he with his natural tenderness, as if he were presenting a gift to the very words he read by speaking them aloud. I know that sometimes our knees touched and that we pulled away from one another, or we did not. I wish I had a picture. We must have been beautiful with the weak light coming through those old dormers, our knees up and backs against either side of the window seat, an awkward *W*, books in our hands.

*   *   *

It became our habit to write letters. Randall wrote every first Sunday of the month. He would tell me what new book he was reading, what he'd marked to show me. I might describe a particular day, such as the time Daddy filled the backyard with water to make an ice skating pond, though we told Mother the pump had broken and it was all we could do to turn the thing off before the rain cellar flooded. Of course, once the sun wore down our imagined rink and we found ourselves blade-sunk and stranded in your grandmother's peony bed, Daddy had to tell her the truth.

She loved her peonies and fretted all that winter that we had somehow damaged the roots, that spring would come and the pinks she had ordered, the ones with the name that rhymed with Frank Sinatra, would have no company. But everything grew and blossomed on schedule, and we ended up calling the peony bed our lake and threatening to flood it every winter.

Randall sent me back a letter about a book he had recently read on the gardens of Kyoto, how the gardens were made of sand, gravel, and rock. No flowers, he said. No pinks. Once in a while they use moss, but even their moss isn't green like we know green. No grass green or leaf green but a kind of grayish, he wrote. You can't even walk in these gardens because they're more like paintings. You view them from a distance, he wrote, their fragments in relation.

The line I can still recall, though at the time I was baffled. I knew we were now at war with the Japanese; we were repeatedly given classroom instruction on the failings of the Japanese character. We had learned of crucifixions and tortures; we understood the Japanese to be evil—not only did they speak a language no one could decipher, but they engaged in acts of moral deprivation our teachers deemed too shocking to repeat. I understood them to be a secret, somehow, a secret we shouldn't hear. Now, oddly, I knew something of their gardens.

*   *   *

The last time I saw him was the Easter of 1944. He was not yet seventeen—can you imagine? the age of enlistment—but would soon be, and he understood that it would be best if he went to war, that Sterling expected him to, that there were certain things that boys did without question. He never spoke of this to me; I learned it all later. Instead, his letters that winter were filled with some tremendous discovery he had made, a surprise he intended to share at Easter, not beforehand. You can imagine my guesses. Daddy had barely shut off the engine when I opened the door and sprung out. I might have bypassed all those narrow rooms and passageways altogether, scaled the tree and banged on one of those filthy windows, but I could feel Mother's eyes. She wanted me to slow down, to stay a part of them. In truth, the drive had been a sad one—Rita newly married and stationed with Roger in California, Betty oddly silent. Our first visit seemed light-years past, an adventure far more pleasant than it had actually been, a family outing when we were still family. We had grown into something altogether different: guests at a party with little in common.

I stood, waiting for everyone to get out of the car, waiting until Mother opened the door and yelled, Hello. Then I ran to Randall's room. I knew the way, could find it blindfolded—through the passageways and up the flights of stairs. I touched the countries in the Gallery of Maps, the danger spots, the capital cities. I picked up the mouthpiece and recited my Roosevelt impression—"I hate war, Eleanor hates war, and our dog, Fala, hates war"—just in case anyone was listening.

When I got to Randall's door I saw that it was ajar, so I went in without knocking. He stood facing the line of dormers, his back to me, his stance so entirely unfamiliar, so adult, that for an instant I thought I might have barged in to the wrong room, that for all this time a second, older Randall had lived just next door.

"Boo," I said. I was that kind of girl.

He turned, startled, and I saw he had been writing my name on the window grime.

He was so thin, rail-thin, we called it. A beanpole. Just legs and arms and wrists and neck. I imagine if he had been permitted to live his life, he might have married someone who would have worried about this, who would have cooked him certain foods and seen that his scarves were wrapped tight in winter. No matter. He crossed the room to me.

"Any guesses?" he said.

"None," I said, blushing. This was the age of movie star magazines, of starlets discovered at soda fountains. I had plenty of guesses, each sillier than the next, but I knew enough to keep them to myself.

He marched me out of his room to the cook's stairway, a long narrow corridor down to the foyer, then pushed on a second door I'd always assumed led to the pantry. It took us back to the Gallery of Maps, where he paused, as if expecting me to react. "So?" I said. He ignored me, taking my hand and leading me to the darkest continent in the Gallery—an hourglass stain near the far end tucked behind the door to the musty unused parlor.

Randall swung the door shut and pointed to a few shredded cobwebs collected in the corner, where Antarctica would have been.

"*Look*," Randall said. And then I saw: a tiny black thread, horizontal, a hairline fracture dividing time remaining from time spent unlike the other cracks in the walls, the veinlike fissures that ran through that old house. "A *clue*," Randall said.

*   *   *

Sometimes, when I think about it, I see the two of us there, Randall and me, from a different perspective, as if I were Mother walking through the door to call us for supper, finding us alone, red-haired cousins, twins sketched quickly: bones, hair, shoes, buttons. Look at us, we seem to say. One will never grow old, never age. One will never plant tomatoes, drive automobiles, go to dances. One will never drink too much and sit alone, wishing, in the dark.

Randall knocked on the wall and I heard a strange hollowness. "Right here," he said. "Right beneath my nose."

He pushed and the wall flattened down from its base like a punching bag. He held it there and got down on all fours, then he crawled in. I followed, no doubt oblivious to the white bloomers Mother still insisted I wear with every Easter dress.

The wall snapped shut, throwing us into instant black. It was difficult to breathe, the sudden frenzied dark unbearable. And cold! As if the chill from all those other rooms had been absorbed by this tiny cave, the dirt floor damp beneath my hands, my knees.

"Randall?" I said.

"Here," he said. Then, again. "Here."

His voice seemed flung, untethered; it came from every direction and I began to feel the panic that comes over me in enclosed places. I would have cried had Randall not chosen that moment to strike a match. He was right there beside me, touchable, close. I sat as he held the match to a candle on the floor. It wasn't a cave at all, just a tiny room, its walls papered with yellowed newsprint, the words buried by numbers. Literally hundreds of numbers had been scrawled across the walls, the ceiling. Everywhere you looked. The strangest thing. Some written in pencil, others in what looked like orange crayon, smeared or faint, deep enough to tear the newsprint. There seemed to be no order, no system to them. Just numbers on top of numbers on top of numbers.

I could hear Randall breathing. "What do you think they were counting?" I said.

"Heartbeats," he said.

It was the slaves' hiding place, of course. I crawled to the far corner, my palm catching on something hard: a spool of thread. Red, I remember, its color intact. There were other things to look at. Randall had collected them, and now he showed me, piece by piece: a rusted needle, a strand of red thread still through its eye, knotted at the end; a leather button; a tin box containing cards with strange figures printed on them, an ancient tarot, perhaps; a yellow tooth, a handkerchief—the initials RBP embroidered in blue thread on its hem—a folded piece of paper. Randall unfolded it slowly, and I believed, for an instant, that the slaves' story would be written here. Another clue. But there was nothing to read, simply more numbers, a counting gone haywire.

Randall held the paper out to me and I took it, feeling, when I did, the brush of his soft fingers. "It must have been the only thing they knew," I said, staring at the numbered paper, my own fingers burning.

"Or had to learn," Randall said.

"Right," I said, not fully understanding.

"Look," he said. He held a comb, its wooden teeth spaced unevenly. "I bet they played it," he said.

"I bet they did," I said. Even then I knew I sounded stupid. I wanted to say something important, something that might match his discovery. But all I could think of was the dark, and the way the candlelight made us long shadows. I pulled my legs beneath me, still cold, and pretended to read the numbers. After a while, aware of his inattention, I looked up. He was bent over, holding the needle close to the candlelight, sewing, it appeared, the hem of his pant leg with a concentration I had only witnessed in his reading.

I leaned in to see. RB, he had embroidered, and now he stitched the straight tail of the P.

He startled. I'm not sure we had ever been that close to one another, eye-to-eye, my breath his breath. The candlelight made us look much older than we were, eternal, somehow: stand-ins for gods. "I thought I'd take him along," he said, by way of explanation.

We remained in the slaves' hiding place until supper, sitting knee-to-knee, trying to count the numbers. We gave up. Randall read some advertisement for Doctor something-or-other's cure-all, which worked on pigs and people, and we laughed, then he took the stub of a pencil he always kept knotted in his shoelaces and wrote three numbers across the advertisement—5, 23, 1927—the date and year of his birth. He stared at the numbers a minute, and then drew a dash after them, in the way you sometimes see in books after an author's name and birthdate, the dash like the scythe of the Grim Reaper.

"Don't," I said, licking my finger and reaching to erase the line. I may have smeared it a bit, I don't know. At this point Randall grabbed my wrist, surprising me with the strength in those fingers. It was the most wonderful of gestures. He brought my hand to his cheek and kissed my palm, no doubt filthy from crawling around on that floor. He seemed not to care. He kept his lips there for a very long time, and I, as terrified to pull away as I was to allow him to continue, held my breath, listening to my own heart beat stronger.

There was one other after that. Visit, I mean. The morning Randall came through Philadelphia on his way out. He was going to ride the *Union Pacific*, in those days a tunnel on wheels chock-full of soldiers stretching from one end of the country to the other—some heading east to Europe, others heading west to the Pacific. Your grandmother would tell me stories of worse times, during the early days of the Depression, when she said that same train took children from families who could no longer feed them. She said she remembered a black-haired boy walking by their farmhouse, stopping with his parents for a drink of water. They were on their way to the train, the orphan train, they called it, sending the boy east, where someone from an agency would pick him up and find him a new place to live. She said it was a terrible thing to see, far worse than boys in bright uniforms heading out to save the world from disaster. She described children in trains, sitting high on their cardboard suitcases to get a view out the window, their eyes big as quarters, their pockets weighted down with nothing but the few treasures their parents had to give them—first curls, nickels, a shark tooth, ribbons—things they no doubt lost along the way. That, she'd say the few times I tried talking to her of Randall, is the worst thing of all. Children given up for good.

But I don't know. I remember the look of Randall stepping off the train. His big, drab coat, his leather shoes polished to a gleam shiny as those fingernails. It was a terrible sight, I can tell you. Mother and I had driven to meet him at the station. I believe it was the only time I ever saw him when I wasn't in an Easter dress. You would have laughed. I wore a pink wool skirt and a pink cashmere button-down, my initials embroidered on the heart. A gift from Rita. I was so proud of those clothes, and the lipstick, Mother's shade, that I'd dab with a perfumed handkerchief I kept in my coat pocket.

But the look of Randall stepping off the train. He had grown that year even taller, and we could see his thin, worried face above the pack of other soldiers. The morning was blustery, and it felt like there might be snow. Other girls were on the platform slapping their hands together, standing with brothers, boyfriends. We were a collection of women and boys. Mother stepped forward a bit and called out to him, and Randall turned and smiled and rushed over to us, his hand extended.

But that was for Mother. When I went to shake it, he pulled me into a hug. He wore the drab, regulation wool coat, as I have said, and a scarf, red, knotted at his neck, and I tasted that scarf and smelled the cold, and the lilac water, and the tobacco smoke all at once.

"Look at you," he said, and squeezed me tighter.

Mother knew of a diner nearby, and we went, though we had to stand some time waiting for a table, the room swamped with boys in uniform. I became aware of Randall watching me, though I pretended not to notice. I had come in to the age of boys finding me pretty, and I felt always as if I walked on a stage, lighted to an audience somewhere out in the dark. Mother chattered, clearly nervous in that big room with all those soldiers, waiters racing to and fro, splashing coffee on the black-and-white linoleum floor, wiping their foreheads with the dishrags that hung from their waists, writing checks, shouting orders to the cooks. Yet all the while I felt Randall's gaze, as if he needed to tell me something, and that all I had to do was turn to him to find the clue.

But there wasn't much time. Too soon that feeling of leaving descended upon the place. Soldiers scraped back their chairs, stood in line to pay their checks. Everyone had the same train to catch. Mother smoothed her skirt out and said she believed we should be heading back ourselves. Then she excused herself, saying she'd rather use the ladies' room there than at the train station.

Randall and I watched her weave her way around the other tables, some empty, others full. We were, quite suddenly, alone.

Have I told you he was handsome? I didn't know him well, but he had red hair, red as mine, and a kind, thin face. He might have had the most beautiful thin face I have ever seen. I should have told him that then, but I was too shy. This is what I've been thinking about: maybe he wasn't waiting to tell me anything, but waiting to hear something from me.

I may have taken another sip of coffee, then. I know I did anything not to have to look at him directly.

"On the train up I sat next to a guy from Louisville," he finally said. "His name was Hog Phelps."

"Hog?" I said.

"Said he wasn't the only Hog in his family, said he was from a long line of Hogs."

I looked at Randall and he shrugged. Then he laughed and I did, too. It seemed like such a funny thing to say.

I received only one letter from Randall after that. It was written the day before he sailed for the Far East, mailed from San Francisco. I remember that the stamp on the envelope was a common one from that time—Teddy Roosevelt leading his Rough Riders up San Juan Hill—and that Randall had drawn a bubble of speech coming from his mouth that said, "Carry on!" I opened the letter with a mixture of trepidation and excitement. I was too young and too stupid to understand what Randall was about to do. I imagined his thoughts had been solely of me, that the letter would be filled with love sonnets, that it would gush with the same romantic pablum I devoured from those movie star magazines. Instead, it described San Francisco—the fog that rolled in early afternoons across the bay, the Golden Gate Bridge and how the barking sea lions could be heard from so many streets, and the vistas that he discovered, as if painted solely for him, on the long solitary walks he took daily through the city. He wrote how he seemed to have lost interest in books, that he no longer had the patience. There was no *time*, he wrote, to sit. He wanted to walk, to never stop walking. If he could, he would walk all the way to Japan by way of China. Hell, he wrote (and I remember the look of that word, how Randall seemed to be trying out a different, fiercer Randall), when I'm finished with this I'm going to walk around the entire world.

I tried to picture him writing it, sitting at a large metal desk in the middle of a barracks, like something I might have seen in *Life*. I pictured him stooped over, with a reader's concentration, digging the pen into the regulation paper in the way he would have, if we were talking face-to-face, stressed a word. I saw him in civilian clothes, in the dress pants he wore every Easter. The same ones, as far as I could tell—a light gray wool, each year hitched up a little higher and now, leg crossed across one knee, entirely ill-fitting, the RBP far above the ankle. He might have, from time to time, put the pen down and leaned back to think of a particular description, fingering those initials he had stitched in red. It was clear to me even then that he had worked on the letter like a boy who wants to be a writer. Certain words broke his true voice, were tried on, tested for fit. They were a hat too big for him—the Randall I knew interrupted again and again by the Randall Randall might have become. The *Hell*, as I have mentioned. A line from some dead poet—*I would think of a thousand things, lovely and durable, and taste them slowly*—I had heard him recite in his room a hundred times, and other words I recognized as words still left to learn. It seemed he wanted to cram everything in.

Still, it is a beautiful letter. I have saved it for years. It finds its way into my hands at the oddest times, and when it does I always hold it for a while. Teddy shouts *Carry on!*, and I curse him. All of them. Then I pull out the paper, one creased sheath, and unfold it as slowly as I would a gift I'd never opened. My fear is that somehow in my absence, his words have come undone, been shaken loose, rearranged; the letters shuffled into indecipherable forms.

But there! My name in salutation, the sweetness of the attendant *Dear*. I'm again as I was, as he may have pictured me when—writing at that desk beneath the window, the metal newly polished, the air fresh, eucalyptus-scented, the sea lions barking—he signed *Love, Randall*, and underlined it with a flourish as elegant as a bow.

2

I heard a story once, told on a radio program by a Japanese soldier who had participated in the battle for Iwo Jima. It must have been an anniversary, or some significant day. I don't know. I happened upon it by chance.

The soldier was talking about a group of Japanese kindergarten children from the other side of the island, Iwo Jima, who had been taken, weeks before the invasion, to view a cave known to be the breeding place of a particular blue-winged butterfly.

The butterfly mated at a certain time of year and always chose this part of the island, this cave, in which to do so, the soldier said. The children had become very interested in these butterflies due to a certain teacher who had apparently brought a book on the subject into his class. The students had read about butterflies all year. Of course, the teacher knew that this was wartime, and in wartime nothing is secure, but he had checked the necessary persons and been given the clearances to gather his kindergarten class at dawn that morning and herd them into a boat.

A picnic was planned and the children carried their bento boxes close to them and walked in straight and even lines when instructed and did not bicker in the way that all children, Japanese, American, what have you, will bicker. They were happy to have a trip planned and a place to go. I tell it this way because this is the way I remember the Japanese soldier telling it.

Once on shore, he said, the children ran around the rocks before gathering at their teacher's command. The teacher told them not to bother the Japanese soldiers who were trying to do their job. He told them to follow him and stay in a straight line. He told them to keep quiet. Then he led the way down the long path that wound around the shore edge through the caves and stony underpasses.

They walked in a deep fog and the path proved difficult. The teacher stopped from time to time to wipe his glasses and to let the children rest. Their excitement flagged. It was hot on the island, and for as much as they wanted to see the blue butterflies they also wanted to sit on the ground and eat their lunch and return home; they were children, after all. But at last they reached the butterfly cave, marked, as the teacher had read it would be, with a small pyramid of stones. The teacher turned and announced the end of their journey with some fanfare as the children applauded.

The teacher entered the cave, slowly, carefully, aware that the sound of his own heart pounding competed with what he barely discerned as the rush of tiny wings. It was there, though, like a burst of water, or some invisible woman catching her breath. He lit the lantern he carried and held it high, and the children stood behind him at the mouth of the cave, waiting to be told what to do next.

The blue he had not imagined! He had seen the butterflies in books and once in a glass jar in his professor's office, but never like this, so close. The teacher took off his glasses and polished them again. He blinked a few times. The blue reminded him of the blue used to slick the cue in billiards. Not a dark, water blue, but a blue that could hold light.

The butterflies pressed against the walls of the stone cave, forming a pattern of sorts with their wings, trembling wings, the whole cave rumbling as if a train passed over them, a great rumbling roar, and then the teacher realized that wings alone could not make such a horrible sound, and that something, something terrible, was happening above them. He called out to the children to come inside fast and to squat with their heads between their legs and their arms crossed over their necks as they had been instructed in school for air raids. The children gathered around their teacher as close as they could, their bento boxes discarded at the cave mouth; above them the blue butterflies fell from the cave walls and batted their wings in ways ungraceful.

This is how the Japanese soldier put it: In ways ungraceful.

He found them there soon after the onslaught had begun, the relentless bombing before the invasion. He was not afraid to admit it now, he said, but he himself had been looking for a place to hide and had stumbled into the cave where they squatted, a mother hen and so many chicks. The teacher and the children were very brave, he said, and his voice hitched up a bit. They promised him they would not move and would stay in the cave though the noise would be unbearable until he returned for them. But the soldier had been wounded soon after and carried off the island in a boat bound elsewhere with men dying. He had been knocked unconscious, he said. By the time he regained himself the battle had been lost and no one, it seems, had seen the teacher or his children.

This is an odd story, he then said, of which I feel responsible my entire life. What secrets men keep, I thought at the end of it. And for an instant, I forgave them.

3

Not so long after we received Great-Uncle Sterling's letter, a package came in the mail addressed in the same slanting, angry hand. Rita, as I have told you, was in California, and we'd receive packages from her from time to time. I'm so *bored*, she'd write, the letters looping and curling around the page, all I can do is sew these gosh darned things. The things of which she spoke were usually monogrammed skirts, or vests. She made Daddy a light jacket once, his name stitched in purple thread on the collar. It was much too fancy for Daddy, though I remember he wore it that Thanksgiving, the last time Rita came home after Roger had returned from Europe and the two were reassigned to Texas. That was a terrible visit, of which I'll tell you more later, the point is, it was clear to Betty and me, slamming through the kitchen door that afternoon and seeing the package sitting on the kitchen table, that this was not something from Rita, nor one of Mother's mail-order dresses.

I held the package up to the light and said the writing looked familiar, though at the time I didn't recognize it.

We knew better than to open the package before Mother came

home from the factory. We were latchkey children, but that didn't mean we were undisciplined, as you might gather from latchkey children now. Quite truthfully, we were probably better behaved. We had certain parameters; certain rules we knew to follow. One being that we knew we had to wait for Mother to come home before opening anything addressed to her, and so we did, sitting at the kitchen table muddling over our homework, looking up, from time to time, at the clock above the stove, or, from time to time, feeling the package, again, to guess.

Mother came home at five o'clock and usually headed straight up the stairs to her bath, but that day she indulged us and came in. She was a handsome woman, not pretty in the way women are today, but handsome in the way they were then, during wartime. She had black hair she curled in the style that was popular, and pale brown eyes that watered. She carried a handkerchief and would often sniff and say, my, my, my and wipe her eyes. We always tried to get her laughing so hard that her watering eyes looked like crying, though the few times I ever saw her cry were terrifying.

She frowned when she saw the handwriting and then tore open the package. Inside, she found another package, one wrapped in thinner, brown paper. A card had dropped to the floor and she retrieved and read it quickly.

This is more for you, actually, she said at last to me. Here, she said, handing me the card.

I read it quickly. It said that Randall had always spoken a great deal about me. It said that Randall had had few friends. This is probably my doing, given the circumstances, Patricia, he wrote. And I remember how odd it felt to read my mother's full name, as if I had somehow spied her as a girl my age, flirting with my father or sitting on a fence post, her legs swinging.

It said that Randall had left this package behind in Maryland, and that he had requested it be sent to me in the event of the unmentionable. It said that he had respected Randall's wishes and had not opened the package, nor would he ask that the contents be shown to him. He would, however, like to see us again, like to see me, again, because he believed we might be a comfort to him at this hour. He had decided to leave the old house and would return to his rooms in Baltimore. There would be an estate sale at the end of the month. I would appreciate the company, he wrote. It will not be an easy day for me. Then he had signed it, your loving uncle, Sterling J. Jewell.

I did not realize that Mother and Betty were waiting for me to unwrap the package. I read the card again, then folded it as it had been folded. Mother had her handkerchief to her eyes and Betty drummed the table. I suppose, in hindsight, I should have examined the package more carefully—it was, after all, a package that had been prepared for me, the string pulled taut and knotted with me in mind—because I could not now tell you what kind of string it was, butcher's twine or the finer white string we used to use for kites. No matter. I tore the string off and unfolded the sheaves of paper and there, bundled together in a handkerchief I did not recognize, were several of our familiar objects. I first picked up his extra pair of reading glasses, spectacles, he called them, with the cracked left lens. They were dusty, of course. They had come from that house, that room. I pictured the last place I had seen them: folded, stems down, in the first shelf of the book shelf near the window seat. He had lost the case, he said, and cracked them who knows how. I remembered how once he had put them on and pretended they were bifocals. I fingered the stems, brass, and so delicate I could not imagine the thin wire frames holding steady such thick glass. No wonder the crack, I thought, and slipped them in my pocket.

What else? An elaborately carved letter opener made out of a sleek white wood that I now know is whale tusk, a certificate of accomplishment in the Great Books program, a children's primer he had never shown me before. It must have been his first. I opened it and laughed at the unsteady letters he wrote, the Qs with their long cat tails, the Ks with shaky angles. It was difficult to imagine him as the child who wrote so clumsily. I suppose I must have always believed that Randall was born writing, or at least with a book in his hand. The sentences in the primer were elemental, Dick and Jane. It occurred to me then that he might have still had his mother at this time, and that she might have helped him trace these letters, holding his small hand in her own, fingering the alphabet.

There was also a book, one with a soft, leather cover, its illegible title worn to nothing, though I knew: *The Gardens of Kyoto.* I may have cried, I don't recall. What I remember is Mother's hand on my back, and the way Betty seemed, for once, patient, waiting for me to examine everything before she looked herself.

Mother kept her hand on my back for some time. I opened the book and saw again the inscription—*For Ruby and child, with affection*—and the professor's signature. X, Randall claimed. Professor X. Clear as day, he said. And in truth I could make no other name from it, the X scrawled across the stained rice paper of the cover page, behind which the ancient cherry woodprint, its thick limbs propped up by strange crutches, stood.

"Look," Betty said. Her patience had clearly worn out and she held in front of me a notebook. "It's his diary."

"Oh my," Mother said.

I had the feeling of not wanting to set anything down, that these things might disappear as quickly as he did, and so I balanced the diary on *The Gardens of Kyoto* and opened it, first glaring at Betty.

Indeed, it was a diary. His diary, though he had never mentioned keeping a diary to me before. He had written his full name on the flyleaf—*Randall Jeremiah Jewell*—along with a warning: *All those who read these pages without an explicit, verbal invitation to do so risk their own lives and the lives of their loved ones!* I smiled and closed the book. It sounded so much like him.

"You're not going to read it?" Betty said.

"No," I said.

"But he sent it to you," she said, swinging a leg up so her foot bumped hard on one of the kitchen chairs, nearly knocking it over.

"Elizabeth Jane," Mother said. "Go upstairs or outside."

"I'm comfortable," Betty said.

Mother looked at Betty and she reluctantly stood.

"Just because he sent everything to you doesn't mean you shouldn't show us. He was my cousin, too," she said, turning and storming out and up the stairs.

"She's just jealous," Mother said, stroking my hair. "And she misses Rita."

"I know," I said, because I did, and because I didn't like Mother stroking my hair, or feeling sorry for me. I wanted to be alone. I wanted to be upstairs with Randall's things so I could look at what else he had sent—I had just caught the spool of red thread from the slaves' hiding place out of the corner of my eye—and reread my name, written in his hand, on the thin brown wrapping paper that had wrapped the whole package. But then I have always wanted to be alone during moments painful to me, and never understood certain social customs—wakes, shivas for the Jews—when neighbors, friends, and strangers alike crowd your house to keep you company after a death. I suppose other people find comfort in the presence of persons who have come to share their grief, though for me, grief is solitary. I wanted solitude then, to be alone with Randall. Randall was clearly there with me, in the presence of his things but moreover in the knowing, as he had known, that I would only see them if he were dead. I asked to be excused and gathered the package—the spectacles still in my pocket—his diary and *The Gardens of Kyoto* under my arm, and went outside, the screen door slamming behind me. I started down the long walk, not sure of where I should go but walking nonetheless. I didn't want to stay inside. I walked toward the red slanting sun, and soon found myself in front of Springfield's orchard. I climbed the fence easily, then ran as far as I could into the orchard, the world blocked out by hundreds of trees spreading in every direction, line upon line, evenly, like rows and rows of soldiers, gnarled beautiful fruit trees, as old, it seemed to me, as that woodcut cherry in Kyoto.

4

My understanding is that a decision was made to spare
Kyoto, that there had been some discussion and that the decision
was reached that, given the gardens and temples, the city of Kyoto
should be taken off the list of possibilities of where to drop the
bomb. Perhaps one of the generals in charge of such things had been
to Ryoan-ji, or viewed it, I should say, since it is not a garden that
can be entered. It has no benches, no paths, no ponds. It has no
lawn, no trees, no flowers. I read about it in Randall's book: how the
Japanese garden was derived from the Shinto shrine and centers on
the worship of *kami*, or spirits. Spirits dwell in specific places—
Mount Fuji, for instance, or a particular pattern of rock you might
find rising out of the sea. Ryoan-ji is one of these places.

The Japanese believe that to meet *kami* there is no need to die
and go to heaven. You can, quite simply, visit the garden.

5

I sat in the orchard a good long while. I can still see me there, a teenager, barely, still a girl as confused by Randall's affections as I had been by his death. I imagine Mother sensed this about me and felt powerless in the face of it. She would have liked to have had something to say, something to give that went beyond her callused hand on my back. But what more could she have offered? I counted clouds, a trick I had developed for whenever I felt scared. I used it sparingly—when Rita banged out the screen door to Roger, who waited in his automobile, leaving home for good; when Daddy broke his arm roofing; when we got the first letter about Randall; now.

I counted to God knows what until my heart settled down. There were storm clouds and thunder much farther west, toward the Springfield house. We were forbidden to enter the orchard. Mr. Springfield was as mean as a snake, even Mother said it, and the rumors were that if he caught you on his property, or stealing even the fallen fruit, he would twist your finger so hard it would snap in two. I wished for this, wished for Old Man Springfield to come charging down the high hill, thunder over his shoulder, and snap all ten fingers one-two-three until they hung like broken things from my hands. Why should I be alive and Randall dead? I felt like climbing the highest apple and waiting, arms outstretched, for the lightning.

I turned over and lay on my stomach, Randall's things in his handkerchief on the stubble of grass next to me. I opened his diary. Randall Jeremiah Jewell. I traced the letters with my finger, nowhere near broken, and turned to the first page. It was dated December 25, 1938; Randall would have been eleven years old. His handwriting looked different than the handwriting I had grown accustomed to seeing in his letters: smaller, cramped, as if he had composed the entry under a blanket in the dead of night, hunched as small as he could go, his eyes blurry. Perhaps this was his way of assuring that nobody would read it. I had a difficult time, and anyone else, I imagine, would have been so daunted at the prospect they would have let Randall's secret thoughts remain secret. I leaned closer to the page, forgetting where I was, forgetting the approaching thunder, the chill that had suddenly sprung into the air from the ground up, as if the roots of the fruit trees had collectively exhaled their moldy, wet breath. It was early May 1945, just weeks after we'd received the news, and yet in that time it felt as if the world had shifted some, tilted off its orbit. Mother and Daddy walked more carefully around us, wrote often to Rita and once, even, drove us to Capetown to make the telephone call, the four of us screaming into the receiver, Rita? as if just by yelling we might better the connection.

Anyway, it would not have surprised me if winter had come before summer that year. If the apples had never changed from green to red. If Mr. Springfield had put on a jester's hat and run like Ebenezer Scrooge through the neighborhood shouting Happy day! Everything had gone out of sync. The cold I barely noticed; instead, I read, pretending that Randall lay right there next to me, reading along, pointing out the passages he wanted me to note for their genius.

My life, it began, by Randall Jeremiah Jewell.

Mother has just given me this for a Christmas present, he wrote. I don't play enough outside. And I'm too thin. I will make a New Year's resolution to eat more. I will write every day. I am read-ing *Gulliver's Travels* and *Bleak House* and enjoying both tremen-dously. I also continue to peruse the *Encyclopedia Britannica: A Dictionary of Arts, Sciences, and General Literature.* Mother bought me the set before I could talk. Eleventh Edition. I have read most of C. Did you know, he wrote, and I felt a shiver of some kind of recognition, as if he were speaking directly to me and not, simply, to the diary, that the Romans invented cement and then lost the recipe for thousands of years? Remarkable. Tomorrow the library reopens. Good-bye. Your friend, Randall.

How odd, I remember thinking, Randall writing as if he were speaking to someone he knew. And a friend, no less.

The rain had begun, though I didn't notice it until it wet the next page of Randall's diary. He wrote of the library in town, where he went after school. How he had become acquainted with a certain Miss Thomas, the librarian, and how together they had composed a reading list. Miss Thomas, he wrote, unfortunately resembles a frog. She seems to have too many chins and her eyes have that pointy shape that indicates ill health in childhood—

Yes, these were his words. Give or take. You will find that cer-tain words stay with you.

And they are very green, he added—this about Miss Thomas's eyes—frog green, which I find pretty. Some day I will build the courage to tell her so.

Raindrops splattered the page and I shut the diary quickly, tuck-ing it beneath my shirt. I gathered the rest of Randall's things and ran back the way I came, now terrified that Old Man Springfield had seen me and was closing in. I scaled the fence easily and turned around. But there was no one there, only the rows upon rows of fruit trees, their gnarled limbs curling like so many corkscrews. In the now-dark late afternoon, clouds bunched, bruised across the low sky, a flock of starlings suddenly lifted up from several trees, swooped then rose in a synchronized pack out of range. The thunder cracked directly overhead and I ran, already soaked, toward home.

Mother waited for me. She hadn't yet changed out of her factory uniform and I remember how, entering the kitchen, I was struck by the smallness of her life. I don't mean to be cruel. I have told you she was a handsome woman, which she was, and kind and hard-working, but I suppose at that age I believed that largeness in life depended on other things.

"You're wet," she said. She may have been preparing supper; I don't know.

"Good deduction," I said. I'm sure I passed through rather quickly on my way up the stairs to my bedroom. It was a room I had, until Rita moved out, shared with Betty, though Betty had moved into the third-floor attic where Rita had previously lugged a cot and a desk lamp and the stacks and stacks of her movie star magazines I would steal when she was visiting Roger. I passed the door, where Betty had tacked a sign that usually read Keep Out. I saw now she had flipped it to the other side: Visitors Welcome, it read. A rare invitation, so I went without knocking.

I heard a scuffle at the top of the stairs

"Betty?" I called.

"For the love of Pete," she said. "Why didn't you say something? I thought you were Mother."

I smelled now the cigarette smoke and, reaching the top stair where I could step onto the floor landing, saw Betty relighting the bent end of a half-smoked cigarette.

"Got another?" I said.

"I'll share," she said.

I stood on the wide-plank floor looking around. Betty hadn't

changed anything, really. Rita had shellacked black-and-white photographs of her favorite movie stars to the walls and they were still
there, a chorus of men smiling out at me. William Powell, I remember. Clark Gable, of course. Frank Sinatra. Some of them were
inscribed to Rita. She paid close to a dollar for these, and waited
weeks after sending off her mail-order form for the stiff manila
envelopes to arrive. I can still see her, kissing the flap she swore had
been kissed, licked, by the movie star himself, though Mother told
her they had stupid girls such as herself to do that kind of work.
When Rita met Roger she said he was the spitting image of Errol
Flynn, that if he hadn't joined the Army he could have had a brilliant career on stage. That's the way she would say it. On stage. As
if it were the same as, In Heaven, or On the Throne.

Anyway, I hadn't been in her room since she left and saw now
that Rita had shellacked some pictures of Roger and herself near the
movie stars. I looked at a photograph of the two of them taken in
one of those booths they used to have at county fairs and in the bigger tourist restaurants: four frames of Rita and Roger, and in the last
they were kissing, Rita's big fat curls obscuring most of her face
though I could see well enough Roger's look of concentration.

"He doesn't look a thing like Errol Flynn," I said.

"Here," Betty said, holding out the cigarette. I took a puff. I was
just starting, and hadn't yet learned how to inhale.

Betty held out her hand for the cigarette and I passed it back to
her.

"So?" she said. She sat cross-legged on the cot, the stub of the
cigarette between two fingers. "What'd he have to say?"

"Who?" I said.

"Your boyfriend, cousin Randall."

"Leave him alone."

Betty frowned. "I'm sorry," she said. "Really. It's just sad, really.
I mean, it's just sad." She had smoked the cigarette down to the nub
and I saw now that the flame was out.

I sat next to her and looked around. I had left Randall's things at the base of the stairs, next to the door to my room. Now I wished I had brought them up. I would have liked to have shown Betty the spool of red thread and told her of the slaves' hiding place and how we had found the walls covered in numbers. But I didn't say a word.

Out the small attic window the last of the smoke drifted up to the rain. It was raining hard, the sound amplified there, in the attic room, that close to the roof. It's a lonely, comforting sound: rain in an attic room. We must have sat there for some time listening to it before Daddy came home, before Mother called us down for supper.

6

What a character your aunt Rita was. She had what they called sparkle: the first to go skinny-dipping, for instance, and once she spent the afternoon at Jacob's Creek pond catching bullfrogs until she had so many in her burlap potato bag she said it practically hopped its way home. She's the one, too, who took a knife to their legs, first stunning them on the head and then slicing clean through until she had more than three dozen.

I wish I could have bottled the look on Mother's face when she came home to the kitchen white with flour, a mound of frog legs keeping warm in the oven. Of course, it was Daddy who had to go to the Jacobs to apologize for his daughter's actions. He did this again and again, at various times, and though he always put on a stern look and once, even, threatened with his belt, I think he loved the spirit his first-born showed, a consolation prize for having had no son.

On the day she married Roger he came down the stairs red-eyed and Rita teased him, saying, was she being given away by Mother or by him?

*   *   *

Who could have known? Roger was handsome enough. He had the regulation haircut and sharp blue eyes. He wore a uniform and could fly a plane. She met him at a school dance—he was Missy Goodall's older brother home from the Army for Christmas. Rita, immediately smitten, asked him to come for lunch the next afternoon, and I remember how the house nearly quivered when he walked through the door in that uniform, this before Randall's leaving, when going to war seemed nothing short of suddenly winning a ticket to living. You won't understand what I mean by this, but any young boy in a uniform seemed larger in stature, heroic somehow. Daddy rose from his chair as if meeting an adult. He shook Roger's hand. Mother blushed. And Betty and I could barely contain ourselves, seeing our older sister standing there next to a living, breathing man. In uniform, no less.

She married him that summer, after graduation. The summer of 1943. In those days it didn't take much time. Besides, Rita had always seemed too old for the boys her age, boys who were now heading into their father's businesses, or college, or talking about enlisting. Here was someone who had already completed his preliminary training, who waited for the orders that would give him an officer's standing. Rita imagined they might be stationed somewhere exotic, possibly Hawaii. She said that Hawaii had been Roger's first choice, and given his record and his general level of intelligence, why wouldn't they grant his request?

The day before her wedding, we sat, the three of us, in her attic room. Roger had told her she could take only half her wardrobe, a genuine heartache for Rita, since she had sewed every dress by hand. Still, an officer's wife should never, Roger said, appear ostentatious—I can still remember her coming into my room asking to use my dictionary to look it up—and they were only permitted to take so much weight in luggage across the country. It turned out they hadn't gotten their Hawaii post, though they did manage California, which Rita claimed was even better, since the food in Hawaii, she had heard, was god-awful.

"For the love of Pete," Rita was saying. "You're gorgeous."

Betty stood with the dress pinching her at the shoulders and beneath the arms. "We'll just let it out some."

Betty looked down at herself and then back at Rita and me, who stared at her in the mirror. "I look like a horse," she said.

I shook my head and Rita rolled her eyes. "Okay," she said. "Try this one."

She held up an emerald green dress with a line of sequins around the bodice. "It's a bit ostentatious for me now," she said, without irony, unzipping Betty's dress and helping her pull out of the grip of the shoulders. Betty, clearly awkward in her panties and brassiere, stepped quickly into the emerald green. "Inhale," Rita said, zipping. In truth, Betty was at least two sizes larger than Rita, though nobody seemed to want to admit this. Betty was what we called a big girl, and though she, like Rita, had blond hair and blue eyes, she might have been more a best friend than a sister. Rita's blond hair truly shone like the spun sunlight you read about in fairy tales; Betty's blond hair lay flat, dull.

Rita pushed at the zipper as if trying to close a too-tightly packed suitcase. Betty winced. "I can't breathe," she said.

"It will be fine," Rita said. "Give me a minute." At last the zipper slipped more easily on its groove and Rita zipped it closed. "It's a question of the in-seams," she said. "I could let those out in a jiffy."

We looked at Betty in the mirror. Though she did not look like Rita would have in the emerald green, she looked pretty enough, stuffed and molded into a shape by the dress's stiff lines. "Gorgeous," Rita said, and Betty smiled.

I can't remember what I received from that afternoon. Maybe a few hats and a pair of slacks Rita had copied from a magazine. I rarely wore dresses. I do remember that we were exhausted by the end of it, and even though Rita had a hotel full of Roger's relatives to return to she stayed, lying with the two of us on the attic floor, staring up at the unpainted beams of the roof. It was rare for the three of us to be together in such a way. Generally Rita had social engagements, sometimes including Betty, sometimes not. I, as the youngest and the least like the two of them, was never asked to join. It didn't bother me. I had my own amusements. Reading, primarily, and helping Mother in the garden. Anyway, there we were, and though the moment may have been lost on my sisters, I remember how acutely aware I was of the moment as a *moment*, as a point in time I would always remember. I tried to levitate, to view the three of us from the attic beams, but the most I could do was close my eyes and picture us as we were, or as we just had been, three expectant faces in the mirror.

Rita continued talking about the wedding, about the god-awful dress that Mrs. Goodall, Roger's mother, would be wearing. "She claims it's ivory," Rita said. "But it's horse-piss yellow. And she's got this matching hat. This *hat*, I told you? I mean, there are certain women who can wear hats, and certain women who have no business even trying one on. Mrs. Goodall should know she's one of those no-business-trying-one-on women but you would think she was Myrna Loy. She goes on and on. And she's got Missy dolled up in teal, which is no teal I've ever seen though she insists, and I can't say a word because she's still angry I didn't ask Missy to be a bridesmaid and I would have, I told her, but I have two sisters and a best friend and I wasn't going to have one of those weddings with the whole darn class."

It was wonderful to hear her speak. She had a voice that infused every story with drama, and whether she was talking about the wedding or about nothing at all, I loved to listen to her, as, I know, did Betty. Betty might have interrupted from time to time. Betty was more Rita's friend and could offer comments or respond. But I was simply Rita's little sister, taking it all in, taking her all in, thinking how I would remember.

There was some mix-up with the photographer and so no photographs exist of Rita's wedding. I find this prescient now, though at the time it was considered tragic. Rita wore a dress with organdy pleats and a high lace neck and lace sleeves cut from one of Mother's Irish tablecloths, sleeves that hung past her wrists and covered her fingers. Every time she reached up to brush back her hair, the lace fluttered, softening the gesture. She had used the same lace for her veil, which trailed out so far that Betty, the maid of honor, had to hold it up as she walked. Roger stood near the minister, still in uniform. Behind him were his younger brother and some cadets from the academy who got drunk at the reception and tried to dance with me on their shoulders.

These would have been the photographs: the boys dancing with me on their shoulders and the lace on Rita's fingers; the way Daddy stood, once they reached the end of the aisle, as if he, too, wanted to marry Rita; Mrs. Goodall, who didn't look half bad in her little hat and ivory dress; Rita at the top of our stairs yelling for all the available girls to gather and turning around to toss her bouquet directly at Betty; Betty catching it with both hands; Rita, dressed now in a pink traveling suit she had ordered through a catalog, running down the stairs as if being chased, Roger at her heels; Rita, without looking at Mother or me or Betty or anyone else, racing outside and jumping, laughing, into the touring car that would take her to Philadelphia, to the suite at the Grand Hotel the Goodalls had reserved and then, we knew, to Atlantic City, where she would spend a week before returning to Philadelphia to board the train for Chicago, and then California; Rita waving from the touring car to no one in particular; the crowd of guests waving back, throwing what leftover rice they had in their pockets; the touring car moving slowly through the guests and down our drive, turning left at the Springfield's orchard and following the same route we had walked, Betty, Rita, and me, on our way to school most mornings; Rita, once the touring car reached the end of the drive, sitting straight and face-forward, as if she were the one navigating the road.

I remember how I wrote about it to Randall. I'm ashamed now to say I wrote mostly of Roger in his uniform and the Army friends in theirs, I imagine to make him jealous. No doubt I gave all the superfluous details, though I may have had the wherewithal not to go on about Rita's lacy veil. He died before I could tell him the end of the story. I suppose I'm grateful for that.

Randall sent back a postcard, the kind that were popular around the time of the First World War. On it was painted a little soldier boy slouched like a tired shepherd against a haystack, a rifle clenched to his chest. "What is just? What is unjust?" Randall had written on the other side. "What is it to be a ruler of men?"

7

Mother decided to take Sterling up on his invitation, or request, I should say, to help with the estate sale. She said he had no immediate family and that with Randall gone it would be a terribly lonesome task; he needed us, she said. She was right, although the idea of returning to that house, to Randall's room, knowing that I would look up at the dusty windows and see nothing but the reflections of oak shadows, made me miserable. I said I would rather catch polio than go back there. Mother looked at me hard. "It isn't easy for any of us, young lady," she said. And I knew, in the tone of young lady, that I would have to keep my protests to myself.

This was late spring, as I may have mentioned, a month or so after we got the news of Randall's death. Coming into Maryland the farms were thick with alfalfa, clover; the wheat knee-high. You still see a few of those old farms today, but then it was pure business. A drive through the country in that season meant the buckle of tractors plowing fields, and horses pulling cultivators through rows of corn so green as to be yellow, and stark Guernseys corralled in bright pastures, chewing, and a general feel of commerce, of production. Business. I suppose it's the same feeling now on city streets, but then country didn't mean a place where nobody was home. Everybody was home and working: old men and boys too young for the war. We'd stop from time to time to buy a soda or to wash our faces; the drive long and dusty, as I remember. It hadn't rained.

We got to Randall's house near sunset. As soon as we turned up the long drive I clamped my eyes shut, not wanting to look. I put my head down between my legs and counted to one hundred. Next to me Betty snored; she had slept all the way from Clarksburg. Daddy stopped the car and turned off the engine. "We're here," he said, as if we wouldn't have noticed. Mother let out a long sigh. I kept my eyes shut and looked up, feeling a sudden slant of light. Something struck the car, a walnut? an acorn? and I opened my eyes, thinking I might see Randall there knocking. But all I saw was what I knew: the oak trees, the brick house. No, that's not entirely right. There was something I hadn't expected, something you wouldn't be familiar with but at the time had become quite common: the red-bordered rectangle placed in the parlor window, the gold star stark in its white center.

We stood at the front door and Mother knocked. I remember thinking that we never, before, had to knock, that Randall was always right there at the front door to greet us. Now the door swung open to Sterling, older than I remembered him, hunched, leaning on a cane I later learned Randall had carved: a snake twisted up its shaft like a magician's wand.

"Sterling," Mother said, and hugged him tight. He shook Daddy's hand and Betty's, and mine he took in both hands and squeezed. His own hands were wizened, this is the only way to describe them, and when I looked up I saw that his head shook slightly, something I had never before noticed. Parkinson's, of course, though at the time this was simply attributed to old age. He wore a cardigan sweater though it was warm, and a tie with a conservative pattern. He had been a well-known judge in Baltimore for many years and had moved to the country before Jeannette, Randall's mother, died, when Randall was still quite small. He was an expert on Jonathan Edwards, the Calvinist preacher, and had been working on a biography. He was a good cook, a master bridge player. He would later be instrumental in influencing the Supreme Court on the state's first desegregation laws, filing a friend-of-the-court brief that was cited in the decision that followed.

These things I learned much later, at the time of his death, when Mother sent me the obituary that appeared in the *Baltimore Sun*. I remember my surprise at the photograph that accompanied the obituary, one taken in the early days of Sterling's judgeship. His head was slightly turned, as if it had been suggested that he look away from the harsh studio light right over the photographer's shoulder. He wore a gown, the regal black of it like a stand from which rose his long neck. He might have been chiseled out of marble and set down in museum storage somewhere: the sharp nose, the high forehead; not the man I remembered at all, and yet, something familiar sat at the edge of my surprise. Randall. A hardened, fleshy Randall. A Randall who might have been an athlete, or a man you watch in a barroom. A Randall chopping wood. A Randall crossing a path quickly, his coattails flying, hurrying to make an appointment. A Randall all grown up: a father Randall or a husband Randall. They were in fact the spitting image; I had never seen this before, or certainly never seen it when the two were alive in the same room, at the Easter suppers when finally Randall and I would join the rest of the family, our clothes dusty, our cheeks flushed. Then Sterling would carve, his old hands gripping the silver knife and fork, as Randall sat by his side, his own delicate hands in his lap, waiting for his father to finish so he could lead the rest of us in grace. This was Randall's job: grace. The point is, there was no resemblance then; absolutely none. Randall might have been his father's employee. Sterling might have been somebody's grandfather, invited to dinner out of the goodness of the family's heart.

I suppose they were too far at either end of the spectrum—Sterling into old age, Randall barely shedding childhood—to view them in the same light, to see them as father and son. But Sterling's photograph was clear proof of flesh and blood.

Sterling led us into the dark house, through the Gallery of Maps and out to the parlor where a dimly lit desk lamp seemed the only light in the room. The furniture was threadbare and rose-patterned, though most of the roses had disappeared, so faded into their own background they could easily have been mistaken for stains. Looking closely, you could still see ghosts of their buds, ghosts of their full blooms, ghosts of the thorny vines that twisted around the arms and the backs of the chairs and sofa. I traced the pattern around my knees, pretending to prick my finger, to suck the blood. Mother and Daddy and Sterling talked about the details of the sale. On the arm of my chair a small white ticket fluttered on a loop of white thread: $5 or best offer. All the furniture, including the desk and the desk lamp, had these white tickets. I suppose this was what had been keeping Sterling occupied during the weeks after he learned of Randall's death. He had made the decision quickly, he explained to Mother and Daddy. He wanted to get rid of the clutter, to return to Baltimore, to his research, his life there. Most of this was Jeannette's, anyway.

Sterling swept his hand around the room, indicating "most of this," I suppose. I pictured Jeannette there, with their young son, Randall. The windows were washed clean, open, the cold air breaking down the smell of ammonia still sharp in the freshly painted room. She stood in the center surveying the furniture, just unloaded, as the deliverymen waited for her to make up her mind. She did so abruptly, decisively, pulling Randall into her skirt to move him out of their way. The men lifted the sofa, heavy with new down and the thick metal frame the salesman had assured her would guarantee its longevity. The roses, red, brightened with the sunlight through the clear glass, the room washed with the cold newness, a morning's expectation.

"Perfect," she said as the men set the sofa down near the bay window, arranging the two wing chairs on either side. She clapped her hands. "It looks wonderful." The boy clapped his hands too and the deliverymen laughed. One stopped and crouched down to jiggle his chin. "Where'd you get that hair, kiddo?" he said, standing and winking at Jeannette.

I suppose I had this fantasy in the way I've had them since I can remember; in the way I still do: so sharp, so distinct, it's like a waking dream. They're often peopled with persons I have never met, only heard of, as if I, with concentration, can bring them back into some visible form, even though they're long dead, their bones rearranged in the graveyards. I remember when you were born how your great-grandmother appeared to me: Vicey, a woman I had only met on a few occasions though one I had heard many stories of; Vicey whose own mother was reputed to be the town whore. You know the story: She was born blind from that woman's syphilis and died so young we barely knew her. But there she was, sitting in the corner through my labor, unseeing, beside her a lamp with a large pink tasseled lampshade, the light from its solitary lightbulb dull.

Anyway, I must have looked as transported as I was, since I suddenly became aware that everyone was staring at me.

I fidgeted and pulled at my dress. Though it wasn't Easter, Mother had still insisted that we wear our holiday clothes, as if this weren't a sad event but a party we were attending.

"Sweetheart," Mother finally said. "Did you hear your uncle Sterling's question?"

I looked at Uncle Sterling. I'm not sure I had ever looked at him so directly. He stared back at me like an old, shaky bird. I have mentioned that he had a high forehead in his judge's photograph. Well, it seemed even higher now that he had lost all his hair, or most of it, though there may have been a few strands he combed across his skull, spotted as his hands and dry. His eyes were hooded with loose skin so that you could not fully tell whether they were blue or brown. His nose, enormous; the kind more often hidden behind a handkerchief as it is loudly blown. I don't need to say he terrified me and so I simply looked at him and waited, hoping he would repeat it.

"Sweetheart?" Mother said.

"I'm sorry, no," I said. "I didn't hear."

"Uncle Sterling wanted to know if you might show him to Randall's room."

My heart went loud in my chest. Did this mean he had never been there? That all these years he had no idea where his son slept? It's an absurd thought, of course, though at the time I thought it might be true, at the time it seemed perfectly plausible. Every visit I had ever made had seemed as if I were visiting Randall in a place all his own, one he did not share with anyone, much less an old man.

"Yes sir," I said.

Mother smiled as she always would when we remembered our manners, and the room seemed to gather up with the expectation of our going. Uncle Sterling made no motion, though, and so I sat back down. Now the conversation ground to a halt and the only thing to do was to watch the dust motes drift in the late setting sunlight. I knew if I stood and pulled the heavy drapes aside, I would see the brilliance of the sunset. I had often watched it from Randall's room. The house must have faced west, because each time I was there it seemed as if the house were the sole audience for the setting sun, sitting square and solid in view of its sinking. Randall and I would each take turns declaiming to the sun—this Randall's word—as we read aloud the end of whatever we had chosen, our voices rising, our dramatic presentation at its most dramatic, lit in the way that is the most romantic, or youthful. If I could have pulled aside the heavy drapes now I might have been inspired to recite "Ode on a Grecian Urn," or something equally predictable. I don't know. Perhaps I would have just looked.

There was something in the heavy drapes, a green velvet that retained the memory of Jeannette. Beside them, a corded tassel hung, long abandoned and certainly intended to hook them back, to present the stage, the players. Is this where Jeannette sat with Randall as a boy, reading? Is this where she stood long after he had been put to bed and her husband had returned to his study, the door closed? Is this where she walked in the middle of the night, restless? Perhaps. Or maybe she was nothing like I pictured her.

I felt a hand on my shoulder and there Uncle Sterling stood, waiting. " 'Bye," I said to my family, who nodded.

"This way," I said, pointing to a staircase in front of us, "though there's a shortcut, too."

"Take me that way," he said, so I led him out of the parlor and through the old cook's pantry and the Gallery of Maps, passing the intercom, oddly hopeful, as if I might hear Randall's voice on the other line were I to lift it from its brass base.

I opened the door to the back stairway and began the climb. I could hear Sterling struggling a bit behind me, with his cane. He had been somewhat crippled as a child, and his limp grew worse as he aged. I waited midway for him to catch up. In the almost dark of that staircase I turned to see his bald head, his old hand on the banister. "They were smaller in the old days," I said.

Then, when he said nothing, I turned back around.

"Carry on," I muttered, though I don't believe he heard me.

No matter.

My initial excitement at leading Uncle Sterling through the same drill I had been led through by Randall dulled as we got closer to Randall's room, and I was reminded, again, of his death. I slowed down my march, feeling Sterling close in behind me, his breath labored. We reached the landing and walked down the hallway. Randall's room was empty, of course, and vast without him. I let Sterling go first and waited to see if he wanted me to stay or to leave him alone.

He clomped past, his bad leg worse, I am sure, with the anticipation. The leg was like a tic of some sort; you could read his mood in it. This I later came to learn, since Randall rarely spoke about his father, and the time before Randall's death had been spent in this house with Randall, only. Now I noticed things about his father. How Sterling leaned heavily on his right side, his left side hitching up a bit when he propelled the bad leg forward. How he swung the leg heavily in front of him, its hidden brace thumping down like an anchor he repeatedly lifted and dropped. How he wavered some now and then, as if the anchor had hit soft ground and would not hold, before reaching the window seat and sitting down, one big hand on each knee.

I stood at the door unsure. I could have shown Sterling some things: the rotted nail at the window in the far corner, how if you took it out the window hung at a pitch; the initials we had carved in the soft molding near one of Randall's closets, the braided rug he claimed his mother had made in one sitting, the secret drawers that ran along the window seat. But he didn't yet ask questions. He simply sat, his head bowed. He might have been weeping, or he might have been asleep. Impossible to tell from where I stood.

"Young lady," he finally said, and I must admit I startled; my mind had been elsewhere.

I walked over to him, wishing for a cigarette. In those days, at least, this is what you often wished for at difficult times, as if the difficult times could disappear in smoke, and when the cigarette was stubbed out, the problem would be solved. I was newly fifteen, believing myself closer to twenty. I'm sure I walked with an exaggerated steadiness. The truth is, I wanted to cry as soon as I set foot in that room.

Sterling patted the window cushion next to him and I sat down; we were side by side, him with his bad leg stretched straight out, his big hands still on his knees, me with my swing skirt and one of Rita's hand-me-down sweaters. I wore my hair pulled back straight and clipped, and socks stretched up to my knees. I'm sure I sat with my ankles crossed. This is what Mother had taught us, saying it took no money to have manners.

We stayed this way for some time and then Sterling cleared his throat.

"Tell me about him," he said.

"Sir?" I said.

"My son," he said.

I pulled my skirt over my knees.

"I don't know," I said. I cringe now to repeat it; he was a father asking about a son.

"He liked to read," I said.

"What kind of books?"

I shrugged. "All kinds."

"Did he ever mention the works of Edwards?"

"Sir?"

"I gave them to him once; I found Edwards useful when I was his age."

"I don't remember."

"I see."

"He told me about a lot of books. He may have mentioned them."

Sterling stood. "Well," he said. He began to walk, again, clumping around the room.

"He liked words, too," I said, as if I had suddenly remembered an obvious detail about him, suddenly remembered, for instance, that he had been a left-handed, champion swimmer, a hero in the state. "See?" I pointed to the words left to learn. They were still there, inscribed in grime. Sterling clumped over and peered at them.

"These?" he said.

I nodded. "Yes sir," I said.

He put his old hand toward them, and I thought, for an instant, that he might add a word of his own, something lawyerly and Latinate, like habeas corpus; instead he X-ed out each word as if a teacher marking misspellings. Then he turned from the window and clomped out of the room. I heard him on the narrow stairs, descending through the house, a pebble going down a drain, clanging here and there. I didn't know what to do and so I sat, listening to his descent.

We stayed that night at a rooming house in Sudlersville called the Dew Drop Inn. Betty and I shared a room, and Mother and Daddy were just down the hall. They went to sleep early, Mother saying she felt exhausted from Sterling. "He doesn't exactly make it easy for us," Mother said. "And I'd like to remind him that it was at his invitation that we came."

Daddy was typically quiet about the whole thing, though I could see that he marked this to time with his wife's family, and that he would eventually demand some kind of payback. It was that way with them. Give and take. I'm not sure, in the end, whether I'd call theirs a happy marriage, though quite truthfully I've seen so few of those I don't know if I'd recognize one. Mother ran the show and Daddy went along.

We ate in the Dew Drop Inn dining room, a depressing former living room with stained carpeting and a waitress who doubled as the receptionist. She had little patience with the four of us, and we were left to pour our own coffee and find our own butter rolls from the sideboard. "I didn't know what to say when he left so I just sat there."

"The poor thing," Betty said.

Mother looked at me and rolled her eyes.

"I didn't see you doing much today in the line of helping," she said.

Betty huffed. "I'm not feeling well," she said.

"Oh, you and your not feeling well," Mother said.

"Anyway," I said, louder. "I just sat there until I heard him get all the way downstairs and then I came down and he didn't as much as look at me the rest of the day."

"Well, he's mourning," Mother said.

"Exactly," Betty said.

"I suppose you might think of a few other things to tell him about Randall," she said. "Maybe something you read about in that diary of his."

I looked down at my plate as if I had never been so interested in Brussels sprouts. I'm sure my cheeks were aflame.

"You might let us in on a few things as well," Mother said.

I shook my head hard. I had only read a few entries, but each one I read was like another piece of him given to me and then taken away; I couldn't bear it.

"All right," Daddy said then. "I'm tired, Mother. Let's go to bed." He pulled back from the table and I heard the two of them leaving. I kept my face down, trying not to cry. Betty kicked me under the table and said I was a wimp.

The little white tag I had seen on the couch in the parlor now hung off of everything. Mother had waked early to meet Sterling; the sale would begin at ten o'clock. I walked through the old furniture dragged out to the front lawn, the bright morning light fading the upholstery even fainter, exaggerating nicks and scratches in the soft wood. Cardboard boxes filled with kitchen utensils and the detritus of the kitchen drawers were stacked beneath signs written in Mother's hand: "Yours for Free!" Stained tablecloths and linen napkins were pinned to a clothesline strung between two oaks, the stains like an outdoor Gallery of Maps. I hid among them for a while.

When we had pulled up, we had seen Sterling and Mother sitting on the faded wing chairs I recognized from Sterling's study, odd against the backdrop of the old brick house, their faces in and out of shadow as they watched us approach down the drive, Mother waving, Sterling's face especially stern. This must have been terribly difficult for him, though he had never liked the house among the farms and had wanted to return to Baltimore for a long time. Still, this was the home where he had lived with his wife and son. Now neither lived at all.

Of course, at the time I knew none of it. I believed him furious at me, a cousin, a friend, unable to offer him anything more of Randall than books, than unlearned words. And what could I give? Randall's hand in the dark? The look of his letters, propped on the salt and pepper shakers on the kitchen table, waiting for me to come home from school and discover like golden tickets? Randall's squeeze good bye? The smell of the boiled wet wool of his coat? The throng of boys crowding onto the train, Randall just one of hundreds of boys, their arms too thin and hands too big, their ears pink from the cold platform, where they had lingered for the last time with the people they loved? How Randall, his red hair orange against his red scarf, had waved from the train window in the way they do in the movies, though of course no one ran along the side, no one broke from the decorum of wishing men, boys, off to war. Nothing as uncivilized as pure grief, only stoicism. We had watched the train depart silently. Girlfriends waved. I know I smiled, wanting Randall to remember me pretty, knowing that smiling I looked pretty.

*   *   *

I stepped out of the car and went over to Mother and Sterling, threading my way through the end tables and floor lamps, the paintings propped against the legs of kitchen chairs, the fishermen's trunks and stacks of *Life* and *National Geographic*, the *Court Reporter,* old newspapers, piles of clothing. I noticed the rose-covered sofa a bit apart from the clutter, as if it felt embarrassed to mingle with the more ordinary items.

"That's reserved," Mother said, noticing my interest. Sterling nodded. I could barely look at him. "An old friend. Someone who thinks she's getting an antique." Mother laughed, though for what reason I didn't yet know; I imagined she was gay with the exhilaration of cleaning. She was this way, Mother. She loved spring trips to the dump, anything to be rid of a mess put her in a lively mood.

"Anyway," she said, heaving herself up. "I've got to get your father to help me move a few things down from the attic. Keep your uncle company, sweetheart." Then she left.

I sat next to Sterling in Mother's wing chair and waited, though Sterling didn't say a word. He had a dark blue shawl over his legs, and his old hands, resting on top of it, looked like two exhausted white animals that had crawled a great distance. I noticed how thin his legs were beneath the shawl, their twin outline descending out of my view, lost to its fringe. He wore his usual cardigan and another tie; he had dressed himself carefully. This might have been the first time he had met any of his neighbors.

They arrived slowly at first, turning into the drive in their dusty Fords; riding tractors, or bicycles. They were older men and younger boys, farm wives. They wore aprons or overalls, hats, some, and gloves, others. A few were dressed as if for church services, though this was Saturday. I believe as many came because they had always been curious about this brick house set back from the road as those who were looking for bargains. They wandered among the things, eyed pipe racks and raked through the piles of clothes, flicked the lamp switches on and off, though the lamps were, obviously, unplugged. Everything about them suspicious, they talked out of the sides of their mouths, whispered as if in a library. Mother ran among them. She had brewed coffee and from somewhere donuts were produced. She treated everyone like an invited guest. "My word!" she would say when some gray-haired woman held one of Jeannette's hats up to her head. "Isn't that becoming!"

Soon there were so many people that the things disappeared within them, carted off like crumbs at a picnic of ants. If you had been driving along that road on your way into Sudlersville, you might have thought that old Sterling had had a sudden change of heart, that he had invited the neighborhood to a garden party. The day had blossomed; the leaves caught the light and glowed. Children ran here and there, playing tag. Men and women, sharp and crisp against the day, carried wooden boxes filled with Randall's shirts and trousers, Jeannette's dresses, hoisting them onto their bicycles. Others shoved trunks, carpets, whatever would fit into their automobiles—their shirtsleeves rolled to their elbows, their underarms stained, suspenders straining—closing the doors the best they could. I remember one young boy, perhaps my age—too young for the war but almost, almost—riding with his sweetheart, a girl a bit younger with white-blond hair who balanced in the well of his handlebars; she held a desk lamp in her hands and laughed as he pedaled them away, swerving to miss the bumps in the drive. The look of the two surprised me. I guess I had begun to think of this as an old, faded place. They were too young for it, somehow. They might have been Randall and me.

By noon most everything was gone. Daddy had been in charge of the money and he carried the cigar box as if it were a collection plate in church. He seemed to be constantly counting, calculating, mumbling something or another to himself as he passed by on his way to make change. Betty had another one of her headaches and so Mother excused her. Who knows where Mother had gone to: here and there, offering cream to the last buyers, refusing to go lower on the tea set.

I sat with Sterling as Mother had instructed. He barely spoke, simply watched as the buyers haggled, occasionally answering a question put to him by Mother or Daddy, but mostly silent and, truth be told, not even watching the hagglers. I was the one watching the hagglers. Sterling looked off toward the empty distance, as if waiting for someone due to arrive hours ago. We had moved to the rose-covered sofa (the wing chairs had been sold literally out from underneath of us); Sterling, with his two long legs posted firmly on the ground, reminded me of Abe Lincoln, or the statue of Lincoln in the memorial, his hands carved marble, translucent stone: bony, veined, no doubt hands that held pens that wrote important words. Funny, now, to remember, since Randall's were so delicate; perhaps they were hands that would have grown to resemble his father's after all.

I don't know how much time passed before I realized that everyone had left, the boxes, and tables, and linens pinned to the line bought and carried off to other places, other homes, so that the two of us, side by side on the rose-covered sofa, were the only interruptions in an otherwise natural landscape. Crows looked down from the old oaks, cawing. In the far distance I thought I heard some music. I'm sure I tried to think of something to say, but I was shy, and conversation never came easily. He seemed not to notice—me, or the awkwardness of our postures. He continued to stare off toward the road, his legs, his hands, his entire expression steady. I picked at a stain on my jumper and patted my hair. I crossed and uncrossed my ankles. I noticed again that the roses had faded to the point where they might be mistaken for tulips or lilies or any kind of flower at all, or no flower, and thought of poor Jeannette, buried not far from here in a local graveyard. Randall had once taken me there, not to show me his mother's grave, but to show me all the funny names on the tombstones: Ichabod Applegate, the very Reverend Archibald Bottomspout, an entire clan of Higgensproofs. The tombstone he particularly liked belonged to Eliza Higgensproof, the matriarch, who no doubt would have rolled over several times had she been able to rise up and read her epitaph. *Here lies Eliza Higgensproof*, it read. *She done what she could.*

Jeannette's grave marked one of the far corners. Her tombstone tilted slightly, Randall explaining that she died during mud season, and though they could have waited for the ground to become more solid before burying her, neither he nor his father had the heart and so they had let the gravediggers put her into soft ground; each day, he said, when they went to visit her grave, she had sunk just a little. Later his father had asked the gravediggers to return, to even the mound. It felt in the end as if they had had to bury her twice. The gravediggers had done their job, though they had neglected to right the tombstone, and it stayed, tilted in the way of ancient tombstones, of the long dead.

She had no epitaph, I remember, simply her full name, Jeannette Olive Jewell, and the dates of her birth and death. Because the tombstone was so low to the ground, green lichen obscured much of it. Indeed, her grave seemed in great contrast to the rest of the place, particularly on the day Randall and I visited, several Easters back. Around us were pots of white lilies at the feet or the head of the dead, and here and there faded American flags stuck where the hands of the dead might have been. Jeannette's grave was like a tiny, verdant mountain, something lofty on a flat plain. I remember that Randall wore a navy peacoat, the kind popular at the time, and that he wrapped it tighter to him against the wind. The graveyard was just off a curve in the road, and every once in a while an automobile would skid by, taking the curve too fast, and we would both look up as if the automobile had news for us, an urgent message. The truth is, neither he nor I knew what to do or to say: a mother buried in ground, there, somewhere directly beneath our feet: what are we in the face of this? The bones of her, the skull, the relic of what she was before: a woman whose extravagance came in the form of sunlight, of too-loud laughter, of allowing her son to waddle naked in the garden against the urging of all of them—her housekeeper, her cook, her husband so much older than herself and still, she adored him, truly. I know this. She adored the hands of him, the bony knees, his habit of reading, of clearing his throat before articulating a difficult position. She loved that often she could clap her own hands and lift the gloom in him. Hang it out to dry. Flap it in the wind, begone! where it fluttered up like so many starlings to roost elsewhere.

Sterling stared out to the road. I thought of Randall at his mother's grave. How he had finally turned and shrugged, signaling for us to move on. "Alas, poor Yorick," he said, "I knew him well."

8

The automobile appeared out of nowhere, the kind you don't see anymore but one that was then considered quite grand: its running board and chrome bumper shined as if with spit. It caught the noon sun as it turned down the long drive—a flash of silver—then bumped along, a panic of dust in its wake. Sterling slowly stood, his two big hands pushed against the faded rose cushions for leverage, then balance. The automobile came to a sudden stop, everything quick about it. Someone who looked like a policeman scurried out of the driver's side and ran around to open the passenger's door. I had followed Sterling's lead and stood. Now I watched as a stout woman emerged from behind the trunk, shaking dust from her dress. Ruby, though at the time I had no idea. She looked out toward us, raising a hand to shade her eyes. I saw an older woman with blue-black hair and high color. Of course, if I had known this was Ruby I might have watched her differently; I might have stared. But to me she was simply a pretty stranger walking briskly toward us, her shading hand now extended.

"Sterling!" she said.

"Ruby," he said, his voice younger, or steadier. I'm sure I must have startled at the name.

Sterling limped forward to greet her and they embraced in the way of old movies, of past times, of days when people who had once loved waited years between encounters.

"This is Tom," she said, introducing the man in the uniform. "He drives for me. They won't let me behind the wheel. It's a tremendous conspiracy because I'm certainly fine but they say I'm wound too tight to stay on the road."

Ruby looked at me and then back at Sterling. "Oh," said Sterling. "This is Patricia's daughter. She was a great friend of Randall's."

"You knew Randall," she said. She held out her hand in a way that made me unsure whether to shake it, or to curtsy and kiss it; she was that kind of woman. "I'm his aunt. Ruby."

"Pleased to meet you," I said, opting to do neither but remaining like an idiot with my hands at my sides, amazed to be there in front of her. Ruby turned away and brushed past the two of us. Tom had disappeared back inside the automobile.

"Exactly the way I remember," she said, standing before the sofa, arms crossed like someone examining a particularly swaybacked mare. "A bit worse for wear but I think I can match the original material. There's that store on Seventh Avenue that specializes."

She turned back to us; we stood watching, transfixed by the storm of her, the efficiency. "Darling!" she said. "Do you remember when she found the set? You would have thought it was—" Here she broke off, as if suddenly remembering something. She sank to the sofa as Sterling limped over to sit beside her. "And Randall, too?" she said. Sterling nodded and took Ruby's hand to stroke. "Better Jeannie never lived to hear," she said. "It would have killed her. Torn her heart in two, baby," Ruby said, and I remember, even then, thinking how strange the word baby sounded. Not an endearment I would ever have heard between my parents, or between the parents of anyone I knew. It was urban. Exotic and smoky and entirely out of place across from cornfields. But then I already knew Ruby was other.

She had come from New York City, where she once worked as a hat designer. In fact, those were Ruby's creations I had seen Mother admiring on some of the younger farm women. She had quite a reputation in New York, her name frequently in the papers before the war when she would make a yearly trip across the Atlantic on the *Normandy* or the *Queen Mary*, there to see the latest fashions, to bring them back to New York City society. She had dated Harpo Marx, it was rumored, though she never married. When I met her she must have been in her late fifties. She wore rings on every finger, and a short strand of pearls she told me she had bought with her first paycheck, back when she was an apprentice in a milliner's shop. I didn't know what a milliner was and I pictured it as having something to do with a mill, poor Ruby standing in an apron grinding wheat into flour, refusing to remove her short strand of pearls.

She stayed for lunch. She didn't have much time. She had driven down from New York the night before and had spent the evening with friends in Wilmington at the DuPont, she said. She had to get back before the next day. She had come for the sofa, apparently having written to Uncle Sterling about this beforehand. Mother remained gracious, though there was a tinge of something, irony, I suppose—did she, too, know?—in the questions she posed to her, as if she understood that some of Ruby's answers were embellished for the sake of the girls, certainly for the sake of Betty, who hung on Ruby's words as if they were the very pearls from around her neck.

Ruby glowed with the attention. Her hair really was glorious, brushed to a sheen and pulled back in a French twist, and blue eyes the color of Randall's. She made a party of the lunch, gesturing for Tom to bring in from the car what she had brought from a delicatessen in Wilmington: sliced meats and deviled eggs and pastries we hadn't seen since before the war. She had suggested we have a picnic on the dining room floor, since not a stick of furniture remained, and even Sterling had gone along. We sat, legs crossed, a tablecloth spread out beneath us and the food piled in the center.

"When I heard the news that Sterling was going to sell this old house and all the furniture I had to come," she said, winking over at me. "I knew he wouldn't give a rat's ass about that sofa and it had been Jeannie's great love." Here she paused. "After Sterling, of course. And darling Randall."

She looked away quickly and bit into something. The silence, or the presence of the silence, weighed us down. It was oddly corporeal, as if at that moment darling Randall had entered the room and now sat on the windowsill watching.

"Remember his hair?" Ruby said, turning back to us, to Sterling, actually. He might have flinched; he might have steadily looked back at her. "The day he was born I thought the doctor would faint dead away. He said he had never seen such a full head. And not just the head! But down the back. I thought he would faint dead away."

Mother cleared her throat. "You were visiting?"

"Pardon me?" Ruby said.

"Were you visiting then?"

Ruby and I both looked to Sterling.

"Ruby had come to be with Jeannette," Sterling said.

"I see," Mother said.

"But what a beautiful boy he was," Ruby said, still looking at Sterling. I had already turned back to her, trying to detect a flush, or some sort of clue that I, alone, might understand. But there was nothing; she fingered her pearls and seemed to be thinking of other things.

*   *   *

Tom drove as quickly down the drive as he had approached, the sofa strapped to the roof with twine and leather belts. Ruby may have waved from the window, or it might have been the tree reflections on the brightly polished glass. The two of them disappeared eventually in a cloud of dust, Mother, Daddy, Betty, and I standing near the front door waving. The whole encounter had the feel of theater, with Ruby slashing the backdrop and stepping in, displacing the rest of us and then, too quickly, leaving the scene, stepping out, stitching up the slash to a point where it was almost perfect— the magician, the seamstress—so that indeed looking closely you might never see the narrow seam through the clouds, the oaks, the long dusty drive, the fields across the way where the young boys and older men who had earlier thronged the front yard now drove their horses, pulling plows that churned the ground black.

Daddy said it was close to the time we should head back to the Dew Drop Inn. It had been a long day. Mother wanted to stay a while with Sterling, though we did not see him—the dining room empty, cleared of the tablecloth, the picnic basket. Even the presence of the silence had left, as if Randall, with everyone gone, had walked out himself. Perhaps it was thinking this that made me realize where Sterling must have been. I snuck away and ran through the Gallery of Maps, up the short maid's ascent to the narrow staircase, turning sideways, groping in the dark but still hurrying and finally pushing through the swing door into the longer hallway that led to Randall's room. His door was closed but I paid no attention. I pulled it open and stepped in.

Sterling sat in a corner of the window seat, looking out. Perhaps he had watched Ruby's leaving from there.

"I thought of something," I said.

Sterling turned to me. His bad leg, propped on the window seat, looked endearingly casual, as if he had attempted to arrange it into a position suggesting leisure. "Come on," I said.

I didn't know whether Sterling would follow me or not, but I went. I heard his awkward clumping and tried to slow down, but I was filled with the dangerous excitement one feels right before telling a secret, when you know that the secret will amaze and astound the listener. I slipped down the narrow staircase, my breath quick, then waited at the entrance to the Gallery of Maps. He caught up, his own breathing labored. "This way," I said, trailing my finger across the continents. When we got to Africa I stopped and located the thin line Randall had first showed me. I pushed with some force until the door gave—warped somewhat by the late spring humidity—and flattened to the floor. "This way," I said. "You'll see."

He went along. In retrospect I understand how extraordinary it was, or perhaps how profoundly Ruby's visit must have affected him, for Sterling to follow so faithfully.

The air felt as dank, as wet, as it had the last time. I crawled ahead in darkness, tempering my breath, willing it to slow: every sound made giant, the darkness so entirely complete that it cut off your hands, blinded you. I think now of those fish I have read about that live in caves deep at the bottom of the ocean. What are they called? I can't remember. The point is the fish have gone invisible from that dark; are erased by it, their skin literally transparent.

This is how it felt in there: somehow possible to disappear entirely. I crawled toward the center of the dank little room, or what I believed to be the center, my eyes adjusting, and found the matches and candle. I lit the candle, though it seemed shorter than I remembered, as if Randall had returned to the slaves' hiding place before leaving for war and sat for a long time looking. Perhaps. I placed the candle back in its stand and scooted away to give Sterling a better view. The truth is the hiding place was minuscule, barely the size of a good closet. Sterling held the candle up to get a better look, and I leaned against one of the walls, my jumper sticky with perspiration and the humidity of the tiny space. Sterling seemed transformed by the room, no longer a person to make me afraid, simply a friend with whom I was sharing my secret.

"There were five of them," I said. "Ghosts. A mother and a father and three kids, I think. He said he'd see them not like ghosts you would imagine, the ones that rattle around, but like people who'd lived here all along. He said it was as if he were the ghost and the ghosts were the ones who belonged here. People who had always been here but ones he never paid much attention to before. Sometimes, he said, he'd walk into a room and they'd be there on chairs or standing together looking out the window and they'd turn to him and then right there, as he watched, they'd fade away like a photograph left in the sun too long."

The words spilled out, as if earlier, having lost my hands, my feet to the dark, I was nothing but words and hearing. Sterling looked back at me through the flame.

"He said they never made a sound and he didn't either, because they were about seeing, they were about being seen. I never knew what he meant by that, but I'm telling you exactly how he told me. He said the first time he saw them they were in the kitchen sitting around the big table and he thought, for a minute, that maybe your cook had some friends visiting. And then they faded. It was like a big picture book, he said. A big family album flipped from page to page. Every room he could remember where he had seen them and how they had been gathered. And he said he never learned their names but that was okay, because slaves' names weren't names at all just things they were called temporarily. Or called for no reason. Like emperors' names, Roman emperors: Cassias, Caesar. He said everything about them was temporary and wrong and borrowed from somewhere else, and that made them more slaves than being slaves made them slaves. Also being bought and sold, he said. Like it wasn't so much being *bought*, he said, it was the possibility of being *sold*.

He read about it. And each time he'd see them they'd be a little stronger, stay a little longer before they faded and he couldn't quite describe what they looked like but he said he *thought* the children were two boys and one girl and it was the girl he liked best because she was the one who sometimes smiled and she had two braids on either side of her face and she couldn't have been more than seven, eight years old and wore a dress and sometimes smiled, oh I told you, and anyway, he said he knew he would find their hiding place, because he knew from reading that this was where the underground railroad went and that probably this family came up from Virginia or Louisiana and wasn't it strange? That you could just go from here to there, from owned to free, from dead to alive, and he said one slave girl had walked all the way up from somewhere south and that she had escaped dogs and men with guns and other slaves who were sometimes cruel to those trying to escape and then she had reached somewhere north where she was free but she didn't believe it and said she would keep walking and she kept walking and she kept walking until she was in Canada and still she wouldn't believe it, that she was free, and she froze somewhere, still walking, and they wrote a song about her, something about how freedom is in the mind not the place and he said yes; he would have kept on walking, too."

I don't know how long I went on. I think for some time.

"He knew a lot," Sterling said when I finally paused. Wax dripped on his old fingers. "He was a wise boy," he said.

"Yes," I said.

"Did he ever speak to you of her?" Sterling said. "Jeannette?"

I rubbed my hands on the dank floor.

"A little," I lied.

"He adored her. Was her shadow. He would follow her everywhere, grab her skirt in great fistfuls if she attempted to leave him." Now I looked at Sterling through the candle flame, his shadow large behind him. From time to time his eyes watered, not with tears but with age, and he would bring up one paw of a hand to wipe them. It struck me how Sterling seemed to be disappearing as surely as that family—the mother and father with their worried expressions (this is how I pictured them), the little girl smiling, her dress torn from the dogs, brambles, and the two boys, their hair cropped short, their dark eyes serious, jostling some for space, twins in need of separate attention.

"I meant to tell him before he left. I owed it to him, knowing what he was about to do. But I couldn't find the courage. What idiocy," he said, and I, stupidly, nodded.

Sterling cleared his throat. "Ruby and I met in New York. I was lecturing at Columbia. Ruby was friendly with someone from one of my classes. She never had any intention of marrying. I tried to convince her. I told her we could stay in New York. She could work. But she insisted this was impossible."

From somewhere I thought I heard the sound of dripping water.

"Jeannette offered to raise the child. She was more that way. Younger by some years. She had aspirations to enter the nursing profession, though they were vague aspirations. Not like Ruby's. Ruby knew what she wanted from the beginning. Fame. Or her version of it."

I wanted to be in the attic with Betty, feet up, smoking cigarettes and staring at Frank Sinatra pinned in black-and-white just above the headboard. In retrospect, I realize I might have helped Sterling with his story, asked him questions or at least commented. From time to time he would pause. But in truth I don't think he expected anything of me; in truth I believe he forgot my presence all together. He hardly knew me, of course; he spoke to Randall.

"Ruby thought it best. She took a leave of absence from her job at the milliner's and returned to Virginia. I'm sure everyone suspected but in those days you never asked. I wrote to her from time to time and her return letters were cheerful. They were knitting a lopsided blanket, that type of thing. I prepared my lectures. I researched my Edwards biography at the New York Public Library

on the weekends, and I suppose you could say I tried to put everything out of my mind. I'm not saying I'm proud of it, just that I'm
not sure what I anticipated about the future. The present seemed
complicated enough. Randall was born just before the end of my
semester, and I asked one of the graduate students to proctor my
exams and took the train there. I had never met Jeannette, but
somewhere along the journey I decided that I would propose marriage. According to Ruby, Jeannette was a straightforward, clear-
thinking girl. A good mother. And she was. A wonderful mother."

He cleared his throat.

"She was a caring wife, and I appreciated her loyalty, to me, to
Randall. If at times I looked at her and wished for Ruby, there were
days, in the first years certainly, when Ruby was entirely forgotten
and we were a real family. She wanted very much to leave Baltimore. The sisters had grown up in Virginia, in the country, and she
wanted to live among farms. For the boy. And so I obliged her, as she
had obliged me, and when she found this monstrous house and fell
in love with it, I agreed. I believe only then did I begin to regret my
decisions. I concentrated on my book and spent less time with the
two of them. I continued my research, kept a room in Baltimore for
the weekday evenings and returned home only on the weekends.
More and more, I suppose, I resented the direction my life had
taken. When Jeannette became ill, I hired nurses to care for her, and
for Randall, and stayed in Baltimore, wishing them away. I suppose
I believed her stronger than she was, more willful. She died so
quickly. I wasn't even by her side."

Sterling's breathing was labored; his words seemed to drift out
of him and rise to the ceiling, pop. He was telling me what he
believed I did not understand: that in fact I had just this day met
Randall's true mother and that Randall had never known. But of
course I knew different. Randall and I would often read the letters
that Randall had found in his father's study: the few Ruby had sent
from Virginia during what she called her unexpected sabbatical, and

the one she mailed from Paris months earlier. Randall had included that letter in his package to me, folding it so neatly inside *The Gardens of Kyoto* that it was days before I discovered it—its lines perfect, as if they'd been traced with a ruler; the embossed crest of the Parisian hotel above the date. That letter he stole from his father's locked tobacco box, I knew; *The Gardens of Kyoto* Ruby had sent to him on his thirteenth birthday, enclosed with a card. Dear son, it read, you have reached the age of truth.

The line he knew by heart, the rest of the note unimportant, he said. She had begged him never to tell Sterling, saying it would kill him; she had sent the book because it was partially addressed to him, because the illustrations were beautiful, because it had been given to her by a man she had met on a passage to Paris when she felt entirely lonely.

Randall burned the card almost as soon as it arrived; he kept the book, he told me, because it would have been a sin to burn that, too.

But should I tell Sterling? Should I reveal that yes, Randall knew, had known for some time? This is what kept me distracted. Should I divulge Randall's secret, as Sterling, now, divulged his own to me?

"I imagine I resented the boy somewhat. I blamed him, after Jeannette's death, for keeping me from Ruby. This was not intentional, but I believe it is how I felt. And I wish I could talk to him about it."

Perhaps it was then that I noticed; perhaps it was later, just before Sterling snuffed the candle and we crawled out, single file. The point is I saw, as I'm sure Randall intended me to see, on the wall where Randall had written the date of his birth how he had returned to scrawl the year of his death, 1945. I don't know what guided Randall to write in those four numbers, unyielding, heavy, random as any of the other numbers on the walls and yet somehow not. He had known. He had deemed it so, somehow, and it puzzled me then as it puzzles me now: what he was thinking; what he intended with this to show me.

· *Book Two* ·

1

I met your father on a cold fall day in late October, at a football game I had been invited to by another boy, Charles, who I knew while at college and liked well enough, in the way girls liked boys well enough to go to football games or dances or to Philadelphia for dinner. In those days you dated boys who were nice, or handsome. When they picked you up, they walked to the door and knocked; they came inside to meet the housemother and your best friends, if your best friends were downstairs waiting to see them. They chewed gum and offered you a stick; they had shined their shoes and wore pressed, crisp shirts and ties.

Charles was exactly that: another nice boy. He had just graduated from Annapolis and wore the standard ensign uniform: a deep navy blue, with thin lapels, and well-shined buttons, and a hat, of course. I can't remember why he had entered the Navy. We probably didn't talk about it. You didn't talk about careers then in the way you do now: you simply tried to have fun. The war was over; the boys were home.

He took me to the Army-Navy football game. I understand now

this must have meant a lot to him. He brought me a mum with blue and gold ribbons and slipped his arm through my coat to escort me down the campus walk. I wore heels, no doubt, and white gloves. I'm sure I had bothered with a hat and a hat pin, and had a scarf tucked around my neck. This was 1951. Girls were neat.

His friend was due to pick us up on the corner and we stood, a bit awkward in the cold. Charles had a flask of something tucked inside his Navy coat and he offered me a sip. I shook my head, though I wouldn't have minded. Girls I knew passed by and stopped to chat; Charles continued to sip from his flask, and by the time his friend arrived his face, including his ears, exaggerated by the thin strap of his hat and the regulation crewcut, were bright red with drink and frost and perhaps the anticipation of the game.

I had been to a few football games with other boys, though I was not aware of the importance of this particular rivalry. We piled into the car, Charles in front with his friend, me in back with the friend's date. She was a girl from Bryn Mawr who immediately told me she couldn't believe she had taken the afternoon off for this, that she had a Russian history paper due Monday morning and that her advisor, a professor such and such whose name I believe she expected me to recognize, had nominated her for the department prize and that if the paper were no good she hadn't a chance in hell to win it, and she had been working all semester, hell, she said, she had been working all year, all her goddamn life, to win the goddamn award because how was she going to afford graduate school without a fellowship and how would she get a fellowship without some kind of honors?

I had no answer to that. I can see me now, vacant and shrugging.

"Anyway," she said, turning away from me, back to the window, "I told him yes. Bill, I mean." She thumbed in Bill's direction. "So what can I do?"

Bill seemed friendly enough, a likely counterpart to Charles, who I saw now had more of a wild streak than I had anticipated. I began to feel a bit uncomfortable in the backseat with Bill's disgruntled date; Charles now drinking from Bill's flask as well as his own. The familiar drive along the Main Line seemed precarious in a way that mocked my earlier anticipation. I had been eager to see the changing leaves, to perhaps stop somewhere for cider. I even thought of suggesting it. Now I said nothing, my gloved hands in my lap.

"So, you're a liberal arts major, right? What's the name of that school again?"

"Saint Mary's," I said.

"I've heard of it. Small, right? Specializing in the men of the surrounding area. Finding them, I mean. Husband hunting."

She laughed, her teeth large and slightly yellow. She was not a particularly attractive girl, though she did have beautiful eyes, grayish, that seemed oddly horrified by the words coming out of her mouth. I understand now she couldn't help it; in those days to be a girl interested in Russian history was not an easy thing to be at all.

"English literature," I said.

"What?"

"English literature. That's my major."

"Oh," she said. She turned and stared at me. "And what are you going to do with that?"

"Perfect the art of dramatic presentation," I said, mostly to myself, though I believe I might have won her over then. Or maybe she just got tired. She slunk back in the seat and pulled her wool coat over her legs. The boys in the front seat seemed to have entirely forgotten us, and we both turned and looked out our windows. In truth, the changing leaves were beautiful. We were driving through older neighborhoods, the houses paint bare, porches sagging. Men were out raking leaves, women, God knows where. A few yards had harvest displays, pumpkins and dried corn stalks. The day seemed newly washed; our spirits should have been lifted.

"How did we find our way here?" she said, turning back to me.

"What do you mean?"

"These morons. Some goddamn football game. I should be in the library, or in bed for God's sake." She looked at me.

"What's your name?" I asked, because in truth I had not paid attention.

"Daphne," she said. "Like the laurel tree." And of course I had no idea.

Daphne and I became great friends. I'm not sure how this happened, except for the fact that the game was a disaster and we had no one else to talk to. By the time we reached the stadium parking lot both Bill and Charles were drunk. They weaved their way through the tailgating parties until they found their friends, all recent graduates of Annapolis. The men were singing Navy songs, girls like extra scarves around their necks. Daphne and I sat on two coolers and smoked cigarettes one after the other. She told me that she actually believed her Russian history professor was in love with her, which was perfectly wonderful since she was in love with him.

"Madly," she said.

Of course he had a young wife and a couple of children and it was doomed. "Doomed," she said. "Bill is my attempt at getting out in the world."

"I'm sorry," I said.

She looked at me, her gray eyes darkening against the clear afternoon.

"Have you ever been in love?" she said, in a way that sounds silly, now, but then seemed like the kind of question that only a girl studying Russian history at Bryn Mawr could come up with, a girl with gray eyes and big teeth and a way of constantly pulling her coat more tightly around her knees.

"Once," I said. "Maybe."

"Maybe?" she said. "Then you haven't, of course. The thing about love is that there is no maybe. If you have to say maybe you have no idea what I'm talking about. No idea whatsoever. I mean, there's no maybe with Professor Taylor. Gideon. That's his name, for Christ's sake. Gideon. I mean, even his name is perfect. And there's nothing he doesn't know, and he wears this sweater. I mean this sweater somebody must have made for him or something. His wife, for Christ's sake. Maybe she knitted it when she was goddamn pregnant or before they got married or something. Anyway, this sweater is brown with these big green diamonds all over it. I mean, it is the ugliest sweater you've ever seen. Terrible. And it fits him all wrong. One sleeve is shorter than the other and the neck is too big and I think it's even unraveling somewhere and he wears it. I mean, the point is, he wears it, do you know what I mean?"

I nodded, because I did.

"And he doesn't just wear it sometimes, he wears it a lot."

Daphne stubbed her cigarette out in the trampled grass and looked across the field. "I wish to God he'd stop wearing that sweater," she said. "Maybe I wouldn't love him so goddamn much if he dressed like all the other bastards."

People were beginning to gather their things for the game. I wondered whether Daphne would even agree to go in. I wanted to stay out here with her, to hear more about, I don't know, the sweater, but I felt I owed it to Charles. I was his date, after all, though he was in the middle of some kind of wrestling match with the other ensigns, entirely oblivious to my absence. But when the announcer started listing the opening lineup, everyone snapped back to life and Charles and Bill stood and walked toward us, their coats open, their blue uniforms muddied.

"Giddyup," Charles said, and we stood.

*　*　*

I believe it was halftime, or maybe just a quarter break. Daphne and I had sat with the midshipmen's dates in the stands. In those days, the midshipmen's dates sat together with other invited guests, and the midshipmen stood, some distance away, singing and shouting and, from time to time, linking arms, swaying left to right, throwing their hats in the air, hoisting one another onto their shoulders. Charles and Bill had left us soon after we entered the stadium. We would look over at them from time to time, as if to watch the behavior of a particularly exotic pack of animals. Here were the things that boys cared about: allegiance, patriotism, alma mater. I barely knew Charles, so I'm not quite sure whether this was the real Charles, or a Charles that Charles believed he had to be in the presence of all the other men in uniform. They were a sea of blue, directly opposite the sea of gray, the West Point cadets. Some girls appeared to understand all this, and many of them stood to be like the boys, pretending they could follow along with the songs.

The stadium was vast, truly cavernous, the sound of the singing and the cheering deafening. We were on the west side and the sun, low, suddenly struck us in shadow. A few of the other guests had the regulation blue wool Navy blankets and we huddled beneath them. Daphne smacked her hands together, blew on her fingers. When she suggested we duck out, I'm not sure where we were in the game, only that Navy was behind. The throng of midshipmen screamed at the players, their faces angry, flushed not as before, the tailgate pink, but a new, crimson purple. Sonofabitch, they shouted—we could hear them even from where we were—or, goddamn Kolowski. Goddamn Polish sonofabitch can't carry a ball to save his goddamn grandmother.

We slipped out, taking the cement steps in a hurry, as if at any minute the entire stadium might collapse under the weight of all that shouting, the roar, the sheer volume. I remember breathing a deep breath once outside; then Daphne and I decided to walk around the stadium to get the last of the weak sunlight on the other side, the

Army side. The thick stadium walls muted the sound of the crowd, though every once in a while we would hear the swelling, the roar.

"I think goddamn Kolowski must have done something right," Daphne said.

"Either that or they're tearing him from limb to limb."

"Putting his head on the goalpost and parading it through the streets."

"Declaring themselves kings."

"That's the thing about goddamn kings," Daphne said.

"What?"

"They're always just regular players who declare themselves kings."

"Absolutely," I said, not understanding.

"I'm a Communist, actually," Daphne said.

I slowed down.

"I know what you're thinking, but it's not like that. They don't eat their babies or anything. I'm just sick of the working people never getting to declare themselves kings. The goddamn Kolowskis of the world."

I listened.

"Gideon says, because he has told us to call him Gideon, not Professor Taylor or any other honorific, just Gideon. Anyway, Gideon says the distribution of wealth will make it evolutionary. Communism. Like Darwinism. He says it's just a matter of time. Like erosion."

I nodded. "I don't know much about it."

"No," Daphne said. "I suppose you wouldn't."

I felt wounded by this, even though it was clearly the truth, and suggested we stop walking and sit on one of the benches along the perimeter of the stadium. I wanted a cigarette, I said. My hands were goddamn ice cubes.

We sat and Daphne pulled her wool coat over her legs and I slipped off a glove and lit a match, Daphne cupping her hands around it to press her cigarette into the flame. There was little sun now, the day blustery; programs and trash blew here and there. The crowd's distant roar seemed to cycle upward, toward the treetops and the maples whose leaves were mostly on the ground, dried brown, though one or two still held stubbornly to each limb. I'm not sure how long we sat there before your father walked up, or from which direction he came, or how he managed to so completely surprise both of us. It was simply like this: one minute we were alone on the bench smoking; the next minute your father stood in front of us in his Army officer's uniform: pinks-and-greens, they were called. Quite striking, really: mauve trousers, a khaki shirt, and a dark green jacket with a cap to match. His hands were clasped in front of him as if for inspection, a curious look on his face.

"Two beautiful women who would prefer to sit alone when the greatest match in history takes place directly behind you?"

"We're sick of matches," Daphne said. "And history." She blew her smoke out. "Anyway," she said. "Aren't you the enemy?"

"I don't know," he said. "Whose side are you on?"

"The good guys," she said.

"Then you're absolutely right. You should avoid me at all costs. In fact, you shouldn't be speaking to me at all." He looked around. "You never know who's watching. There could be spies in the trees."

Your father smiled then, and introduced himself; I remember how impressed I was that he had a lieutenant before his name.

Daphne blew her smoke out. "Weren't you too young for that war?"

"Which war?"

"You know, the one we fought to end all wars. No, sorry, that was the war before."

"The one to make the world safe for democracy?"

"Was that it?"

Your father shrugged. He held out his fingers and scissored the air. "Aren't either of you going to offer me a cigarette?"

Daphne narrowed her eyes. "What's it worth?"

Your father sat down between us. He looked at me hard, then turned to Daphne. I'm not sure what he said then, but I know she laughed. I realized, in fact, that it had been the first time I had heard her laugh, a laugh that was entirely wrong for her, girlish and sweet, not the laugh of a Communist.

There was something about the ease of them; I felt immediately jealous, in a way that must have been an indication of how I felt about your father. They say this does happen, though you'll probably find it amusing; the truth is I fell in love with your father at first sight. I know that's an old-fashioned thing to say and saying it, now, makes me particularly sad.

"Daphne was just saying how she's a Communist," I said, trying to get his attention. Your father nodded.

"I wouldn't expect her to be anything else," he said, and I knew, quite suddenly, that he felt as I did, but for Daphne, not me.

I'm not sure how either of us made it safely home. Charles and Bill were furious about our absence, claimed to have been worried sick, though I'm sure they barely noticed. Navy lost, needless to say, and they sulked their way back to where we had agreed to meet them afterward, a restaurant called the Comfy Couch. Your father had left us some time before, saying he knew better than to be caught outside the stadium when the Navy boys unloaded. He made a gesture I will never forget, tipping his green cap to both of us, clicking his heels like he might just vanish into thin air instead of turning around and heading back toward the stadium. We walked to the Comfy Couch in silence and found a booth inside.

"He was nice," I finally said.

"*Nice?*" Daphne said. "See, this is what you don't understand. He wasn't nice at all. Charming, yes. Debonair, yes. But nice? No.

Not nice. Army. Entirely Army. I know these types. They spend their day shooting at targets and then read Machiavelli before lights out."

She looked around the room: it was the kind of place where people write their names on the walls or carve their initials into the tabletops; it smelled like stale beer and cigarette smoke. A few other girls waited near the door for their dates and a table of men in midshipmen uniform sat morosely drinking beer.

"What are we doing here?"

"Waiting for our ride," I said.

She waved down one of the waitresses and ordered coffee; then she lit another cigarette and leaned back against the grimy wall. Above her, the graduating Annapolis class of '49 smiled out in black-and-white; someone had put some money in the jukebox, and a song Rita used to love began. I put Rita out of my mind and concentrated on your father, his thick eyebrows and the way, when he stood, he cocked his head to one side, listening even when there was only silence. He had something quiet about him, something wise. He was older than the boys I was used to; we had learned that he was a lieutenant in the reserves, that he hadn't been to any wars to speak of, that he had graduated from West Point some years back and gone to graduate school, actually, Yale Divinity, though it looked like, with the situation in Korea, he might be asked to go to war soon. In fact, he had said, it looked like he might be asked to go very soon, possibly within the month, and that it would do his heart good to have someone to *correspond* with. He said the word correspond as if it were somehow inherently funny, and I remember that Daphne laughed, understanding, and that I didn't, imagining, instead, our correspondence and, our reunion, our embrace, because I had already begun to imagine your father as someone I might embrace in the way of Ruby and Sterling.

He held out a worn leather address book and asked us each to write down our names and addresses on one of the blank pieces of paper inside. "Corresponding with the enemy," Daphne had said, writing. "Could be dangerous."

"I hope nothing less," he said, smiling, tilting his head some. Daphne passed the book to me and though I knew that he preferred her I wrote my name down anyway, and the address of my dormitory on campus. For some reason still unclear to me I also added my major, English literature, as if he would appreciate this far more than Russian history. He stared at our addresses for a moment and then shut the book, sticking it into his back pocket. Then he gestured as I've described and turned and walked away. When I looked back to Daphne to see what she'd say next, she seemed to have forgotten my presence, as if your father and I had left together. She was looking off into the distance, away from the stadium, blowing on her cold hands. Her eyes, that gray, even darker, were in tandem now with a sky that had lost almost all its color; it looked like snow.

"My mother was a Ziegfeld girl," she finally said, then she turned to me. "She went nuts when I was born. Absolutely goddamn nuts. My father didn't know what to make of her and so they, you know, committed her to memory, so to speak. I don't even know if she knows where I am. Right now, for instance, she doesn't even know where I goddamn am."

I touched her shoulder; it seemed like the right thing to do.

"I bet she does," I said stupidly. "I bet she knows."

Bill and Charles eventually met us at the Comfy Couch and we ordered hamburgers and more coffee before getting on the road. We were all quiet on the drive back, the dark outside reflected inside. We dropped Daphne off at Bryn Mawr and Bill insisted on walking her to her room, though she claimed she could go alone and would prefer. As she got out of the car she told me she would give me a call in a few days and maybe the two of us could have lunch. Saint Mary's wasn't too far away and there was a trolley at the time. I smiled and said I had enjoyed meeting her; it was a natural reflex for me, politeness, and she rolled her eyes and told me we were friends, weren't we? And I said, yes, we were.

Charles walked me to my dormitory and I let him kiss me good night because it seemed too much trouble not to. I was thinking of your father, wondering when he might first write. I suppose I thought of Randall, too; it made perfect sense. In some ways, I saw Randall in the character of your father, in his stance, the way he listened. I don't know. I waited months for that first letter and it never came, of course. I forgot about him. I forgot about Daphne, whom I assumed had gotten involved with her Russian history prize, and the professor, and everything else in her life that would take priority over a friendship with me. I had plenty to do. This was my senior year. I had to study hard to keep my scholarship and I was on several committees, what else?

But one day, many months after the game, I walked back to my dormitory, one of several stone houses that had been donated to the college, to find Daphne in the living room, sitting on one of the floral couches as awkwardly as a child. It was already spring, brilliant the way springs were in Philadelphia. The forsythia had passed their prime, but the dogwoods and the lilac were in bloom and the windows were open in the living room and I could hear, in the distance, the sounds of other girls at their sports. Daphne looked odd inside on such a beautiful day, sitting in a ball reading as if it were raining and bleak. She wore a plaid skirt of some sort, and a loose sweater with big green diamonds.

"It's me," she said.

"Hi," I said. I put down my books on the secretary and went in. "Hi," I said again. I was glad to see her.

She looked down. "Recognize it?" she said, stretching her sweater out.

"No," I said.

She looked up toward the composite photograph that hung in the hallway showing all the girls who lived in the house.

"Why does everyone look exactly the same?" she said.

I shrugged.

She looked back at me. "It's his. Gideon's."

I had to search my mind to remember, and then I did.

"Your advisor," I said.

"My *lover*," she said, and I must tell you my heart raced with the word. It was spring, after all, and this was something out of Colette or Flaubert. Daphne stood and flounced across the room, plopping down on the piano seat.

"Don't act so goddamned shocked. It does happen, you know. All right, so he's married. But he's leaving his wife." She looked across at me. "Maybe."

I sat next to her on the piano bench; the other girls of the house were elsewhere, sports, as I have said, or studying at the library or meeting with one of the endless clubs we were encouraged to join. I don't know how it had happened, exactly, me going along with the activities they promoted for us. There were rules to follow and expectations, though most of the girls would be engaged by the time they graduated; if you weren't at least pinned your education had failed, or at least this is what we were led to believe. A few made it quite clear they had no intention of marrying. Most of them had old lady aunts who were role models, women who had gone to one of the Seven Sisters and then on to graduate work in New York City or Boston. These women would come to visit from time to time, no doubt to buoy the spirits of their young nieces, whose spirits, to judge from their appearances, were in need of buoying: they were odd ducks, all told, girls who stayed in on Friday and Saturday nights, who had permanent library carrels decorated with optimistic quotations—missives on the rights of women from, say, Eleanor Roosevelt or Carrie Chapman Catt.

The maiden aunts appeared on certain Sundays, and the girls would invite some of us to join them for brunch. The aunts had names like Elizabeth, or Judith—full, beautiful names that evoked worlds we would never step into, worlds we had collectively denounced as too terrifying to even consider. We had made our choices and we twisted the pins on our lapels, or wrote the names of our boyfriends over and over again on the restaurant napkins, as if the boys were talismans against the threat these women posed: to live alone in a big city, to step onto the sidewalk in heels and smart coats, hands up hailing taxis, ring fingers conspicuously bare.

Daphne played some scales, the long sweater sleeves she had rolled to her wrist slipping over her fingers.

"I'm sorry," I said.

She stopped playing and looked up at me, her gray eyes clear; it was that time of day when the lights should be turned on inside but are not, as if in refusal to acknowledge the coming night. It was also getting cold, the weak spring sun long since obstructed by the thick stone walls of the neighboring house. Our living room faced a stone wall where ivy grew over the mortar lines. I would often try to study in this room, my mind distracted, looking instead out the lead-paned windows at the stone walls, the branching veins of ivy.

"For what?" she said. "I'm perfectly fine. I'm exactly fine. He gave me his goddamn sweater because I told him how it made me cry in class and he said he didn't want me to be so obvious. So obvious, he said, like he thought I would just run down to the podium and throw my arms around him and weep. He didn't understand it at all, why it made me cry. He thought I meant something entirely stupid. Something so, I don't know, girly." She pushed back the sweater sleeves and folded her arms. In the dining room, a clock ticked loudly.

"We meet at a goddamn motel called the Enchanted Forest, if you can believe it. It's one of those one-story ones where you can park and go in and avoid the receptionist all together, not that she would notice. The kind with dirty screens so you don't even want to touch the windows, and sheets that prickle and the whole thing smells like mold because the enchanted forest is just a few goddamn pine trees that block all the sun. The place is always dark and so goddamn gloomy before, during, and after we make love I want to cry, even though it's *him*, for Christ's sake, Gideon."

She drew her hands up to her face.

"What am I going to do?" she asked from behind them, and then she sniffled and wiped one of those long, woolly sleeves across her nose, looking at me like I might know the answer and of course I didn't. I had no idea what she should do. None of the girls I knew would make love in a place called the Enchanted Forest; none of the girls I knew would make love at all.

She shook her head. "Look at you," she said. "Look at this place." She stood and walked around the living room, turning on table lamps, fluffing pillows. "And I thought the motel was gloomy." She laughed, and I did, too. She had her back to me and turned around suddenly. "You know, I didn't come here to tell you all that. I'm sorry. I didn't, really. I'll be fine. Gideon will pass me with flying colors, give me the history prize, and I've already got my admission to Radcliffe, anyway, and he'll go back to his perky goddamn wife and that will be that."

She smiled; she really did have a beautiful smile. "We'll all be fine," she said, in a way that should have made me wonder, but did not.

"Look," she said then, pulling something out of her skirt pocket and walking back over to me. "It's from him."

"Who?" I said, because I saw now she had a letter of some sort.

"The enemy. Remember?"

She unfolded a sheath of paper and passed it over to me. The letter was dated February 1952, Kumwah, Korea. My dear Daphne, it began, and my heart, immediately, floundered. I passed it back to her without reading further.

"It's to you," I said.

"Oh, don't be such a nincompoop," she said. "I'm sure he has no idea which one of us is which. He just picked some name and wrote. He's probably picturing Debbie Reynolds."

She pushed the letter back at me and I continued reading.

They've got us digging trenches and when we're finished we get to live in them. Not exactly great compensation. The rations are pretty bad, and after two months here I dream of tomatoes. Yesterday I saw someone leading a cow toward the colonel's barracks and decided that the time had come to introduce myself and to practice my Korean. Most of the other boys are Ethiopians. The Ethiopians are the best fighters and so that's fine with me, but they tend to keep quiet and so I've taken to reciting the last World Series plays, inning by inning.

Anyway, I introduced myself to the colonel and he must have been pretty lonesome too because he invited me to dinner. This was the first time I had had fresh meat in months and I should have been delighted but the funny thing was all I could think of was tomatoes.

I remember our meeting at the Game and you and your friend were prettier than all the other cadets' girls combined. You may write to me at the address below and that would be better than tomatoes. God Bless America.

Your friend,—

I folded the letter and gave it back to Daphne.

"You like him," she said, stuffing it into the envelope. I wanted to ask her if I might look at the postmark and the stamp, if I might study the way he had addressed her name, but I did not.

I shrugged.

"I hardly remember," I said.

She looked at me and put the envelope in front of us on the music stand.

"You be me," she said.

"What do you mean?"

"Write him back. Sign it 'Daphne.' He doesn't know the goddamn difference. He wants a pen pal, that's all. He doesn't remember me from you from a hole in the wall. I don't have time. I've got to study for my orals and figure out a way to get out of the enchanted forest." She smiled. "You know what I mean?" she said.

"I suppose so," I said.

"Anyway," she said, "you're the English literature major. I'm the Communist, for Christ's sake. I can't write a Communist killer. It's against my higher principles." At this she stood. "I've got to get back before dinner. I took the goddamn trolley and you know what that's like." I didn't, actually; I never left campus except in a boy's car, and then rarely. Mostly I stayed in the dormitory, or the library. Vacations I took the train back to Mother and Daddy's house, though lately I had been avoiding even that, explaining to them as best I could how my exams required too much library research, how it would be better if I stayed at Saint Mary's through the holidays. Since Rita's death and Betty's departure, I couldn't bear the hungry way they looked at me, as if they each wanted to take a spoon and swallow me whole.

2

I have always pictured our Professor X—Randall's and mine, and Ruby's, I suppose—as a small man, bookish in the extreme, with an owl's face and an urgent, hurried manner: a horticulturist employed at a midwestern university where a wealthy alumnus endowed a greenhouse on the roof of the university's tallest brick building, poorly maintained until the professor's arrival. The professor saw to it that the glass was newly caulked, and the greenhouse became a tropical alcove in the middle of a blizzard. There were times when three, four feet of snow lay on the ground and high above, over all of it, Professor X's students walked about in their shirtsleeves, spritzing orchids with shiny copper watering cans, sponging palm fronds. He followed them, nervously cataloging, sketching. The students didn't mind; they generally adored him in the way you might adore an eccentric uncle, one who shows up on your doorstep from year to year carrying gifts he's gathered from his travels abroad.

Near-deaf from time spent in the trenches in France, Professor X survived the First World War, he would tell his students, by concentrating on the flora of northern France, sketching the shapes of leaves and the strange wildflowers that were so unfamiliar to him, a boy from Boston, that at first he felt like he had been dropped onto a separate planet. His hands shook, he said, from the shelling, but this had helped him find the line, since he knew about as much about drawing as he did about the flora of northern France.

In no time, he said—and here is where the students drew close, because they knew these stories, had heard them all before, Professor X's deafness somehow affecting more than his ears. It was as if he lived in a world entirely without memory, so that every time he told his story it was as if for the first time, the words disappearing once spoken into air.

His students loved him anyway; they drew close because here was the best part of the story, the hardest part, and it frequently brought tears to Professor X's eyes.

In no time, he repeated, the other soldiers, the good men, started calling him Leonardo, after da Vinci; it was mild teasing, nothing cruel, he said; they liked me well enough, as well as they liked anyone.

Here Professor X might straighten his glasses a bit, for emphasis; he might pull the handkerchief from his breast pocket and wipe his forehead. He insisted on wearing a suit jacket in the greenhouse, though the students were more often clothed for the beach—you can imagine the temperature, not simply from the sun, but from the reflection from the snow. Professor X maintained his formality, though after hearing his story, a well-meaning student might take to calling him Professor Leonardo; this quickly abated once the student observed the panic in the professor's eyes, his entire manner hobbled by such hubris.

Professor X kept a firm grip on his handkerchief and continued. Paper was scarce, so he would draw on anything he could, anything any of the other soldiers gave him. These good men took it upon themselves to help me, he said, to find me scraps so I could continue. Here he looked up at the throat of a particularly lurid orchid that hung from the metal transom supporting the glass. We were short everything—food, medical supplies, ammunition. I think they wanted us to fight the Germans with our teeth. We would have. Anything for honor.

In time the good men started bringing me the letters, he said. Letters taken from the corpses. They wouldn't bring me the clean ones, no; those they would send on. It was the decent thing to do. But the bloodied ones, he said. Those they passed along to me.

At this point the greenhouse went terribly quiet and it seemed as if even the drip, drip, drip of moisture dropping from the glass roof paused to let the professor finish his story. The students knew about corpses; they knew about Germans and war. Many had brothers, cousins, who were there now. But the men they knew who had returned—even their fellow students, the soldiers who came to classes on the GI Bill and sat in the back, their stubble beards and dirty fingernails a testament to the quonset huts erected for their living quarters—kept to themselves; they never spoke about bloody letters.

Some of the boys would tear off the blood-stained edges, he said. But others wouldn't. They'd toss the letters at me. Here you go, Leonardo, they'd say. For your collection.

Professor X wiped his eyes. A few students, the newer ones, looked away; he was their professor, after all.

I used all the paper. I felt it was the right thing to do. I never read the letters, though. Ever. I just drew a big X through the writing so I wouldn't be tempted, and then, on whatever blank space I could find, I documented my flora, keeping records of where and when I had first observed it.

Mind you, he always added, these were terrible, terrible days.

It was around this time he would straighten up and clap his hands, as if to bring himself, the plants, indeed the entire landscape, out of a trance. Back to work, he'd say, and the students would scatter to their individual duties, taking with them the professor's story to tell again at dinner, or in their dormitory rooms—to anyone who might not have already heard. They knew the rest of it from other sources: how the professor had returned to the States and been hospitalized for depression, how he had published his drawings as *The Silent Victim: Flora in Wartime* and been made a minor celebrity by the women who were leading the postwar pacifist movement, how one of them, a suffragist whose name was known in every household, held his book high in the air at an international disarmament conference in Amsterdam and shouted that if this book couldn't end the manmade institution of war then nothing, *nothing* could, how all that attention had only frazzled his nerves to another breakdown, delaying his plan to take the Trans-Siberian railroad, to continue east to view the gardens of a certain city in Japan where he was sure, he had told particular classes, peace resided—he had seen it once or twice, in a combination of stone and bough. And he had found it there, he said. Peace. And he would have stayed forever had the monks not been evacuated and interned during the early days of the war preparation. He had left on the advice of an elderly teacher. Sailed home just in time to read the news of Pearl Harbor.

Of course there were also those students who suspected Professor X of being a quack, a phony in their midst. Flora of northern France? It was out of print, wasn't it? Even the library had lost its copy.

But I've strayed from the point. The point is that the city of Kyoto had declared itself open during the war years, which meant that the Japanese promised, and promises were sometimes listened to during wartime, that there were no military facilities within its walls. During most of the war, this meant that there would be absolutely no reason to destroy it; with the atomic bomb, however, all bets were off.

Professor X found himself privy to this—that deliberations were being held on where to drop a bomb more powerful than any other—and, worried that the government might target his beloved Kyoto, he managed to request, and secure, an audience with the men deciding such actions in Washington.

I imagine he had several sleepless nights preparing for what, exactly, he could say to convince them. These nights, when he shut his eyes, he saw again the famous suffragist shouting at the gathering of pacifists, women, primarily, in hats and woolly coats, applauding her, applauding his little book. It shamed him. Simple drawings sketched in the margins of stories he'd never read, words of men long dead, forgotten by the persons they'd addressed so passionately, because if nothing else there was passion there, in the muck and mud of that terrible place. He'd saved the letters. This he'd told no one. He had every one, his own graveyard in a simple sailor's chest. But he'd never read them; he was too afraid.

He could tell them about this, but he doubted the men's interest in such stories. They wouldn't see the point and, truth be told, neither did he, exactly. No. He had to speak as an academic, as someone who had studied a culture for nearly twenty years, as a horticulturalist and published author, as a former resident of a city, a place they had no knowledge of: Kyoto. Even the name was beautiful. He could tell them of the narrow back streets, the arched bridges, the cherry trees. He could tell them of the artisan's shop where the paint pigment, brighter than any color he had seen here in the Midwest, glistened when wetted in thousand-year-old wooden bowls, and of the brushes whittled from ebony and jade, their bristles stiff pig hairs bound with leather cured on mountaintops. That everything had a reason: vegetables wrapped in brown paper; apples kissed; children rouged. Bare-footed monks in, yes, saffron robes, plucked weeds from the gardens of moss, simply moss, before the sun rose, and poems of one, two stanzas were composed over lifetimes and the graves of unborn children were as honored as those of grandfathers.

He could tell them of the Imperial Palace, built during Charlemagne's rule; how just south of the ceremonial hall the garden sits, a field of raked gravel empty but for the two gnarled trees that flank the stairs of the hall, pine, he believed, older than the palace itself. Or the other, the garden of Ryoan-ji near the Dragon Peace Temple, composed of fifteen rocks, one rock hidden when the garden is viewed from any point along the veranda. Why? No one understands, though the Zen priests believe it invites contemplation, the viewer left to fill in the landscape.

Thinking of what to say to the men, he grows sleepy. He remembers walking through the gardens at Toji-in late in the afternoon, the shadows deep, the camellias and azaleas in bloom. He carries his sketchbook—the brushes he had bought earlier at the artisan's store and the pot of black ink in his wicker basket—and stops near the pond that forms the Chinese character *shin*, heart or spirit. He has been studying with an elderly teacher who, just yesterday, complimented his progress; this has encouraged him and though he cannot afford them, he has bought new supplies at the artisan's store. Now he allows himself to imagine that he too might draw as well as his teacher, that he might, as his teacher assured him, find the gesture in quiet places.

He unwraps the pot of black ink, unwraps the brushes, tickling the back of his hand with the pig-hair bristles, breaking them out of their stiffness. He uncorks the pot of black ink, its color so rich, so entirely without light, he imagines he might slip into the ink and find it bottomless, a well toward the center of, what? He shrugs as if someone else has asked him the question and looks out toward the pond; beneath its surface carp lay like carved wooden things against the mud, their small fins fluttering in the currentless water, their gills, panting, their tiny eyes colorless among the copper coins. Carp clogging the *shin*—the heart, the spirit. He must remember to tell his teacher this, the irony of it, though he is unsure whether his teacher appreciates irony. He is far from home, he knows. Far from

Boston, far from France, far from the Brooklyn hospital where boys younger than he were put in straitjackets, their gaunt faces twisted into expressions impossible to forget.

He dips the brush into the black ink, blotting it on the cork. Positioning the sketchpad against his legs, knees up, he leans against a pine, the smell of its resin striking him as something familiar: hiking expeditions in the White Mountains with his father, a man as shy as he, as cautious, who never got over Woodrow Wilson's betrayal. *He kept us out of war*, his father would say, as if words, alone, were culpable.

The professor wakes just as he is dreaming that he quells his hand to pass the brush over the paper. It is always this way: the anticipation, so real in the dream, that he might steady his tremor to draw as well as his teacher, and the inability to see, before waking, whether he has succeeded. In life, of course, he did not; he left Japan before he could even imagine it.

In the morning the professor boards his train. The journey will take several days and he has packed plenty of papers to keep him occupied; still, he finds that as soon as he sits he becomes far more interested in looking out the window, in thinking, than he is in the work in his valise. Because of his deafness, he does not hear the conductor knock on the door to his compartment, nor does he hear him slide it back. He simply feels a tap on his shoulder and understands that he has been daydreaming. He gives the conductor his ticket as they pass through Indiana.

I imagine that the professor slept soundly on that journey in the way he did not, could not, the days and weeks before leaving; he was on his way, the first leg of his mission, and he realized, finally, that the preparation for his statement to the men had been made, that he could stand before them and tell them things that might convince them to spare Kyoto: the carp in the pond at the center of Toji-in, how in late afternoon the monks who rake the moss with their bamboo rakes come to the edge of the pond and whistle, and how the carp, perhaps because they believe they are to be fed, or perhaps because they too want company, rise to the water's surface in great seething packs, like the stray dogs in France who fed off the poisonous corpses of men. Poor pups, the Frenchmen said. They were good pups. The monks lean on their bamboo rakes and watch as the carp boil to the water's surface, open-mouthed, their scaly, thousand-year-old tails beating the water to froth; the *shin*, the soul, whipped into a torment. Is this the reason the monks call to them? To see for themselves the misery, the carp-froth, of other men's souls? But, no. He will not tell the generals this, nor will he tell them of the letters he keeps in his sailor's chest, nor how a certain student once led him, breathless, to a plant left in her care, the blighted one given up for good that had suddenly, miraculously, grown a new shoot—a leaf of pure, brilliant green.

3

It was getting close to graduation. Mother and Daddy seemed to write every day, something about needing to double-check the details, confirm the plans. But there was little to do. I would wear the long white dress that all the girls wore, or my variation of it. Mother had fitted me the summer before, draping the material over my shoulder so that I looked like a latter-day Greek statue standing on our old ottoman in nothing but shorts and a T-shirt, a heavy swath of white cotton, poplin, across my shoulder.

She turned me this way and that, pins in her mouth; she asked about spaghetti straps, was I interested? I shrugged. "Sure," I might have said, or some other lackluster variation. I wasn't interested. In spaghetti straps, or pleats, or a tea-length, or a Grace Kelly bodice. I kept trying to picture myself among all the other girls processing down the campus green the way I had seen the seniors the spring before, their hands gripping single red roses, their smiles stiff against the squeak of the bagpipes. This was a Saint Mary's tradition. A trio of bagpipers leading the girls, the girls walking single file across the stage, the nuns arranged in chairs according to rank, their crinkled faces barely discernible within the round black cinch of their habits. I tried to see myself among them, not the nuns, of course, but the other girls. I could not. It all seemed so pointless, suddenly. The diploma, the handshake, Mother and Daddy watching from their folding chairs, programs accordion-creased, fanning themselves during the long-winded commencement speech delivered by one of the career-girl's spinster aunts.

I had absolutely no idea what I would do next, whether I would return to Chester and teach at a local high school, as Mother hoped, or whether I would go on to secretarial school in Philadelphia. Either option dispirited me.

Anyway, I stood there as Mother pinned, looking at myself in the mirror from time to time, watching Mother. She might have sensed my lack of enthusiasm because she said little, simply worked. Or she might have fallen back to her own thoughts. It was an expression she used more and more these days. "I've fallen into my thoughts," she'd say, as if her thoughts were quicksand, difficult to step out of once she'd stepped in. In truth, since Rita's death, Mother said little; she had lost her job at the factory soon after the war, replaced by one of the returning boys, and though at first she pretended she would welcome the break, the time in the garden and the house, I often found her sitting in the rocker in the front hallway, staring vacantly, as if half expecting a visitor, or waiting for the sun to drop. She said she never knew time could move so slowly, that she had so much more to do when we girls were little. I tried to get her interested in the books I was reading, or to pick up another hobby. Cross-stitch, I remember suggesting. But she seemed too distracted to concentrate on anything new. I'm too stupid, she'd say when I pushed her.

She and Daddy had been looking forward to my graduation for months. With Rita dead and Betty doing God knows what, they turned to me, to my life, for conversation. Sometimes it felt a burden too heavy; I wanted to run away, to escape their long looks the few times I went home my senior year, taking the trolley to Chester, waiting on the cold platform for Daddy to pick me up, my books held tightly against me as if for warmth. To their incessant questions I often gave quick answers, pretending not to see that I deflated them. Daddy would suggest we three take a walk after supper. Old Man Springfield had passed away and nobody seemed interested in purchasing his orchard. A family of osprey had somehow found themselves off course, he said, because they nested in one of the far pastures, in a particularly old pear tree he'd like to show me.

Too tired, I said.

Mother and Daddy exchanged looks. I say exchanged because it really did seem this way, as if one held a look out for the other to take, to consider, to return. If I had been a child they would have shrugged over my shoulders. But I wasn't a child, nor was I a teenager. I was a selfish young woman, and if I could have it to do over again I'd like to be back there with the two of them, sitting in the dining room at the good table Mother liked to set for my infrequent dinners at home, the linen napkins and tablecloth she had spent the morning starching and ironing folded across the oiled oval, its leaf removed so the table, once expected to seat five, sat three. If I could have it to do over, I'd be animated, gracious. I'd tell them about the books I had read that semester, the papers I had written. I'd tell them about the girls I lived with and our housemother, Pickle Smith, whose nickname was a constant source of mystery and amusement to all of us. She swore she'd never reveal its origin, though she seemed proud of it and would, in introductions, pronounce the Pickle with a kind of a twist. We knew her real name to be Beatrice, and those among us more daring than I would sometimes address her as Miss Bea, to which they'd get a raised eyebrow—a raised eyebrow, I could have added in the telling, that the more daring could imitate with perfect precision. This would have amused Daddy, I'm sure. I can imagine him laughing and asking me to do an imitation; my sorry attempt would have amused him even more. Mother might have at first disapproved; Pickle Smith was our housemother, after all, and we owed her the respect we owed any of our mothers. Still, I would have won her over with my imitation and the three of us might have laughed in the way we used to laugh as a family, when Rita was alive, and Betty still at home.

I don't believe I ever told them a thing about her, Pickle Smith; I can't even remember introducing them at graduation.

Graduation turned out to be a beautiful day, though there had been weeks of rain beforehand, and the crocuses and early spring bulbs looked like fossils in the mud. The girls stood around in their white dresses, boyfriends, fiancés at their sides, smiling for their parents' cameras and the cameras of their friends' parents, everyone posed for a portrait, clustered too close. After the procession there was a picnic on the freshly mowed Great Lawn, all the greener from the rain. Long tables with white paper tablecloths were set around the perimeter, and waitresses— the junior class girls in black skirts and white blouses—served plates of roast beef with horseradish, potato salad, sliced tomatoes. I remember how embarrassed I felt that Daddy tucked his paper napkin into his collar and that Mother said Good for you! every time she met one of my friends. I wanted them to be like all the other parents, men and women from the Main Line whose children were not the first in the family to receive a college diploma. We were poor, as I've told you, and though I am sure in retrospect I was not the poorest student, I certainly believed that I was, believed that everyone noticed Mother's twenty-year-old suit, her hands, still callused from her years in the factory, her standard-issue stockings, as they noticed Daddy's napkin tucked into his collar waving like a flag of difference.

*   *   *

We were halfway through lunch when Betty, too abruptly, arrived, saying that her train had been derailed or some such thing, though I am sure she simply wanted to miss the procession.

She looked around at the scene: the white paper tablecloths, the bagpipe trio in the center of the Great Lawn, the girls and their families. "How quaint," she said, and sat down hard.

Mother held out her handkerchief, the one she had no doubt earlier cried into as I crossed the stage and accepted my diploma from the president's outstretched hand.

"Wipe some of that off, young lady," she said.

Betty took the handkerchief from Mother and dabbed at the thick red lipstick outlining her lips. She looked garish in the broad daylight, and I wondered whether she had done this for my benefit or whether she in fact believed she looked beautiful.

"And your cheeks," Mother said.

Betty rubbed her cheeks, though this just made them redder.

"For the love of Pete," she said. She slipped off her gloves and motioned to one of the juniors to bring her a plate. "I'm famished, and the last thing I need is an etiquette lesson. What'd I miss, anyway?"

"My graduation," I said.

"Your sister did beautifully," Daddy said. He lifted the ends of his napkin and dabbed at some horseradish on his chin. Betty reached over and snatched the napkin out of his hand, loosening it from its tucked-in place and handing it back to him, whole.

"Thank you," Daddy said.

"Don't mention it," Betty said.

Daddy smiled; he adored all of us.

Betty looked down at the plate that had been set before her. "You'd think they could heat something up."

Mother shrugged. "You'd think someone could have made a point to be on time."

"Someone," Betty said, her mouth closed but full, "had to work until two A.M., and then someone had to take a train."

"Please," I said.

"You do not have to work until two A.M.," Mother said. "Nor do you have to talk to your mother that way."

Betty put down her fork. I looked to Daddy but his face had already adopted the expression it reserved for when Betty and Mother were fighting, as if he had resigned himself to the fact that the two were like cocks in a ring and, depending on the weather, the sleep the night before, the conditioning, one would eventually take the other down. I, usually silent during their sparring, must have felt particularly adult this day, or particularly desperate. I slammed my hand down so hard the glasses shook and water spilled onto the table, wetting the tablecloth.

"I mean it," I said, as if I had previously said something forceful. The two looked at me; I'm sure I flushed in the way I always do whenever I express an idea that might be met with some resistance. The white dress Mother had sewn for me must have set off my flush in a startling contrast. I felt that everything I would have truly liked to have said, about Betty and Mother, about missing Rita, about Daphne, had clogged in the too-narrow passageway of my throat.

"Fine," Betty said. She wiped her mouth and set her napkin on her lap, punctuating the closure. Mother looked at me and smiled. "Delicious roast beef," she said. To which I, stupidly, replied, "Thank you."

I had seen Daphne just a few weeks before. She had, since March, been sending me your father's letters. She would tuck them inside a larger envelope and include a note of some sort, *studying like a god-damn dog*, etc., never anything too detailed. No mention of Gideon, the Russian history professor, for instance, or the Enchanted Forest.

She sent your father's letters unopened and would often scratch out her name in the address and write in mine, or something funny, like Debbie Reynolds, or J. Edgar Hoover, or Sister Clarice, who was the president of Saint Mary's. Everything about Daphne felt slightly blasphemous and I remember worrying that the letter addressed to Sister Clarice might somehow find its way out of my possession and into a letterbox, arrive on Sister Clarice's desk, and I would be forced to divulge the whole story, the entire lie, as she sat there listening, her thick fingers already clasped in prayer for my hell-bound soul.

But the last letter came with a longer note, one that suggested, by its tight, cramped script, lines between the lines. She wrote that she had to go away for a while, that she in fact had to leave before Bryn Mawr's graduation, though who cared, really, she wrote. Her father was still in California and wouldn't be able to make it; her mother, God knows; her aunt, infirm. Anyway, she wrote, I've asked that all my mail be forwarded to a P.O. box off campus.

A tiny silver key had been taped to the inside of the envelope, along with instructions as to the number and location of the post office box. It seemed odd to me that she wouldn't have mentioned where she had to go, or why something would be so important that it would necessitate missing graduation. I knew that Daphne didn't take much stock in ceremony, but I also knew that she would have wanted, no, relished, the opportunity to stand when her name was called as the winner of the history prize, to nod to the applause. I knew enough about Daphne to know that.

I took the trolley that afternoon, changing three or four times until I had finally found the right route. I'm not much of a traveler, and in those days, certainly, I believed because Saint Mary's was where Mother and Daddy had deposited me, Saint Mary's was where I should stay. To simply buy a ticket and step on a trolley elsewhere felt reckless.

I arrived at Bryn Mawr near dinnertime. Girls were everywhere, streaming from the various buildings toward what appeared to be the dining hall. They seemed different than the Saint Mary's girls, not more sophisticated, as you might guess, but smarter; they looked like they had books in their heads, foreign languages, historical dates, theorems. I remember walking by what must have been the library, a boxlike contemporary building constructed primarily out of glass where girls hunched at reading desks, the light from inside the glass box yellowish, warm. I pictured myself among them. I could have been. I certainly had the grades. But when the time had come to apply for scholarships, Mother and Daddy wanted me to go somewhere smaller, Catholic. No one in our town had ever gone to a place like Bryn Mawr; it seemed too far away, though it was no farther than Saint Mary's. Funny how certain things turn out.

Anyway, it took me some time before I finally found Daphne's dorm and asked the proctor, a well-dressed woman in her thirties or early forties, for Daphne's room number.

"Daphne?" the woman said.

"Is she at dinner?" I asked.

The woman looked up at me from the newspaper spread across her desk. She tapped her nails against the oak top.

"Why are you looking for her?" she said.

"I'm her friend," I said, feeling ridiculous; the woman seemed suspicious in a way I could not understand, as if Daphne were an inmate, or a princess.

"Sixteen East Oaks," the woman said, looking back down. "She moved off campus in January."

"Off campus?" I said. I had never heard the expression.

The woman looked up again, and squinted. I felt as if I had Saint Mary's tattooed across my forehead. Were Bryn Mawr girls mind readers? Did they never ask such obvious questions?

"Walk to the west gate, turn right, second left is East Oaks. It's not far," she said.

"Thank you," I said, and, hesitating, turned toward the door.

"Give her our best," the woman said as the door closed behind me, which at the time I didn't recognize as odd.

Off campus, I thought. Off campus. Second left, I thought. Second. Her directions seemed to be a test of my intelligence, a test of my ability to follow instructions. I wanted to return to tell the woman that I, too, could have gained admittance to Bryn Mawr, I might be here right now, that I, too, might be off campus, or in the library sitting high above the passersby reading, oblivious to their looks, oblivious to everything except the words on the page, that I, too, might have earned a scholarship to Radcliffe to study Russian history, or comparative literature, or philosophy, even.

I found the west gate with little difficulty and turned right, as instructed. Off campus consisted of a neighborhood of Victorian houses, primarily faculty houses and some stray departments. The Department of Child Study, I remember reading on a bronze plaque on one red-painted door.

I turned left on East Oaks and looked for 16. The numbers were quite high, the walk farther than the proctor had indicated, perhaps eight, nine blocks. The houses, too, had begun to change. Several had mangy dogs chained to stakes in their front yards who sprung to their feet and lunged as I walked by. Guard dogs, no doubt. I ran a little, passing a tree hung with Easter eggs of various colors, faded a bit from the rains. I would have stopped to take a closer look—I had never seen such a thing—but I felt frightened, off-kilter. Who was Daphne, anyway? A Communist. A girl I had twice met. Someone whose mother had lost her mind. She was no one I knew, no one like me: she made love in a motel called the Enchanted Forest with a married man. She used words I had never heard.

When I finally reached 16 I had worked myself in to a kind of terror. The yellow house had a front porch with two rocking chairs and a couch. A calico cat balanced on the railing and looked out to me, somewhat welcoming. I took the steps and knocked too loudly on the front door. An old man in a bathrobe answered and for a moment I thought I might run, that this might be Gideon, the Russian history professor, that I might have caught the two of them in the middle of a rendezvous.

"I'm looking for Daphne," I said, realizing, abruptly, that I couldn't remember her last name. I tried to picture one of your father's letters addressed to her, but all I could picture was Daphne's own handwriting: *J. Edgar Hoover, Champion of the Human Race.*

"Jesus Christ," I heard. Daphne stood at the top of the stairs in the shadow of an upper hallway. I couldn't see her that well but I knew, somehow, that she looked terrible, that something had gone horribly wrong. "It's okay, Mr. Rawson."

The old man opened the door wider to let me in; then turned, wordlessly, into a door off the foyer. I started to laugh, I am sure out of nerves.

"I thought that was Gideon," I said.

"Gideon?" Daphne said. "For God's sake, give me some credit."

She stepped out of the shadow to halfway down the stairs, and she did look terrible. She had on a baggy shirt and socks, her face so gaunt I thought at first that she still stood in shadow until I realized, stepping in, that she simply had dark smudges around her eyes, as if she'd been crying for months. She wore glasses, which I found curious, because the other times we had met she had not. They were heavy black-framed glasses—the kind more typically worn by a man, an Eastern European or some other immigrant intellectual—that made her seem frail, dwarfing her face, exaggerating her gray eyes to the point where the gray seemed all behind the thick glass, her face a smear of white, her hair as straight and black as charcoal lines. I found myself wishing for Gideon's sweater, something to add color.

"I know," she said. "I look like hell."

She reached the bottom step and hugged me. I could feel her ribs, the thinness of her arms. "Thank you, anyway," she said. She pulled away and pushed her glasses up with a nail-bitten finger. "Do you like them? I'm blind as a bat but vain, too. I bought them last month. I don't know, I think they're very Lenin."

She smiled. She really did have a beautiful smile.

"Mr. Rawson said he thought they were sporting. That's what he said. 'I think they're sporting, Daphne.' Isn't that wonderful?"

I nodded, suddenly aware of the smell of the house: dampness, cats, a smell I associate with certain types of buildings—the ones closest to railroad lines and highway overpasses whose windows are often boarded with plywood, whose front doors have grates. I followed Daphne up the stairs. A faded wallpaper creased the wall and I noticed a line of grime at shoulder-height similar to a collar stain. Daphne remained temporarily cheerful; she told me that Mr. Rawson was actually a fine old goat and that he had given everyone in the house a pair of mittens last Christmas, mittens he knitted himself, having taken up the hobby when his wife died three years ago. Mrs. Rawson had been a painter in Paris before the war; Mr. Rawson was on a ship that had docked somewhere in the south of France, or something, she couldn't get his part of the story straight, it was her story, Mrs. Rawson's, she loved. Originally from New Orleans, of the New Orleans Tates, Daphne said. Or that's how Mr. Rawson put it, as if everyone would know who the New Orleans Tates might be; she, the soon-to-be Mrs. Rawson, never wore the same color shoes, always wore one red and one black, or one black and one yellow, and that wasn't even extreme, Daphne said. Somebody else in the *arrondissement* had a pet cheetah.

Anyway, Mrs. Rawson, or Constance Tate, wouldn't give Mr. Rawson a second look, so the only thing he could do was return to the little gallery she had set up along the Seine every morning and pay her to draw his portrait. He did this throughout his entire leave, and then the days following, since he couldn't bear to get back on the ship and never see her again. At forty-six portraits, she agreed to meet him for a glass of wine; at fifty-three, she invited him to the room she shared with a poet from Harlem; at sixty-two, they were in love.

Here Daphne stopped on the stairway and turned toward me; we had actually been climbing quite a while. It turned out she lived on the top floor, in a one-room studio with tiny shed windows. "That's how he always says it," she said. "'At sixty-two, we were in love.'" I looked up at her and saw that her glasses had slipped again—they must have been quite heavy—down her nose. She turned back around quickly, continuing the climb. "He's got all of them, the portraits, lining the walls of his crummy apartment," she said. "They're terrible, actually. Which makes the story even better."

She opened a door one would have imagined led to the roof and I followed her in; the studio was impossibly small and bright. There were tiny shed windows, as I mentioned, and I instinctively went to one to look at the view: the gothic spires of campus above the tree line.

"You can see school from here," I said, as if she wouldn't have ever noticed.

"Exactly," she said, "why I need shades." She plopped down on a sofa covered with a piece of corduroy and I sat on a folding chair beside a tiny wooden table. There were carvings in the tabletop and penned doodles; on the windowsill a banana, flooded in sunlight, rotted.

"I went there looking for you," I said.

"And what did you find?" she said.

"Smart girls," I said. "Smart girls studying."

She laughed and reached for a pack of cigarettes balanced on the arm of the sofa. She lit one and gave it to me, then lit another for herself, standing to walk to the window I had just looked out of, jimmying it open. A breeze lofted our smoke, though everything else remained still. Light shone through a row of green-glass wine bottles. Dust waxed the table; I divided it with my finger.

"How's our lieutenant?" she said, still facing the window.

I blushed. "He's fine," I said. "I mean, he tells me, or you, he's fine."

She turned to me and blew a few smoke rings. "Glad to hear it; the last thing we need is a dead lieutenant on our hands." She crossed the room and stubbed her half-smoked cigarette into a clogged ashtray. "I'm sorry," she said.

I shrugged, though I doubt she saw me. "I'm not myself, really," she said, sitting down on the sofa again. She drew her legs up to her chest, her thin arms clasped around them, locking hand to wrist. "Or, I'm more than myself. Or, I don't know, beyond myself, beside myself."

I waited. My cigarette burned in a little porcelain saucer I still so vividly recall. I suppose I felt that if I looked at her she might stop talking and so I watched the long, cylindrical ash of the cigarette, its nicotine marking the porcelain brown. Ivy vines twisted around the saucer's rim, leaves outlined in a staccato gold. It had the air of something once grand, valuable, someone's heirloom carted to the street or to the consignment shop, where surely Daphne had found her furniture, her dishes; or perhaps this had once belonged to Constance Tate of the New Orleans Tates; Constance certainly would have approved of porcelain dishes, crests, teatimes taken beneath the cedars.

"I'm pregnant," Daphne said, or rather, exhaled. For an instant, borne to France the way I had been, I thought I might have imagined these words, that she might have said nothing at all.

"It's Gideon's," she continued. "Everything is. Gideon's. Everything. He doesn't want to have a thing to do with it. Not now, anyway. At first, I don't know, he said he'd help."

I looked at her. You have to understand: In those days to be unwed and pregnant was the end of your life.

"He'd heard of some nurse who would meet you anywhere. He arranged it. Last week. The Enchanted Forest, of course. He waited in the goddamn car. I mean, it's not like he could have walked me in, waited. He said, no. He said he couldn't bear the smell of blood. Gideon, the Communist. That's what he said. So he waited. I was in the room with the dirty screens and the pillowcases in yellow plastic. Did I tell you about it? I can't remember. I lay there staring at the spruce outside and the nurse knocked and I thought maybe it was Gideon having changed his mind and I said come in. She didn't look like a nurse at all, she just looked like, I don't know, somebody's nasty neighbor. She had this little suitcase and inside were what looked like bits of rubber hose. I could see because she held up one and then another as if measuring and I wanted not to look, I wanted to concentrate on the spruce outside but I couldn't, really. I couldn't."

Daphne rocked a bit as she spoke, her arms still wrapped around her legs. She was talking to no one in particular, certainly not me. "The nurse said she'd have to give me an internal to check my size and then she'd put one of these things in. She didn't tell me. I asked. She wouldn't have said a word. She said one of those pieces of rubber would get it going and it might take all afternoon and it would hurt like hell and if anything went wrong I should not go to the hospital because they'd arrest me. They will arrest you, she said, measuring one of those pieces of rubber like somebody's garden hose cut with bad scissors. But don't worry, she said. We'll get it going. Where? I said, and I think she thought I was making a goddamn joke because she crossed her arms and said, This isn't funny, and I said, No, it's not, and then I walked out. I told Gideon I couldn't bear the smell of blood and he said he didn't find that amusing. Everybody thought I was being so funny."

She looked up at me and pushed her glasses back against the bridge of her nose. "He paid for this dump, said it would be more discreet than on campus. Now, I don't know. I haven't been to any classes. I haven't heard from him."

"What are you going to do?" my voice sounded wrong, too earnest.

She stood and walked over to a desk shoved beneath one of the windows. In the top drawer she found an envelope that looked, even from where I sat, important. "Four hundred dollars," she said. "My father sent me a graduation present. Pearls. I'm sure he felt guilty because he made no effort to be here. They were beautiful, really; worth twice as much." She put the envelope back in the drawer. "I'm going to Europe. One of the girls here said her sister went to Yugoslavia, said the doctors will do anything for cash." Here Daphne shrugged. "It might even be legal there."

The bagpipers were strolling now, families turned in their seats to watch. They were three men in kilts and berets, kneesocks. The nuns seemed to enjoy them the most and applauded every time they passed their small groups among the graduates and guests. The bagpipers nodded to the applause and continued; they were, at present, heading directly toward us.

"I can't bear it," Betty said, and, placing her napkin on her plate in a way Mother would have forbidden at home, stood. She gestured to me to follow. I told Mother and Daddy that I needed to show Betty the ladies' room, that I would be right back. Betty linked my arm in hers, a rare sisterly gesture I found comforting, and we walked away.

"Don't they drive you nuts?" she said.

"The bagpipers?" I said.

"Well, yes, but I meant Mother and Daddy," she said.

We were passing other families, some of whom I recognized as the families of friends. I felt both proud and ashamed to be with Betty; she looked so, well, loud in the middle of that setting, yet defiant. "Sometimes," I said.

"Sometimes?" she said. "Daddy sitting there with that bib on and Mother practically biting my head off at anything. When did she get all high and mighty?"

I shrugged. "She misses Rita," I said.

"Rita, Rita, Rita. I'm so tired of Rita being the excuse for every-thing; you'd think the two of us just dried up and shriveled away. I mean, I wrote Mother and Daddy about my promotion and I didn't hear boo."

"What promotion?"

"Exactly."

"I'm asking."

Betty pulled up a bit. We had reached the edge of the Great Lawn, near the wide stone steps that led to McCalister Library. I seemed to always head toward McCalister whenever I was walking; it had become a habit of mine, a secret destination. As seniors, we were given keys to the library, and sometimes, in the middle of the night, I would pull on some clothes and take a walk here. It was my favorite place, not modern the way the library had been at Bryn Mawr, more like a wealthy man's library, a vast stone fireplace, never lit, in the front room, around which were gathered the green leather reading chairs. The chairs had been donated by the semi-nary that served as our brother school and were pen scratched and worn, leaking stuffing; still, they suggested contemplation, poetry, or this is what I would think when I'd enter McCalister after mid-night, knowing the reading room well enough to cross it in almost complete darkness. The globe in the corner had once been illumi-nated, but had broken years ago, or simply shut off; the story went that it happened on D-Day, as if the globe had wanted to aid the Allies' secrecy. This is at least what Sister Pat, the librarian, had told us, though Sister Pat also kept a stash of hooch in a locked drawer just beneath the checkout desk; on afternoons when we were bored studying, we'd take bets on the number of times she would cloak it in one of her long sleeves and take a swig before dinnertime.

Here Betty and I found ourselves, Betty practically breathless. "Clarence Ledger," she said. I noticed that a fleck of lipstick nicked her front tooth.

"Clarence Ledger?" I said.

"Clarence Ledger, *Esquire*," she said. "One of the partners. He made me his personal assistant." She tugged at one side of her skirt to straighten it, eyeing me, and I had the odd feeling that she expected me to salute, or to do something equally officious.

"Congratulations," I said.

"Congratulations?" she said. "Do you have any idea? First of all, Clarence Ledger looks like Gregory Peck. No, better. He wears these suits and a hat and he's the youngest partner the firm has ever had."

"And you're his secretary?" I said.

"God, no. Do you have any idea? His secretary is this old hag that's been at the firm for six zillion years. She's very kind, but. God, his secretary? No. I'm his personal assistant. I take care of gifts, arrangements."

"Gifts?"

"For his wife, his kids. If somebody's getting married."

We stood at the base of the steps up to McCalister; I would have liked to have taken her inside, to have shown her the green leather chairs and the dead globe and how a fire was laid in the fireplace, though it had been stone cold for years, and how a dictionary too heavy to lift sat on its own pedestal near the pencil sharpener. But she seemed to be entirely elsewhere. She yawned and covered her mouth and I saw now that her fingernails were filed to long, rounded points and painted pink. "And I'm beat," she said, a little too proudly. "Last night I took the trolley to his house in Locust Hill. He asked me for help with wallpapers and drapes." She winked. "He's surprising his wife."

I wanted Betty to stop talking; I wanted to be in McCalister reading one of your father's letters in the dead of night, because these are what I brought with me on my walks. Your father's letters—there were eleven of them, including the original—he wrote every week. On Sundays, I believed, or imagined, since I thought of war as work, somehow, with Sundays off. Each was dated Kumwah;

each sent on the regulation blue airmail paper; each addressed to Daphne at Bryn Mawr.

I told Betty congratulations, again, that it sounded fascinating. Then I said I had to say good-bye to someone, or good luck, and that I would meet her back at Mother and Daddy's table. I put my hand on her shoulder, still warm, still my sister's, and told her I was proud of her, that I was sure Mother and Daddy were proud of her as well, they just didn't know how to say it. For an instant, Betty looked as I remembered her, like we were upstairs in the attic room, her feet on the dresser Rita had shellacked with movie ticket stubs, her hands behind her head, imagining where she would go when she left. She had no intention of college. She couldn't earn a scholarship and Mother and Daddy couldn't afford to send her without one. This never bothered her; it was understood, from years before, that I would be the one to go to college. She thought at first she might go to New York City, or that she might join Rita in Texas. But then, after Rita died, she said she would no longer do anything she had thought of when Rita was alive and so she looked in the Philadelphia newspapers, in the want ads, and left. I don't believe Mother and Daddy had any idea what she had found, or where she intended to stay; they were too shocked to worry about one of their living daughters. I had already been accepted to Saint Mary's, and spent most of my free time in the orchard, anyway; Betty simply went away.

I cannot, quite truthfully, remember saying good-bye.

Betty looked back at me and smiled. "Next time you might do something a little less virginal," she said, snapping one of my spaghetti straps. I curtsied and stuck my tongue out, then lifted the hem and ran up the steps to McCalister. I had to drop my hem to pull open the heavy door and I turned around and saw Betty still watching me. She waved a little and I waved, too. I knew she wouldn't return to Mother and Daddy's table; I knew she'd go from there back to the world she had decided to build for herself, a world with high fortress walls and rows and rows of defenses, a world she remained in for the rest of her life.

I pulled on the brass ring that opened the heavy door to McCalister, stepping in to the immediate coolness of the vestibule. The pair of arched wooden doors that led into the reading room had been propped open, perhaps as an invitation to any of the parents who might want a tour of campus; but the room was empty, or I believed it was. I went in and headed for my favorite chair, the one that sat closest to the fireplace beneath an oil painting of a fox hunt, the horses arrested in their chase, dogs at their heels, as the fox, a splash of red, lounged in the foreground. The painting had the look of something valuable. It hung in a place of prominence in a heavy gilded frame. I had often wondered about it, whether the painter intended the scene as a joke; after all, didn't the fox bare his teeth as if he were smiling? Weren't the horses and dogs and hunters heading in the entirely opposite direction? A plaque screwed to the frame, bronze, in need of polishing, simply read, *The Pursuit*. I peered at it again; it seemed a great puzzle to me, one I should be able to solve. Only then, while I was examining the painting, did she step out of wherever she had been and stand next to me. How she had known I would eventually find my way to the library I never got a chance to ask her.

"God-awful," she said. Daphne, of course.

"You're here."

"For an instant."

She looked better, fresher than before; she still wore the glasses but they seemed to fit her face more snugly. Perhaps in honor of the occasion, she wore a blue shirtwaist dress that took the edge off the paleness of her arms, her face, the thick black frames. "I didn't want to leave before delivering this," she said. She held out another letter from your father. "It arrived yesterday," she said. "He must not have gotten your letter about the post office box."

"No," I said. I am, as you know, a terrible liar.

She crossed her arms and stared at me. "You've never written him, have you?"

I shook my head. I felt suddenly cold, a child: my dress sleeveless with darts I couldn't fill.

"You're such a goddamn moron," she said. "He could have been in love with you by now."

"In love with you," I said.

"Me, you, what's the difference."

I felt the weight of *The Pursuit:* the horses and dogs jumping, the men with their guns drawn, the fox in the foreground smiling.

"Look," Daphne said. She crossed the reading room to Sister Pat's checkout desk, unlatching the little wooden gate to get behind the desk. I thought, for a moment, that she might know about Sister Pat's stash, but she came back with some lined notebook paper and a pen. "No time like the present," she said.

"My parents are waiting," I said.

"As are the butchers of Yugoslavia, wherever the hell that is."

"You're going?"

"Do I have a choice?"

"Yes," I said. I had already tried to convince her of this back at her rooming house. I had told her of Randall and Jeannette, of Sterling; how Ruby had simply moved away for a while, how it could be done in quiet, that there were places she could go. I would find one for her, I promised.

But she had been adamant. Radcliffe started in September, and she would have to forfeit her scholarship if she waited a year. No, she had said. Her mind was set.

Now she sat at one of the long desks in the middle of the reading room and switched on one of the amber-glass lamps. I stood next to her, though she didn't appear to notice. She bit a fingernail and looked away, as if searching the oriental pattern of the carpet for the words.

May 18, 1952

Dear Darling,

   I keep your letters close to my heart, where I also keep my goddamn books, unfortunately. All I can say is I'm sorry I haven't written sooner. The road to hell and all that. I know you're out there in the trenches making the world safe for democracy, and I am here in the cradle of it, sleeping peacefully, but you have to understand that these nuns are slavedrivers—

I tapped Daphne on the shoulder. "This doesn't sound like me," I said.

She looked up, annoyed.

"He doesn't know what *you* sound like. Anyway, I like the business about the nuns. He won't know who he's writing, and it won't matter." She pushed her glasses up her nose with the pen and returned to the letter.

—I graduate today and I'll have more time and the first thing I'm going to do is knit you a sock, though I know I'm a little late, and if I could I'd pack up a dozen tomatoes—

"That's good," I said.

—and some fresh ears of corn. Anyway, darling, I hear the bagpipers practicing, which means soon we'll have to march like lemmings to the stage and say our how-de-do's. I think of you every night before lights out and kiss the seal you kissed. God bless you.

She folded the lined paper and gave it to me.

"Now you won't break my heart if you toss the goddamn thing out entirely. This was just a lesson in how it's done. Not too adoring, not too coy, a little tutti-frutti. He'll love it," she said.

I nodded and took the letter. "Thank you," I said.

"Don't mention it," she said.

I wanted to think of something else to say, some parting wisdom I could give, but I couldn't seem to.

"Good-bye," I said.

"Good-bye," she said.

That was the last time I saw her.

4

May 2, 1952
Kumwah, Korea

My Dear Daphne,

I have begun to give up hope that you will ever write,
though around here there are sometimes rumors of letters
being intercepted, of planes going down with sacks and
sacks of mail, and I suppose this keeps me going . . . the idea
(the prayer?) that your letters are on that plane, the ship in
the typhoon spun off course and left in the doldrums of
Cape Horn. We give great leeway around these parts. We
think the best. We refuse, suffice it to say, to believe that we
have been forgotten. Have I been forgotten?

This will be a long one, forgive me. There's been little
sniper fire, and it's a sunny morning, and I can almost
picture you listening, sitting across from me in a restaurant.
We have ordered a great bottle of wine and you look as
beautiful as the day we met and you are patient because I
am just returned and have a thousand stories to tell. I will

only tell a few of them now and save the rest for that
restaurant, that day (you will join me for dinner, won't
you?), and I'm afraid the stories I have today are not the best
ones, but you'll understand, won't you?

I know that my other letters have been filled with
weather. This is the first break we've had from the cold, and
though I never thought I would be able to feel my fingers
and toes again they have thawed remarkably well. It is
ironic, mostly, that now, warm fingered and toed, my spirits
should dip so low. This is their intention, of course. We look
up at them from our ridge and they look down at us from
their ridge and we both know that even if we were to take
their hill we would not be able to hold it. Hill 854 is the
current objective. (We have given up on the clever
nicknames. Did I mention to you the twin peaks we called
Jane Russell Hill? After they'd leveled it we renamed it
Katharine Hepburn Hill.)

The Chinese have the high ground in front of us and
we'll be asked soon enough to take it. For what? To impress
the brass who've been driving up here for the last month. It
makes me madder than hell. The colonel says he's talked to
the military men who came up with this idea, but no one
seems to be stopping. They've got lookout stations for the
generals and their guests. I remember hearing that they did
this during the Civil War, that men and women would pack
picnic lunches and ride out to the edge of battle, make a
party of the day. And here we are, nearly a hundred years
later, the same soldiers entertaining the same fancy people.
They say taking 854 will help with the negotiations. I say
hell. They've been negotiating over a year now, remember? I
thought I'd be coming home some letters back and nothing's
changed. All night long they blare the Dixieland music from
the loudspeakers and last week they had some woman with

no trace of a Chinese accent I could hear telling us we were
stupid. We were stupid to be here, we should be home. We
belonged with our families, she said. Again and again. And
some of the boys got real down and I have to say I did as
well and I'll admit it now when I thought of family I
thought of you as much as anything, because that's what
happens here. We had a bad spell then and we're still not out
of it. One of ours, Air Force, got shot down just beyond 854.
It was near noon and we saw he was in trouble, saw the
smoke like if this were anywhere else, at the seashore, we
would have expected to read somebody's love letter in that
plume, a Will you marry me? Or Jackie, I'll love you forever.
The smoke went into a flame more like a glare than
anything else, a daytime shooting star, and he was gone.
Somebody thought they might have seen a parachute but we
said no, he bought the farm. God wish it were so. A few
hours later we saw the Chinese were up to something. Ted
P., the lookout, said Jesus Christ and passed the binoculars
around but we didn't need the binoculars. He wasn't so far
away, the goalpost to our center field. Still alive, the poor
son of a bitch. They had nailed him to a cross. We heard his
moans throughout the night, and God I wish I could think of
anything else. It's what I've been thinking of and trying not
to think of and not being able not to think of since then.
He's still there, though birds have swallowed most of him. I
told the colonel you can't make us take goddamn 854 when
that poor son of a bitch is there like somebody's mascot.

I'm sorry, Daphne. I can't write this to my folks and I
don't know what you've become to me, an intimate
stranger. Perhaps you don't even exist. Perhaps I concocted
you out of my imagination that day of the game, perhaps I
spoke only to the air.

But I can still see you. Flesh-and-blood Daphne. A

beautiful name. You are sitting across from me in this
restaurant and sharing a bottle of wine. I feel it already. My
toes, my fingers warm.

God Bless You —

5

Professor X arrived in Washington, D.C., and made his way to the government building where the deliberations on where to drop the bomb had, for months, taken place. Apparently there were certain men who suggested that the Japanese—the emperor and generals who could make the decision to surrender—be simply instructed to turn west, to look to the Sea of Japan, where, at a particular hour, the Americans would drop the bomb and the Japanese, presumably, would witness the horrible evidence of what might be used against them. I have always found it interesting to consider their flag in light of this story, prescient, somehow: the round red sun against the pure white sky, or this is how I see it. Think of rows and rows of Japanese standing on the beach, shading their eyes against the blast like tourists in awe of a particularly beautiful sunset.

At the appointed hour Professor X stood before the men in a suit jacket and tie, his socks pulled high to his kneecaps, his shoes, earlier, polished by a Russian refugee at Union Station. He kept a handkerchief in his pocket and too frequently pulled it out to wipe his hands. At times like this, his nerves showed in his hands, and he felt grateful, at least, that this was not an overhead projector presentation, where his tremor would have been illuminated.

He delivered the words he had prepared and the generals took notes. Or at least pretended to take notes. The professor's nerves had gotten the better of him; he stammered. The men tried to make him comfortable, asking if he would prefer to sit, or would like a glass of water. They humored him the best they could, their decision already clear. It had to do with topography, with the fact that Kyoto was a city ringed by mountains, a perfect bowl, a perfect valley. What better place to test their weapon? What better place to contain its effects? Kyoto had been chosen months ago, the natural target, really, the site almost expectant: a pair of hands cupped and held open to the sky.

The professor soon lost his place. He spoke of a particular pond in a particular garden of Kyoto, how this pond he knew well, would often visit in the late afternoons. He told them how the pond had been created over a thousand years ago, designed in the form of the character that means heart, or spirit, and how the emperor who had ordered the construction of the garden took his tea in the temple adjacent to the garden and kept his concubines in rooms off the temple he would visit at midnight, believing that the moonlight on his spirit, his heart, kept him virile, and that if he were to visit any of them in the middle of the day, in the stark sunlight, the women would see him as an old man and turn away from him disgusted, though he was an emperor and they were his concubines. This was a story repeated to show how generous the emperor was, the professor told them; to show how sentimental. And it was this same emperor who stocked the pond with beautiful goldfish, one for every year of his life, believing, since goldfish were fabled to live forever, that he might too, though of course he died as all men die, even emperors.

Here the professor cleared his throat. Perhaps he waited for the men's comments, though of course they had none. He went on. He told them that the carp still lived in the spirit of that garden; he told them that we, in this country, could not understand the beauty of such a legend, since we had no legends, really, except parochial ones: George Washington cutting down his cherry tree; Betsy Ross stitching her flag. None of our legends spoke to our spirits, he said; they simply spoke to our good deeds. At this, the man in charge interrupted the professor, thanking him for his comments and concerns. The professor looked down and gathered his papers into a brown leather valise. He shook the hands of the other men on his way out, first wiping his own with the handkerchief.

It is spring in Washington as Professor X leaves the meeting, though still winter back on campus; he walks slowly. In truth, they gave him little time, and he has come so far; what else is he to do? He thinks of all the notes, all the points he didn't make, and sits for a while on one of the benches in one of the parks that city is known for, shuffling through the papers from his valise, trying to persuade himself that in fact he might have actually articulated his position clearly, he might have stood with poise, his hands steady; he might have, yes, persuaded them. Around him soldiers back from Europe walk with girls in cardigans and wool skirts, arms linked; it looks like a painting of a time that might have been, earlier, a Sunday afternoon, a picnic day: a painting of a time before.

He shuts his eyes and takes a deep breath; he tries to clear his mind. He does not want to think of the hospital in Brooklyn; he does not want to think of the dogs in France. He thinks, instead, of his old teacher, and the teacher's granddaughter, a young girl—sixteen, perhaps seventeen—who cared for her grandfather as a supplicant might care for an idol on the altar. When he visited his teacher, the grand-daughter, Suki, would serve tea wordlessly then slip behind the rice paper door; he watched her shadow, always, and he once, even, dared to adjust her obi, the wide-ribboned bow that cinched the waist of her kimono. They lived on a narrow street of peach trees; one of the rivers flowed behind their small wooden house, and his teacher would often suggest that they take a walk, after tea, along the river, where he would tell him that he was so old he could remember the days when dyes from the silks washed and cured in the cold river water turned the river the color of dragonflies—green, red, yellow. Sometimes he would step out of his house and believe that the river had disappeared entirely, replaced by bolts of silk, the kind you could still see drying in the winds, he said, gesturing up and out toward the mountains.

But now Kyoto stood still, windless. Suki rolled out tatami rugs, laid the fans by the pots of inks, the brushes.

He felt the old teacher's hand on his own and tried to remember, tried to focus, on what the teacher said. Suki, he knew, sat in the corner. Perhaps she watched; perhaps she stitched, embroidering the scroll he had admired on the first day he had met her. She would be very steady, and if she watched she watched in a way that would reveal little interest. She kept her head down, her needle moving. If she spoke, she covered her mouth; if she laughed, as she had when he adjusted her obi, she blushed. She was a child, after all, sixteen, perhaps seventeen.

He concentrated, feeling the teacher's skin, its papery dryness, on his own; in front of him arcs of ink, still wet, were slowly absorbed into the grainy paper. It was not necessary, the old teacher said, to keep his eyes open; everything could be seen in the dark. He listened to his teacher's words; they were unlike any teacher's words he had ever known, or perhaps, because he was now an adult, but still, a student, he could hear his teacher in a way he could never hear a teacher before. The teacher wanted to show him how to thread together the lines in a pattern that already existed here, in this darkness, or in all things. *A priori.* His task was to recall, simply. To pull the knowledge from the hunch. He let his breath out slowly; this required enormous effort and he could smell Suki nearby, the powdery smell of her hands serving tea, her milky breath.

The professor shakes his head and opens his eyes. They are there, still: his old teacher, Suki in the corner. Is there time to warn them? Letters are forbidden, packages returned. He has tried. He sent paints and brushes, a tin of sugary almonds at Christmas. Perhaps his teacher is already dead, his ashes cupped in an alabaster bowl, the ancestor's bowl, and placed on an altar where Suki, a mother now, offers tea in the same jade cup from which he drank his tea those afternoons.

She will burn, of course. They will all burn, the wooden houses dry as dead twigs; the water as if material, silk.

The professor gathers his papers back into his valise and snaps it shut, disgusted, oblivious to the stares that the Secretary of War, Stimpson, draws, out for his customary stroll after lunch, walking, though a civilian, with a cadet's purposeful gait. Is this, then, when they meet? Does Stimpson choose, just at the moment the professor gathers his papers, to join him on the bench, to make small talk, eager for a distraction from the enormous tasks at hand? Or does he meet the professor later, in the lobby bar at the small hotel where the professor secures a room, too tired to take the night train back as had been his original plan. Is it here, then, that the two speak, here where Stimpson seeks the company of other civilians, men who do not recognize him, who talk to him honestly of things other than war, their travels, for instance; the places they long to return to.

6

I went back to McCalister that night after graduation and reread your father's letters. Most of the other girls were gone, the underclassmen having left soon after their exams the week before, and the seniors driven by their parents, or fiancés, other places after the ceremonies. Mother and Daddy wanted me to return with them, but I said I had too much to do and couldn't possibly. I assume they knew I was lying, but they were gracious and said they understood. I told them I would telephone as soon as I was ready.

I ate dinner by myself in the dining hall, refusing the offers of some of the friendlier faculty to join them. There were pockets of foreign students and other girls I vaguely knew who were staying on for the summer program, but my friends were all gone. I had said good-bye to them hours ago. Returning to my dormitory, I let myself in to the empty house with my key—even Pickles Smith was elsewhere, visiting her sister in Milwaukee.

Upstairs in my room I continued to pack, halfheartedly. I kept composing letters to your father in my mind; long, beautifully written letters. I pictured him reading them, his cold fingers on the thin airmail paper I had bought weeks ago at the school store. He would read them quickly, as I read his, and then read them again, more slowly, as I read his: everything about him mirrored me, except, of course, everything about him. He too had become an intimate stranger, one I would frequently, wordlessly address; one who watched me cross the stage to get my diploma, who sat next to me in classes, impressed by what I knew. He stretched his long legs from time to time, uncomfortable in the small chairs, his chin on his hand, mildly cynical, mildly bemused by all this classroom learning. He walked me out and we slowly crossed the quad together, lingering before the next class. This is how I thought of him: picturing me even now packing in the half dark.

I lay down on my twin bed and fell asleep for a time. When I woke, I was still in the clothes I had changed into after graduation, the room entirely black, the house still. For an instant I thought I might be back home in the attic room and then my eyes cleared and I saw my suitcases, my old desk still stacked with books.

Long past midnight I let myself out of the house, the key on a piece of yarn around my wrist. No lights burned in the other houses; everyone already elsewhere. Hours earlier this empty space had been filled with parents and girls and music from radios and shouts of greeting, good-byes. How quickly we were gone.

I crossed the Great Lawn, the long buffet tables a giant maze to negotiate. I don't remember any stars, nor the crickets that had, a few weeks prior, begun their incessant chirping. It seemed a dream, almost, the empty campus, the white-cloaked tables, the crisp shorn grass wetting my ankles. I climbed the steps to McCalister as I had done so many other nights and entered the reading room. Someone had left a light on, one of the floor lamps, but I was alone this time. I pulled the letters from my pocket. I had most of them in memory, but still. I liked to hear the sound of your father in my ears, even if the voice was mine. I tried to picture him though his image had long ago faded into that of the entire day, the game, Daphne sitting at the Comfy Couch, the boys driving us home. Often I pictured him as Randall. I know this will sound silly, but it's the truth. I did.

I knew I would never write: how could I take part in such a game? But I found that I had, oddly, come to believe that he meant for only me to read his letters, not Daphne, that he wrote to me, not Daphne, that I was, indeed, his intimate stranger.

Are these the questions you asked? I can't remember. You need to know about your father, I understand, and I imagine I've disappointed you. Suffice it to say that that evening in McCalister I came to the end of something, trying, as I had promised Daphne I would try, to compose a letter back to him. I gave up, and in a fury took your father's letters and cut them with one of Sister Pat's sharpened scissors, cut them as a schoolgirl might to make dolls, with a kind of a precision, first scissoring out Daphne's address as if I were removing the heart and then slicing lengthwise ribbons, pale blue regulation paper ribbons that fluttered down to Sister Pat's desk. It all seemed horribly violent and appropriate. Daring in a way I was not, nor have ever been. I knew I'd regret the action, though perhaps I did not fully comprehend how much. I cut line after line: words from sentences, letters from words. The all of it severed, forever mute but for what I might now remember.

Eventually I found myself scissoring air, the scissors making the metallic sound of blade against blade. I put my finger there and sliced some dead skin from my cuticle and then, moving my finger closer, cut the skin, once, twice, the wounds superficial, yet still, they bled in a satisfying way. Or simply, they bled: drops of fresh, red blood on Sister Pat's oiled desk, on the tissuey remains of your father's letters.

I wiped my eyes with my sleeve and with the same arm brushed the scraps of letters into my good hand and dumped them into the trash can. I bent down and found a few ribbons that had wafted to the floor and held them against my finger to staunch the bleeding. The blood soaked through, darkened, and then I did something for which I have absolutely no explanation: I walked to my favorite chair next to the cold fireplace and pressed my finger—your father's letter stuck, still wet, to the skin—to the corner of *The Pursuit*, near to the fox but not so close as to cover him. In truth, it looked, when I pulled my finger away, as if another, smaller fox, as red-orange as the original, had suddenly appeared in the scene, one that perhaps, before this, had been hidden by the brush grass or one of the fallen logs that littered the field.

There is a Japanese folktale Randall told me a few times; he found it amusing. He had read it in some book and then copied it over in his diary under the heading What to Remember. It was odd, and never made that much sense to me, though I laughed along with Randall when he told it. It's called an endless story, and begins with the rats of Nagasaki, who get together and decide, since there is nothing left to eat in Nagasaki, to board a ship and set out for Satsuma, the city across the bay. On the way over, they meet the rats of Satsuma on board their own ship and on course for Nagasaki. The two ships of rats exchange greetings and ask how things are, only to discover that there is nothing left to eat in either Satsuma or Nagasaki. Since there is no use in going to either city, they decide to jump into the sea and drown.

Now this is the way it went exactly: The first rat began to cry *chu chu*, and jumped over with a splash. Then another rat cried *chu chu*, and jumped over with a splash. Then another cried *chu chu*, and jumped over with a splash . . .

Randall would repeat the ending, well, endlessly. Don't you find that curious? In the middle of something he'd suddenly say, "Then another rat began to cry *chu chu*, and jumped over with a splash." I always found it strange, though I pretended, as girls would at the time, to understand.

8

The summer passed quickly enough. Despite Mother and Daddy's objections I moved to Clarksburg, near Chester, and took a few rooms in town. My job teaching at the high school would begin in September, and I needed, I told them, to study, to write lesson plans, to think. Of course, it was far quieter out on the farm than in town, which they knew, but they accepted my decision in the way they had come to accept most of the decisions of their girls, with a resignation that I viewed as their weakness but which, I have come to understand, was their strength.

It must have been October when your father finally found me. School had started and the days never seemed long enough. I would wake before light to review my lesson plan, prepared so carefully in the summer months and now worthless. The routine I had anticipated did not run as smoothly as I had imagined, comedies did not always follow tragedies, and so forth. We were in the middle of *Othello*. I had imagined the class acting out certain scenes and had assigned parts, unknowingly giving the role of Desdemona (she offered) to a young woman who had a less than stellar reputation.

You'll find this amusing, of course, but I was mortified; she had decided a modern interpretation of losing the handkerchief would be to lose her panties and so she brought in several pairs and left them hanging in obvious places, draped over locker doors, balled underneath desks. The other faculty found it quaint and, I believe, rather creative, but I found it disrespectful and for those early months, at least, I was most concerned about respect.

Anyway, I got up before dawn and never went to bed until midnight. I kept anticipating the students asking me a question I couldn't answer; I kept imagining myself, blushing, sitting in the front of the classroom, the student's question hanging in the air. What would I have done?

But, October. The days had begun to get a bit better. Far less often would I find myself in tears in the teachers' lounge, pretending to stare out the window to where the boys' soccer team practiced. Sometimes I went to that field to sit in the bleachers and watch them, or rather, to be alone. I had made no real friends among the faculty. They were all older than myself, tired of teaching, tired of life, it seemed, drained of curiosity. Many knew the years and months remaining until their retirement.

Lunchtime I would sit outside, the soccer boys in the cafeteria, their coaches elsewhere; the school had been built on the edge of the town, its playing fields carved out of cornfields and woods. In the near distance an aspen grove among the ubiquitous oak and maples had just turned a bright yellow; a splash of pure color within the mottled browns and reds in a way entirely magical. Light appeared to be drawn to it, but I knew this was just an optical trick in the way that light seems to seek water. I go into such detail because this is the day I first walked into the grove, and it was magical, somehow—as if by passing through my real life suddenly began.

*   *   *

I would later learn that the aspen grove had not sprung up on its own but in fact had been planted by a biology teacher and amateur landscape gardener, a woman who had taught at the high school most of her life, who had never married, who was, by all accounts, beloved by her students. She had become something of an eccentric and had read about a recently rediscovered checkerboard forest in Belgium, planted by the squire of something or other in the late sixteenth century. What a find that must have been! To walk through great blocks of color. She would talk about it all the time and eventually decided that her students should try something similar; it was even better, she told them, that they wouldn't be able to enjoy it for years. She would be long gone, she said, but they could return, if they were so inclined, to look in, to see. And every once in a while a student would. You'd spot him tromping around the aspens, wistful, his hands deep in his pockets, an old man; others, the old women, mostly, leaned against a particular tree and stayed longer.

But I knew none of this at the time, I simply knew that the spot would be special. I crossed the field toward it and cleared my way through the maples, my hard, teacherly shoes crunching dead leaves, sinking in the softer ground, my coat, one of Rita's, actually, pulled tightly around me, wrapped, with my hands, like a shawl. The grove began at a point and was a somewhat irregular triangular shape; still, a human spirit thrived within it. The teacher must have known this, known that when her pupils—grandfathers and grandmothers long past the age of learning—returned, they would remember her, that she would be what they thought of while wandering through, or simply leaning, the aspens narrow-trunked, impossibly straight, their leaves small, the size of half-dollars, and ringed with serrated edges. The aspens were full grown but still appeared young, coltish; there is a delicacy about the tree, a grace you don't find in ornamental or fussy species. Out among oak, maple, sycamore, they seem regal, aloof. Or at least these did. You should have seen how beautiful they were.

I walked within them, a figure eight, kicking their fallen yellow leaves into a great pile on which I lay down, feeling silly but entirely hidden, safe. I had lately begun to talk to Randall, and I found myself once again addressing him. I suppose, with all the classroom preparation, I had found myself transported back to the time when Randall and I would pace his room declaiming, or Randall would read something to me that had a great significance, the like of which I couldn't see until he emphasized a word, a phrase. He was my first teacher, truth be told. So no doubt I spoke to him of Othello, or Iago, my favorite character from the play, something banal and obvious, something he would have understood from a first reading but perhaps I had just come upon, having recited the entire thing that morning, before dawn, in the front room of my tiny apartment, a blanket wrapped around my knees. The point is, I might have heard your father had I not been talking, his steps too loud to be mistaken for squirrels. He had looked for me in the teachers' lounge and been told that I often ate my lunch on the bleachers; he had seen me there and called, but I had already made up my mind to explore the aspen grove and, with a determination he would later tease me for, set out across the field. He was, by his estimate, several yards behind me the entire time, though he claimed not to have been spying, that he did, indeed, honestly attempt to get my attention.

I lay in the aspen leaves, my eyes closed, thinking of Randall.

"Ellen?" your father said, and I startled. It was as if it were the first time I had ever heard my name. I stood up too quickly and stumbled; he caught my arm.

"I'm sorry," he said, laughing, and I shook my head and laughed as well.

Oh, your father then! He wore his Eisenhower jacket and trousers, a dark wool cape draped around his shoulders. He stood like a prince in the wood; I must have blushed the color of the maples, my coat stuck with aspen leaves.

"Henry," he said, holding out his hand. "Henry Rock," he said, as if I'd forget.

"I remember," I said, shaking it. His hand felt cold, dry, as if this were already the dead of winter. I held it too long, still unsteady. The truth is my knees shook.

"So, you've come back," I said.

"You spoke to Daphne?" he said.

He knew nothing about it. I suddenly understood this: he knew nothing about what I knew of him.

"Yes," I said. "Well, no, not lately. Would you like a cup of coffee? It's cold, isn't it?"

He blinked awake from somewhere else, his face regaining its familiarity and still, he looked older than I remembered. "My God, I'm being rude," he said. Then, "It's just, I've been looking a long time, you know?"

"Yes," I said, though I had no idea.

9

That night I invited your father upstairs to my tiny apartment above the Woolworth's. I should say that Mother and Daddy thought this somehow low-class, to live above the Woolworth's, but I found it oddly liberating, bohemian. You'll laugh, but in those days there were so few ways for a good girl to stretch her wings, and to be able to slip downstairs on a Saturday morning and have a coffee and a cigarette at the Woolworth counter, my hair still unbrushed, my shoes halfway on my bare feet. I felt the closest I would come to leading a different life, one where I would be strong enough to go farther from home. It was not in my character to truly break away, as Betty had, but those Saturday mornings were glorious. I knew a few of the regulars and they knew me. We'd share the newspaper and they'd ask about my students. I liked to talk those mornings. I felt happy. My cigarette would burn down in one of the green-glass ashtrays set in the cluster of salt and pepper shakers, napkin dispensers, ketchup bottles, and I would often let my fried eggs get cold.

The waitress I knew from the time I was a little girl, when certain special weekend mornings Daddy would escort his three brides, he called us, to this same Woolworth's for pancakes. She remembered Rita best from that time. Shirley Temple, she called her, and pulled at the curls Rita had spent hours perfecting in front of the mirror. Rita humored her, said she felt sorry. Anyone who ends up behind the Woolworth's counter ought to be pitied, she announced one day, somewhat out of the blue. From time to time, when the regulars had left and I had no one but that old waitress to talk to, I'd wonder whether Rita would have said the same about someone ending up on the other side of the counter. But in those days, at least, I tried my best not to think of Rita.

Anyway, your father had suggested he pick me up after school. I had some meetings to attend directly after classes, so it was already almost dark, the playing fields abandoned, when he pulled into the circular drive and parked at the front entryway. I had been waiting just behind the big glass doors, hoping he would arrive before all the other faculty had gone home. They knew the story of Rita, of course; these were small towns. And they most likely understood that I sent some portion of my paycheck to Mother and Daddy each month. I wanted to surprise them, to let them in on my secret life, and so when your father drove up in his wide convertible, the top down, his arm casually draped across the back of the white leather front seat, I bounded out the door far more cheerfully than what is generally in my nature, laughing as if someone had just told me something I still found amusing, entirely convinced that, despite the emptiness of the building behind me, people watched from the windows, wide-eyed, curious, impressed by your father's military uniform—his face still clearly handsome in the near dark—and the way his hand held the white polished steering wheel.

We drove to the most exotic place I could think of, an Italian restaurant with red-and-white checkered tablecloths, candles stuck into bottlenecks, and cheaply framed prints of the Amalfi coast on the walls. Ropes of dusty garlic, crisscrossing the ceiling, threw off strange shadows, and I remember thinking how the couples at the other tables might look at us and imagine us just like them, in love, or even, married. We sat close, the tables small, and your father listened to me with the acute concentration I believed at the time was common between husbands and wives. I was talking about Daphne, telling him everything I could remember that I knew, answering all his questions, trying, as best I could, to please him. He told me he had written her several letters. One a week. And had never had a reply. Did I know, he asked, whether she had in fact written, whether her letters were, in fact, lost? This is what he suspected, he said. Well, he said, this is what they all suspected. The mail, if you thought about it, not only had to travel across several oceans and seas, but through a damn war zone.

"Maybe she didn't even get my letters," he said, and I kept my eyebrows raised, still listening. "She might have had no idea I wrote every week. For all I know they were burning the paper for fuel somewhere and we were the dupes writing and writing."

"I doubt it," I said.

"What?"

"I doubt it. They wouldn't do that, would they?"

"I don't know," he said, as if he truly did not. "You see things, hear things. You get so paranoid you think there's somebody standing behind you making monkey ears. We had a reporter come from *Life* magazine—"

"Really?"

"—to the front. You know. That kind of story. Well, we sat there with him for weeks and nothing happened. Not one thing. We stared at the Chinese and the Chinese stared at us and that goddamn, excuse me, woman on the loudspeaker—we had named her Veronica for reasons I can't even remember—this woman told us all day long we were stupid, that we should go back to our wives and our families, that we would never win. She called us her idiot American boys. And all the while this reporter sat and scribbled in his notebook. Then he shook our hands and left. A few months later somebody gets an issue of *Life* in the mail and the reporter's made up some story and put us in the center of it. Tilsie, most of all, just a guy like the rest, he turns into a hero and nobody, none of the brass deny the story, they just let it alone and what could Tilsie do? I heard he got some kind of parade thrown in his honor when he went back home, somewhere on Long Island. Tilsie, of all people. Just like the rest of us."

Your father looked around the restaurant.

"Nice place," he said. "I'm boring you."

"No."

The waitress brought us plates of pasta. I could barely taste mine; my leg shook in the way it always has when I tell a lie. I didn't know where to begin, or whether to begin at all. What was the point? I felt like Tilsie in the middle of his parade, the crowds throwing confetti, applauding, the high school band leading the way. What could Tilsie do?

"I'm sorry, really. She's just a girl I knew, not even very well," I said.

"They told me she didn't stay for graduation. They gave me her aunt's address, but her aunt said she didn't know where she'd gone and if I found her to let her know. I guess she's always been a free spirit."

"I guess," I said. Pasta slipped off my fork. I put my hands in my lap and kneaded my napkin.

"I just wish I knew about the letters. You feel like such a fool— you know?—to think you wrote nobody."

I tried my pasta again and chewed. I had earlier eaten an olive and now kept the pit tucked in the corner of my mouth, feeling it there from time to time, ridged, hard as a little pebble.

"Oh, but this Veronica. We came to love her, really. Sometimes,

God knows why, she took a break, and the silence would be unbearable. We'd shout out, 'Where's our girl? Where's our girlfriend?' Trying to drive them as crazy as they were trying to drive us. And when
she'd come back on she'd say, 'Stupid boys,' and we'd applaud and
applaud and whistle, cat calls, like she was some beauty who'd just
shown up in, I don't know, black lace."

Your father had stopped eating, his focus backward. "I'm sorry."
He put his fork down. "I talk too much."

"No, not at all."

"These were all the things I was going to tell her," he said. "I
wrote to her that I would take her out to dinner and we would share
a bottle of wine. And you, what about you?"

"I like wine," I said. I felt the olive pit like a little stone I might
carry with me all the time, tucked there in the side of my mouth, a
reminder of other things.

I'm not sure whether either one of us finished our dinner. I know I
coughed the olive pit into my napkin before we left the restaurant;
I know he guided me out by my elbow and that all the warmth of
him, of the candles on the restaurant tables, seemed focused there
on that hard bone. When we got into his convertible, he asked if I
were cold and I shook my head no, though I was, and crossed my
arms over my legs and pulled a scarf over my head in a way faintly
glamorous, or I believed so, and turned my face into the wind. We
drove the back way to town. He wanted to show me something in
the constellations, he said. We found the stars in no time, in those
days you could, and he pulled to the side of the road.

"Cassiopeia," he said. "My favorite."

I closed my eyes and nodded. The truth is, I wasn't interested in
learning; I simply wanted to listen.

"Thirteen stars, and the five brightest—look—form a chair."

"Yes," I said, my eyes closed.

"I used to imagine I was sitting in that chair. Way above everything. The Chinese. The Ethiopians—we had an Ethiopian platoon behind us, nasty sons of bitches—believe Cassiopeia ravaged Ethiopia, or Poseidon did, because of Cassiopeia's vanity. A sea monster or a typhoon. It didn't matter to me as long as she washed my feet. She did, is the funny thing. Sometimes you think you're crazy. I would just take myself there whenever things got too god-awful and sit looking down at the fireworks, at the fires, at the poor sons of bitches who had to stay below at the goddamn thirty-eighth parallel."

I opened my eyes then and saw that your father wasn't looking, either. I mean at the sky, the stars. He focused straight ahead, his hands still holding onto the steering wheel as if he were steering us somewhere, the headlights flooding nothing but the side of the road, the ragweed and goldenrod and Queen Anne's lace that grew in the drainage ditches, the moths in white light. I heard cicadas, the last of them, and other night sounds, but now your father had gone quiet. I waited a moment for him to begin, again. I had thought I might tell him about the rats of Nagasaki; thought it might make him laugh, as it did Randall, 'Then another rat cried *chu chu*, and jumped over with a splash,' I'd say, but when I looked over I saw that it would be best to not, best to simply suggest we go.

Here are some of the things I would rather not tell you. It was considered common, or bad behavior, to invite a boy you hardly knew, a man, to come upstairs. But he had nowhere to stay. He said he might find a motel off the highway and I said nonsense in a voice that sounded nothing like my own. We stood at the door just to the side of the Woolworth's window. We had, for a time, looked at the window display, jack-o-lanterns and orange and black crepe paper and skeletons draped across cardboard tombstones. He stood with his hands in his pockets, his face pressed, almost pressed, to the glass, the weak light from the lighted store pooled at our feet. This was a small town. One traffic light blinked yellow as it would at this time of night. No cars passed, no one looked out the window. It might have been snowing for the deathly quiet.

"Nonsense," I said in the voice not my own. "You'll stay with me."

He might have said yes, or he might have said nothing. I couldn't hear for the buzz in my ears, my heart, quite literally, pounding. He followed me up the rickety wooden stairs that led to my apartment door. I held on to the banister as if I'd never bounded up these same stairs before, hands full of books, groceries. I opened the door to my rooms with somewhat of a flourish. I had never even had a friend visit.

"*Voilá!*" I said, turning on one of the lamps, aware, quite suddenly, of the dead daisies in the crystal vase that had been my great-grandmother's, of the books scattered over the floor and the way the radiator clanked. I pulled the drapes to shut out the yellow blinking light, and offered tea, which he accepted. My kitchen, a range and a tiny refrigerator crammed in what had once been a coat closet, seemed a great relief. I took more time than I should have preparing, reassuring myself that here was a veteran with no place to stay, a friend, after all, so what did I have to be afraid of?

Picture me walking back in, my coat still on, my scarf. I set down the tray with the teapot, sugar bowl, cups, and laughed. Are you cold?—he had asked. He sat on my threadbare sofa, one I'd recently found at the Salvation Army. It seemed fitting, somehow, to see him there, his legs crossed, his jacket unzipped. He had picked up *The Gardens of Kyoto* from the end table, where I kept it as one would keep, I don't know, a Bible, or an album of family photographs. He smiled when I said, no. I was, in fact, warm. Tea?

"Thank you." We were suddenly polite, self-conscious in a way we had not been in the car, or the restaurant.

"An interest?" he said, holding up the book.

"It belonged to my cousin," I said. "He's dead, actually."

"I'm sorry."

"Oh, no. It's not. He was killed."

Your father looked at me strangely.

"I mean, I didn't know him well. He was killed on Iwo Jima."

I poured him a cup of tea and one for myself, then sat, awkwardly, across from him, first slipping off my coat.

"Oh?"

"Yes," I said, standing, too suddenly, to hang up my coat, forgetting the teacup balanced on the arm of the chair, spilling it onto the floor. It shattered into what seemed like a thousand white shards.

"Damn it," I said. "Goddamn it." He quickly helped, brushing the shards into a pile with his hand. I squatted next to him and when he started to laugh, I laughed, too. "Poor little teacup," he said, still laughing. "Poor little thing."

"It was so helpful," I said. "It was only trying to do its job."

"Poor thing," he said. "Poor little thing."

I watched him sleeping, I'm ashamed to admit. I couldn't sleep myself and so I slipped out of my bedroom, ostensibly for some milk, or a glass of juice. This I thought I would say if he woke up, if he found me there, standing next to the Salvation Army sofa. I had brought out a pillow and one of the quilts Mother had made for me after losing her factory job. He slept in his clothes, or most of them, his Eisenhower jacket folded into a square, no doubt regulation, and placed to the side of the sofa. I pulled back the curtain a bit so I could see him in the flashing yellow light. He seemed peaceful enough. I sat across from him, suddenly sleepy though not, somehow straddling the waking-dreaming line. Did I sleep at all? I don't know. I dreamt a Daphne story, I know. I saw her walking on a strange street, alone. She found a place to stay as she had said she would. I'll be fine, she had said that last day I saw her, don't be so goddamned frightened of the world. We stood on the steps of McCalister, Daphne leaning against the big stone urn that held Sister Pat's collection of impatiens and geraniums.

I'm not frightened, I said.

Bully for you, she said. I'm terrified.

I sat there most of the night. If I walked back into my bedroom, if I pulled the curtain and left him, again, in the dark, he might disappear as Randall disappeared, a note on the pillow for me to find long after he'd gone, *Sorry to have been a bother*, or something equally obsequious.

He breathed in the slow, even rhythm of a man sleeping. I unlaced his boots and slipped them off, pulled the quilt firmly around his shoulders in a nurselike gesture, smoothed his hair, dared to, then, touch the rough black stubble of his beard, to feel the faint pulse in his neck. I took his folded jacket and unfolded it, searched the pockets for anything and found a flask, and my name and address written on a piece of lined blue paper. I opened the flask and drank, though I'm ashamed to tell the truth of it, the bourbon— why not? Anything seemed possible: your father in a room that had before this been only mine. I tucked my bare feet underneath me, back in my watching chair, and pulled my own quilt into a cocoon, waiting. There are times when you understand that your life is turning somehow, propelled by circumstance. Earlier I had walked, disheartened, into an aspen grove; now I sat here with him. I was restless. I stood and drew the curtain again, fidgeted until the dark became impenetrable. If I had lit a candle, I might have seen the numbers on the walls, thousands of them, big, orange numbers in a random sequence, or at least a sequence I couldn't understand.

"Can you hear them?" Randall whispers.

"Who?" I say.

"Shhh," he says. "I'm listening."

I shut my eyes, catch my breath.

"I don't hear anything," I say.

"No, you can't," he says. He holds my hand, pressing my fingers, one by one, to his lips. "They're counting," he says.

"Why?"

"Shhh."

He puts one of my fingers into his mouth. I feel his tongue, warm, and want to pull my hand away but I do not want to at all. I clamp my eyes tighter, squeeze the darkness there into a red, burning light.

"Yes," I say. "I hear them."

"Yes?" Randall says, kissing my wrist now, where the veins are, where the skin stays translucent.

"Yes," I say. He has reached my neck, my face—his leg to my leg, his thin chest to mine. Soon he will tug me in an easy way to the cold, dirt floor, push my good Easter dress above my hips.

I wake to find your father near me. Who has drawn back the curtain? The room is bright with moonlight, or very early morning. It is still quiet. He is on his knees and kissing my shoulder where the bone curves toward the neck, and I have never, quite truthfully, been kissed there, and his finger hooks my sweater like a fish hook, pulls it out of his way and he smells like something vaguely sweet, bourbon, and his head is outlined in light the way a shadow will be sometimes and he is too close to tell the color of his hair or whether his face is thin or round or what, exactly, he's saying, because it might be anything until it's Daphne and it doesn't matter then because I'm already sinking, washed over by the tide of him, his hand now on my skin beneath my sweater so that I feel if I turn too quickly he might break me in two, my watery insides draining out the way they're already draining, the way he's already broken me when he pulls what is left, slipping, slippery in his hands, to the floor.

· *Book Three* ·

1

I knew much of Ruby's life before Sterling's confession. Randall and I had fit it together from the clues we found exploring the house, the letters Sterling kept in a locked tobacco box in his study. Our favorite was Ruby's from Paris—the one Randall had included in his package to me. I would read it often the summer following the news of Randall's death.

Ruby had sailed to Paris. Well, not to Paris, actually, and not sailed, this was 1926. She took the *Mauretania,* which held hundreds, or it looked like hundreds in the newspaper clipping included with the letter, grainy, the size of my palm, cut from a newspaper that had long ceased to publish. August 21, 1926. The *International* something. It said they had docked at some port in France I never heard of, though I imagined gray, narrow streets and laundry hanging out to dry: sea birds taut on the line. Their *destination,* it said, was Paris, destination a word as glamorous as baby, or milliner, or the name, Ruby.

The newspaper clipping came away on my fingers in dust. This that summer, when I did little else but shuffle through Randall's package, believing I might have missed something, that I might find a diamond ring looped to the spool of red thread or taped to the back cover of *The Gardens of Kyoto.*

I looked for Ruby in the newspaper photograph, hoping to find her among the waving passengers thronged onboard the *Mauretania,* her grand hat dotted with confetti, summer snow; but she was absent from the crowd.

Of course, I had already searched the photograph, nearly as many times as I had read the letter. Once, even, Randall took the magnifying glass his father kept in his study with the *Oxford English Dictionary* and, holding it up to his face like a detective, announced that the hunt could officially be declared over: he had found her.

He passed the magnifying glass to me and pointed with one of his slender fingers to a spot where a woman in what appeared to be a fox stole held a parasol over her head, presumably against the sun, and stared out toward the water away from the crowd.

She would have had no interest in the huddling masses, he said.

I peered at the woman with the fox stole, who looked nothing like Ruby, the Ruby in my mind or the Ruby I eventually met.

She's too old, I said.

She was older than my mother, he said. She could have been forty. When I met her she looked like she was a hundred.

You were two years old, I said. He had told me all this before: how she had come for a Christmas visit, how she had brought a train on a real track and smelled of snow and perfume, how after she had gone, Sterling boxed the train and track, insisting it be saved for future Christmases, though Randall never saw it again.

I remember everything, Randall said, and I knew, from the magnified expression on his face, that it would be better not to ask how. He seemed to be considering the same question, then he shrugged and said I was right, searching for Ruby on the *Mauretania* would be a futile exercise, that he hadn't the foggiest idea what she looked like.

You, I said, though I instantly regretted it.

She would be dressed to the nines, stepping up the gangplank to join the other passengers as streamers curled to the brackish harbor water below. In the distance the outline of the Statue of Liberty stands against the mist soon to be burned clear through by an August sun that has scarcely risen or set, everything conspiring to be a part of the theater: passengers in evening clothes, though it isn't yet noon; men and women who have come from parties, from cotillions, from jazz clubs and restaurants uptown, from dinner engagements, the opera. She maneuvers through them with the urgency of someone late for an appointment. She will not linger here with the noisemakers; she will go straight to her room. Her head aches and she feels the tiredness and nausea that have become too familiar. Perhaps it is lunacy to make the trip, to insist on this annual crossing as if nothing has changed, as if she were still simply Ruby, a successful single woman, a member of the Cosmopolitan Ladies, a New Yorker. No. She will get to Paris and conduct her business. And now she will smile for the press thronged at the base of the gangplank, shouting at her to look their way, to hold her hand up just a bit to right her hat—what did she call that one?—against the hot, dead wind.

It is then, perhaps, that he first notices her, though several days pass before he summons the courage to introduce himself.

They have been seated next to one another in the dining room, this not uncommon, as they are both traveling alone. The other guests at the table appear to know him, though it seems no one has gotten his name. They call him Doctor, and, one or two, Professor.

He speaks in a kind of mumble, swallowing his sentences before they are completed.

The boat lurches and he spills his wine.

"Apologies," he says. "Please."

"Don't bother," she says, dabbing the wine with her napkin. She sounds rude though that hadn't been her intention; she feels weak; conversation is a great effort. She hasn't much of an appetite, nor interest in wine. Indeed, she has so far spent most of the trip indoors, in her cabin, sketching. The sketches are tacked to the thin, pine veneer of the walls and she often lies on her narrow bunk, widening and narrowing her eyes for different perspectives, staring at the charcoal lines. On the darker days of the crossing, she believes she has lost all talent.

"What?" he says.

"I'm sorry?" she says.

"You said something about a child's drawing."

"I did?" she says. "My God. I really should have stayed below. It's nothing. Truly. I was just thinking out loud."

He does, on closer inspection, have large eyes; luminous in the shaky candlelight.

"Are you an artist?" he asks. They serve fish: thin slices of salmon and new potatoes, someone says. She might blanch. She waves her hand over her plate. "No, thank you," she says.

"I'm sorry?" she says to him.

"I thought you might be an artist. There are so many onboard— you haven't noticed?"

She hadn't.

"Final chance for the Expo, I'm told. Last night I met a Japanese gentleman who bends bamboo into the most extraordinary shapes. He couldn't get over his good fortune. Said they had invited him and paid his way. His shapes are poetry, I believe. Or some form of it. I plan to go there after. Japan. Once I'm through with this. One was called Pebble in a Pond and you could almost see the ripples. A basket. But I'm babbling and here I asked you the question, didn't I?"

"I'm not an artist," she says. "I design hats."

"How extraordinary."

"Not really. No, not at—"

The group at the end of the table shout to him; they are attempting to amicably settle a debate, they call, on the genus of hydrangea.

He answers their question and slightly bows to their applause. His tuxedo seems too large, too broad in the shoulders. He wears it as one wears an overcoat, shrinking within, although anything would seem too large on him. He has the gaunt look of someone who has recently recuperated from a long illness, though he has shaved—all the men do for dinner—and his cheeks are flushed and smooth. He blushes as they applaud, the blush deepening as he stands, again, at their insistence.

Perhaps she then notices the wine stain on his sleeve.

"I have no idea as to the right answer," he whispers, sitting. "I just wanted to be done with it."

In the corner of the vast room a string quartet tunes their instruments. Soon the dancing begins; waiters clearing dinner plates, pouring a sweet German wine, rolling dessert carts among the tables—chocolate éclairs, ginger snaps and sorbet, strawberries, scones, crème fraîsche—braking the wheels against the rocking sea. The ship cleaves waves, rides high then thumps hard on the flat black water. He points to her empty plate. Perhaps they should step outside, he suggests. From here it looks an almost full moon. Waxing full. The air might revive her.

This has taken enormous courage, which she recognizes.

"I'm exhausted," she says.

"Of course."

He stands, all the men do, as she excuses herself. Someone from another table calls her name. Earlier she had promised him a dance, hadn't she? "Tomorrow," she says. They have all begun to blur: the men in their tuxedos laughing, smoking, arguing; the women, fading beside them, their rhinestone-studded dresses tinkling loud as these chandeliers would in storms. She grips a chair and steadies herself, though no one notices until she folds to the floor, lying cold between two tables, her ankles oddly crossed, modest in her descent. Waiters rush to her, as do those seated at her dinner table and the professor, who someone again mistakes for a doctor. He goes along. He knows her well enough, doesn't he? He lifts her to a chair, unbuttons the top buttons of her dress. He asks the others to move away and holds the water glass to her lips, watching her eyes, beautiful, flutter open. He would like to touch her thick, black hair.

She drinks the water. It's nothing, she says; she must be over-tired. Still, she agrees when he offers to escort her back to her cabin and, still faint, lets him guide her.

"I think they're very good," he says. He stands with his suit jacket off, his back crisscrossed by suspenders, his hands deep in his pockets, staring at her sketches, moving from one to another as if he were in a museum.

She watches him from where she sits, feet up. "Really," he says.

"They help me think. They're not intended for viewing."

"The line is strong."

"I thought you were posing as a doctor, not a critic."

"I'm not posing as anything. I'm just a passenger on a boat to Paris."

"I didn't mean to suggest—"

"I like to sketch. I did quite a bit during the war—"

"I'm sorry."

He waves it away.

"I published a little book. It's the reason I'm here. They want me to speak at the disarmament convention in Amsterdam."

"So, you're a pacifist."

"No. I'm a horticulturist who happened to publish a little book that is beloved by pacifists."

She smiles. He is a bit like Sterling. Bookish that way.

"Well, thank God that's over."

"Yes," he says. "Thank God."

He crosses the cabin and sits next to her and she thinks she might press a better crease in his trousers, that she might soak the sleeve of his white shirt in salt water to remove the stain. "I could find you a real doctor, though, if you'd like. I thought I should get you out of the dining room as quickly as possible."

"There's nothing wrong with me. I'm in a delicate way, and the smell of cigars no longer agrees with me."

He raises his eyebrows.

"Please don't look so shocked, it's depressing."

"I don't look shocked."

"Yes, you do."

"Well, I'm not."

"Of course you are. Anyway, let's not discuss it. Tell me about your little book, as you call it. What's it about?"

"Flowers," he says.

"Flowers?" she says.

"Yes, flowers," he says. "And please don't look so shocked. It's depressing."

Who knows the truth of it? Randall and I had read the letter countless times, memorized the name of the hotel embossed in the faint gray crest at the top of the stationery.

Made a new friend on the Crossing, it began,

who has introduced me to this wonderful little hotel in the Latin quarter. A professor of something; a horteculturalist (sp?) who is off to study Japanese gardens. Apparently he stayed here during The War for a while, in the same corner room with the same corner window that looks onto the same square in which bubbles a broken fountain, its statue that of cupid, he claims, though I believe it might just as easily be a forest nymph. Don't be jealous, baby. He seems to have no interest in women, nor men, for that matter. Claims The War beat it out of him. He is one of The Damaged, as you would say. The kind you have so little tolerance for, frightened as a lamb. Terrible to watch him drink a glass of wine. But a professor, a man who loves flowers. Truly. I like him. You would, too.

On warm days like this one she puts her toes in the cool fountain water and reads a book or writes a letter. This is where she is now, she writes. If she looks up she can see the window into her own hotel room, its window box of geraniums; inside, water drips incessantly from the bathtub faucet, but she cannot bear to give up her corner spot or the yellow porcelain tiles of the bathroom floor. She would like to bring some of this porcelain home, but that's Paris, isn't it? Always wanting to carry it back with you in your suitcase.

The streets, this square, smell of fresh rain, the rest of the city, the Parisians, buoyant, the talk only that of the Expo. The future. Modernism. They say it's the first time they've felt hopeful since The War, though I don't find much to admire in what's left of it along the Seine. I'd rather just stare at the bridges. To me, everything shrieks and is far too large, like an overgrown brat nursed on heavy cream; the Huns were behind it, naturally, though they've again done something to anger everyone. I can't remember what. Of the amusing things I found a glass fountain that appears to have sprouted from the ground, and a fabric designer with whom I have literally fallen in love. I have indulged in an outrageously expensive bolt of brushed linen with the most vivid, hand-painted roses, a gift for Jeannette, who adores roses.

It went on. She had come up with one or two good ideas, inspired as always by the city. Just the look of it! Fruits and breads and cheeses in the shop windows, buckets of flowers at the Saturday market, freshly ironed antique lace along the Boulevard Saint Germain. You should wash it in milk, she'd been told, as you should wash in milk wool worn by children.

But she had news, this the reason for her letter. She was pregnant, she feared. No, in fact, she knew. She wanted to tell him, to give him time to think about it before she returned. They would discuss it then.

And there, surely, Sterling must have heard her refusal, his heart sinking at the abruptness of her disclosure as it would sink on seeing her again when she returned from Paris. He had waited with the rest of the crowd for the passengers to disembark, but she was not among them. She lay below, knees drawn to her chest. When she stood at last she stumbled a bit then got her footing; so odd to lack motion, to feel the boat at rest.

"I'm fine," she said; Sterling had appeared at the door of her cabin, having bribed a steward to let him onboard. She gripped the edge of the top bunk and smiled. Thin, she looked. What had he been expecting? A pregnant woman, round, cheerful. A wife. She shook her head as if to say, I'm sorry. And for an instant they simply stood, Randall somewhere between them, no more a boy than a fish with wings.

I fold the stationery, dropping the newspaper clipping's broken corner into the crease, placing the all of it back inside *The Gardens of*

Kyoto; then I join Betty on the porch steps. The summer after Randall's death is a particularly hot one, and Mother has forbidden us to
leave the house, or to visit with any of our friends. Marjorie Winn,
our next-door neighbor, came down with polio in May, her father
bringing her home from the hospital and carrying her inside the
house as we stood at the end of our walk, waving, Mother hissing
from behind the screen door that if we didn't get ourselves back
inside that minute it would serve us right if we ended up in an iron
lung. The farthest we could go was the porch steps, she said, marking it with her toe, as if we couldn't tell for ourselves where the
porch steps ended and the gravel of the walk began. I don't even
want you gardening.

Mother, Betty had said. You would think it's carried in the air.

It might be, Mother said. It might very well be.

Then I won't breathe, Betty said, pursing her lips until her face
went bright red.

Good, Mother had said, leaving.

"Hey," Betty says now, kicking her leg out into the gravel.

"Hey," I say.

I sit next to her and stretch my own legs out.

Betty turns toward me with a sneer. She might mind Mother
and sit on the porch steps, but she wants to touch everything that
has been forbidden, to scour, provoke. She has half a mind, she's
told me, to swim in Jacob's Creek, where Rita stole the frogs; or she
might pull off all her clothes and run around Old Man Springfield's
orchard, drive the tractor in circles.

"How's your boyfriend?" she says now, cruelly.

"Dead," I say. "Yours?"

2

There were several colored soldiers on the ferry—their uniforms the same as the white soldiers' uniforms, though they were directed to sit in back in the colored section. I watched as one, tall and skinny as Randall, helped a woman who looked to be his grandmother up the metal stairway to the second-floor deck. She held on to his skinny arm and walked so slowly that the colored line hardly moved. The white line went fast, all the white people already sitting in the uncomfortable wooden pew beneath the deck awning, watching the slow-moving colored line and the confusion—men and women stepping out of the order of the line to wonder about the holdup, other soldiers saying they would like to get to Baltimore before sunset—as if watching the screen at a picture show. You couldn't touch or get close or help the colored people; they were in their line and we had already come through ours. These were the rules back then and for whatever reason people followed the rules.

I was on my way to visit Sterling. He had sent ferry fare with a cryptic note made all the more mysterious by his wavering script.

Given my fondness for his son, Randall, he wrote, he believed I might be interested in some recent accidental findings. I should meet him at such and such a date, on the earliest ferry. He had signed it, Your devoted Great-Uncle, Sterling, a gesture so at odds with my memory of him that I half-expected to arrive greeted by a stranger, someone spry and handsome, someone who might, upon seeing me, drop to one knee and fling his cape to the sand.

Perhaps this is the reason I took such care with my appearance. I wore Mother's old linen wedding suit, which had been brought down from the attic the week before and still smelled of mothballs. The shade of green looked better with her coloring, she said, eyeing me, but it would do fine under the circumstance. The circumstance, of course, was that we were poor and soon we would be poorer, Mother knowing that any day she would get a tap on the shoulder from the foreman. She had already seen it happen to the women in the higher positions, the ones whose jobs were the most appealing to the soldiers returning from Europe. She rightly knew that it would happen to her next.

Anyway, this was a *nice* linen suit, she told me. It had been purchased at Bergdorf's in New York City on a buying trip her rich Great-Aunt Maude, Sterling's sister, had taken her on a few months before her wedding. This was in '24, she told me. The summer. We took the train, Mother said, Maude insisting I sit next to the window and look out because you never know, she said, when your life might take a turn and you won't have anything interesting to see again. But then, she loved travel, Maude. She'd been everywhere. Women did in those days.

Mother stepped back and squinted at me, pins in her mouth. Then she stepped up again and bent to the hem.

That was the first time I met Ruby, she said, still looking down, her voice a bit garbled by the pins though I heard her clearly enough.

Ruby, Ruby? I said.

Ouch. Stand still.

I'm sorry.

I stepped closer.

She was a designer in this little hat store in Greenwich Village, she said. Can't remember the name, but the hats were the cleverest hats I had ever seen. Sterling had given Maude the address. He knew she would adore Ruby.

Did she?

Of course, Mother said, straightening. Everyone did.

Mother smiled, then, confirming my suspicion that my secret was known to her.

Maude was very impressed. Ruby fluttered around that store like a nervous Nelly, hat to hat to hat. She couldn't decide, she told us, which to take abroad. The shows, she said, as if we would understand. What did we think of the blue?

I stood very still though Mother seemed to have lost interest in my hem. I believe if she had been less caught up in her own story, she might have seen the odd look on my face.

There was a particularly flamboyant one, Mother continued. Red, I remember, with the widest brim I had ever seen and gold mesh netting. I said, Not the blue. I said, That one. And Ruby snatched it up and kissed me. You're a genius, she said. You must come back and work in the store. No question, she said. It could only be red.

Mother looked back at me then, as if suddenly remembering I was there.

Of course Maude explained to her that we were in New York on a buying trip for my *wedding*, that I wouldn't *need* to work. Funny, isn't it?

I didn't know what to say and so I looked down and stretched out my arms. They're uneven.

You're slouching.

I locked my knees and straightened my shoulders.

Oh, I said.

*   *   *

I looked out to the Chesapeake and tightened my hold on my suitcase. It seems strange, now, in thinking about it, that Mother let me travel alone, that she let me go at all. Several months had passed since Sterling had sold the house and moved back to Baltimore; still, I believe Mother must have felt, as I did, that there might be more we could offer him. I remember how, during the estate sale, she insisted that he put his bad leg up on a footstool she carried outside expressly for that purpose, how she propped his foot on a cushion and pulled his drooping sock up to his ankle.

Anyway, Sterling had written that he would meet me at Sandy Point, and that we would from there commence forward, which I had, at the time, assumed meant to Baltimore. Mother and Daddy drove me as far as Love Point, waiting in line with all the other automobiles to get on to the ferry before turning off at the ramp. I was on my own for the crossing, a journey that would take less than an hour.

The ferry engines fired and the great boat shook as if to split in two then settled into a steady drone. We pulled out on the bay. Around us the Annapolis men practiced their drills in sleek blue sailboats—crisscrossing the paths of the uglier victory ships heading north—and fishermen pulled in their hauls of rockfish and crab, the water as crowded as a city road. I shoved my suitcase underneath the wooden pew and stood, wanting to join the group clustered at the railing, seagulls over their heads like a pack of dogs in pursuit. The early morning, the smell of the water and the fresh, cooler air, had somehow lifted my spirits and made me bold; I was terribly shy then, and normally to join a group of strangers would have been impossible. But I did. I joined the others, my hands gripping the gray-painted metal railing against the breeze of the crossing as if I were in some danger of being blown backwards, as if I might skitter across the bay like a dry leaf. I closed my eyes and tasted the wake spray, imagining that when the boat finally bumped the wooden dock of Sandy Point it would be Randall waiting next to the automobile, leaning against the hood like some kind of movie star, his hand up to shade his eyes from what would then be the near-noon glare. I'd wave, one hand in the air, the other gripping my wide-brim red hat, its gold mesh casting a net shadow across my face.

But it was only Sterling on the other side. He stood stiffly next to one of the few automobiles parked at the landing. I waved as we got closer; not the wave I would have given Randall, of course. A simple wave. Shy, because I was again shy as soon as the engines of the boat were cut, the sound now just that of the seagulls and the quieter *chuck chuck* of the readying automobiles. Most of the other passengers had driven on to the ferry and would simply drive off again, continuing down the two-lane road to wherever it was they were going.

Attendants jumped to the dock to knot the thick lead ropes to the piers; everyone frantic in the way of arrival. I was in no rush. I took the steps down slowly, thinking how I hadn't the slightest idea what Sterling and I would talk about, and though I had been initially curious as to what he had to tell me, I was not so naive as to not know that he was simply a lonely man, a man who would want to bring the conversation around to his son, again.

And so I must have seemed rather reticent at our reunion. Of course I am sorry about that now.

Mother had prepared one of her pineapple upside-down cakes and I immediately presented this to him. He nodded and placed it in the trunk along with my suitcase, then guided me around to the passenger's side of the automobile, the tips of his fingers on my elbow as cool as chicken skin, his limp more pronounced, the leg that was sometimes in a brace, sometimes not, shriveled to mere bone, twisted, I knew, beneath his loose trousers; Randall had told me.

Please, he said, opening the door.

I sat down on the hot leather seat and watched him limp around the front to the driver's side; it seemed to take forever and so I rolled down my window and leaned out to smell again the salt air of the Chesapeake.

"You've grown," he said, getting back in with some effort. He took a pair of leather gloves from the dashboard and carefully pulled on one and then the other. I remember thinking how the leather gloves matched the seat, wondering if the gloves had been purchased with the automobile, which was fine: the steering wheel a highly polished cherry, chrome instruments along the dashboard. The gear shaft, a monstrous thing, stuck straight up between us, its handle sheathed in black leather.

"I'm five feet, seven inches and a half," I said.

"Taller than I remember," he said.

"Yes sir."

"When did that happen?"

"A full inch since spring," I said, straightening my shoulders.

"And how old?"

"I'll be sixteen in January."

"Sixteen."

"Yes sir."

We were driving now, climbing the hills that were, on the other side of the bay, less common.

"Do you recognize this?" he asked.

I looked at him but he simply stared out at the road.

"The road?"

"The landscape, yes."

"No sir."

"Your parents came here once, when you were just a baby. Rita must have been five or six. You stayed with your sisters and Randall at our Baltimore house; poor Jeannette elected to keep an eye on all of you."

So I had known him as a baby; I had even met Jeannette.

"Funny. Somebody died. It was the reason for the visit and now I can't think who."

We passed signs for clams, lobster. A giant billboard read "Fresh Peas, California-Style," with a picture of a red pickup truck loaded with tiny green peas and two children, a boy and a girl, standing beside it, their teeth blackened to missing.

"Stupid business, getting old," he said. "Dumb and stupid."

"Yes sir."

We drove in silence after that. I counted the fenceposts that lined one particular pasture and attempted to count the horses clustered near a salt lick, but we were going too fast. Thirty miles an hour, maybe forty; real driving in those days. The dust kicked up from the road.

I wanted to think of something to say, something clever. Rita would have known what; she would have chattered all the way to Baltimore. But I liked the silence in the automobile, the occasional bump as we hit a rock in the road and Sterling broke the yellow-painted line dividing one direction from the other. Every once in a while, an automobile would approach heading back toward the ferry landing and Sterling, or the other driver, would honk, and the two would raise their hands just so slightly in greeting.

It was after about twenty, twenty-five minutes of driving that I felt Sterling shift down, the automobile slowing.

"Look there," he said.

I couldn't see what he pointed at; it seemed to me just another field behind some trees, a kite on a flagpole.

"The kite?"

"That's a wind sock. That tells you the direction."

He signaled a turn with his hand and we drove down a long gravel road through a narrow line of trees, past the wind sock and up to a low, rambling building. It looked at first like stables and I thought that perhaps Sterling wanted to show me a horse; Jeannette, I believe, had been a rider. But then I saw the silver glint of the wings; this one had a turquoise body and silver wings.

"Always wanted to do this," Sterling said.

He turned off the engine and sat with his hands on the beautiful cherry steering wheel.

"Are those your flying clothes?" he asked.

And then, of course, I understood.

We found the pilot tipped back in a chair behind a wide aluminum desk in an office papered with calendars of months past—the stillness there almost matching the stillness we would later feel in the air. He was an old friend of Sterling's who had been called up from the reserves to finish the job in Germany, Sterling said. I don't quite know what he was doing in that office, whether he flew his biplane during the week to dust the crops of the farms that spread in every direction around us, or whether this was simply a place he had found for himself and his plane after returning from Europe. He seemed singularly alone, and I imagined that he had flown that plane back from Germany west over the Atlantic, landing here, on the eastern shore, to stretch his legs and his arms, to shrug and move on.

I'm sure he had a name but I have long since forgotten it. What I remember best is how his face looked like scratched glass and how strong his hands were as he lifted me to squeeze in next to Sterling. I willed myself not to be afraid as the pilot patted one of the wings, still scorched with sun, and swung himself up behind the controls. The propeller spat into motion, circling then steadying into a low whir.

"See?" Sterling said, and I nodded, or attempted to nod. He was too close to turn to and besides, we were suddenly in a rush of air, racing faster than I had ever raced, the plane bumping then hovering, bumping then climbing, the trees a black outline beneath us so quickly I barely had time to catch my breath. I had to strain to keep my eyes wide open, the sky all around me a vast portal elsewhere. We flew directly through the clouds. That was what was most astounding. Below us the woods fell away to fields divided by roads; I saw the outline of a circle sliced as neatly as a pie, an irrigation unit, I later learned, though at the time it seemed a farmer's whimsy. Silver silos caught the glint of sun and signaled back to us. All of it language, somehow, spoken by what had before had no voice, the water loudest as we swooped low over the Chesapeake, buzzing the ferry that now carried its load of passengers back across to the mainland, then climbing higher, losing the bay's roar to the silence of that pure sky, that bright light.

It was then, I believe, that Sterling took my hand, and I felt for the first time his fingers like loose die in my palm, never before having touched this man whose son I loved, because I did, truly, love Randall. Cousins sometimes do.

3

It was too warm for a cardigan, but Sterling wore his usual dress shirt buttoned at the cuffs, and suspenders. We stood outside the foundation, near the stone step that had once led to the front door of Randall's house. Now it rose to nothing. Nearby the few remaining oaks cast their full leaf shadows. If the house had been left to stand it would be cool inside; the way Randall liked it. He never liked the sun much; he always claimed he would have been better suited for England, where they stay indoors all day and read, the weather too lousy to do anything else. A light drizzle, Randall would say, is perfection.

I shivered, something eerily dead about the scene. We had reached the house, or what had become of the house, in no time, landing in a clearing in the field across the road then steering, bumping up the drive.

"Did you know?" I yelled at Sterling as soon as the propeller wound down. He nodded and I might have pummeled my fists on his chest if he had not been such an old man, if his expression as he struggled to get out of the narrow body of the plane had not been one of such deep regret. The pilot lifted me free, then disappeared somewhere; the truth is I could pay little attention to anything but the wreckage before me: piles of brick and shattered glass and upturned roots and a suddenly monotonous view of the neighboring fields, the swath of woods that had once divided Randall's house from the surrounding farms razed to tree stump after tree stump. Oddly, a single wall from the Gallery of Maps still stood—as if the destruction were a result of a tornado not a wrecking ball—its water stains and spidery fissures untouched, oblivious. I thought of Randall pointing out the various cities he planned to visit. If it were Europe he'd say Verona and Venice. For Shakespeare. If South America he'd point to Chile. Bolivar.

And did I know that the soldier was a champion tennis player?

I did not.

Or was I aware that Bolivar was in love with a woman from Connecticut? That letters were exchanged? That there was talk of her following him, though she died as she had lived, a librarian in love with a revolutionary?

I had no idea.

Strange, now, remembering. The place so clearly contained him, though there was no Randall's room nor windows with what's left to learn, the dusty mullions dividing lines among those long lists illuminated by the setting suns, one every day to remind him, he would say, though at sunset he rarely felt in the mood.

Had I ever heard the word *corpuscular*?

I had not.

No dining room where we would sit, side by side, hands freshly washed and waiting to be excused. No parlor to race through, no wing chairs to maneuver in the living room, its smell of wet fires still strong, the cooling ash thick in the belly grate of the andirons, their heavy prongs twisting into worn lions' heads, the crest of some Elizabethan lord. We'd pat their heads for good luck as the Medicis patted the snout of the great bronze boar in the Florence market, Randall said, wanting to impress the commoners for reasons I was still too young to understand.

And did I know that the king's fingers were on display in Rome, hacked off by the commoners and laid out like ten white pencils on a black velvet cushion?

I did not.

No Sterling's study in which to hunt for clues, his heavy books lining the walls, the volumes smelling of pipe tobacco, his Bible there on the highest shelf, where Randall would reach to find the tiny key hidden on its ribbon in the back fold. He'd climb back down and dangle it in front of him, in front of me. "The key to his heart," he'd say, rolling his eyes.

It unlocked the tobacco box on the secretary where he'd found the letters we read so many times, stacked and tied exactly as we'd left them: the cheerful few sent from Virginia during Ruby's sabbatical, the best from Paris: it Randall's favorite, of course, the one he'd save for last. He said he liked the sound of it in a girl's voice and I was the only girl around. I'd read about the geraniums, the business of the poor little lamb, the bolt of fabric with the hand-painted roses, the something she had to tell him. Afterward, Randall kissed the colored wax that sealed the flap. "How very, very," he said, fanning himself with the envelope before locking the tobacco box and returning the key to the Bible.

And did he show me *The Gardens of Kyoto*? Did he tell me she smelled of snow and perfume?

He did.

The heat had reached its noon peak, triggering the cicadas.

"Don't look so low-down, please," Sterling said. "It's a business concern. They wanted the land."

He limped ahead of me and we walked through what remained

of the foundation, stepping over rubble to reach the Gallery of Maps wall, which I recognized now as Asia Minor. The next panel would be Africa, I knew, wondering whether the ghosts of the slaves might still appear here from time to time, clustered in what had once been the kitchen. "The reason this did not topple," Sterling said, "is because someone long ago reinforced it with a cement base."

He looked at me but I must have stared back blankly.

"Randall was correct," he said. "The station masters always gave one wall extra weight so that when you knocked upon it, it would make a louder sound. Here," he said, "where the slaves hid." He tapped the wall. "Think of it as a telephone." He tapped, again. "Of course you need to be on the other side to hear. There were codes and the like." I thought of the secret room, the slaves huddled there listening to the knocks on the cemented wall, each number corresponding to a different letter, the clusters of numbers we had seen written across the walls actually words spoken between those on the side of freedom and those still running for their lives.

"But that's not the end of it," Sterling said. He turned and limped out of the foundation, swinging his bad leg forward then steadying it on the rubble. I followed him, past long, neatly stacked rows of tree trunks with sheared limbs. The land, as well as the house, desecrated, shorn bald. I couldn't think of what Randall would have said, seeing it this way. I know he hated change, things rearranged. Even the dust that covered the desk in his room seemed an indispensable part of the whole.

"It's a shame your cousin never liked the out-of-doors," he was saying. "He might have discovered this for himself. They found it when they cleared the land."

Sterling had stopped, though nothing seemed particular about the spot. He tilted his head slightly, as if listening for horse hooves, then smoothed his hands over his trouser legs and leaned with some effort into what appeared to be another mass of bramble, removing the crisscrossing branches and dead sticks that I now saw had been placed this way to hide something quite large: what looked, at first, like an elaborate trellis on which thick vines had been trained to grow, though slowly emerged into the form of a cage too big for any commonly hunted animal, its bars the same black iron as that used to shoe horses. Rusted shackles hung from the top rungs, and a strange studded paddle Sterling later told me was used for flogging served as a kind of lock on the door, or what had once been the door. When Sterling pulled the lock free it fell off its rusted hinges.

"The bounty hunters used them to transport the fugitives back to where they had run off from, Virginia, most likely, or even Kings County," Sterling said. He struggled to lift the door back into place and though I offered to help he waved me away, jamming down the flogging lock to hold it, his breath short. "They must have known the house was a depot. Kept watch."

"They must have," I said; I was thinking of the ghost family: the way Randall said they always stood so close together, huddled, the man's arms straight down at his sides, the woman with a scar as thick as a finger around her neck—he thought it a scar, though the family faded so quickly it was difficult to know for sure: it might have been a rope; it might have been a necklace.

We heard the drone of the pilot in his beautiful plane somewhere overhead: we would spend the night at the Dew Drop Inn; the pilot would return for us in the morning.

"I find it the greatest of ironies, as an Edwards scholar, that I lived in this house those years entirely unaware of its history, or even the suspicion of its history," Sterling said, looking past me as if he were opening a lecture before a classroom and it were not simply I, there, in the razed wood alone with my great-uncle listening, but a collection of students already versed in great ironies. But the lecture ended almost as quickly as it began. Sterling steadied himself against the cage and turned toward the fields that could now be seen in all directions, the cage like some kind of iron haystack from a hideous fairy tale before the yellowing, soon-to-be harvested wheat.

"What I have always admired about Jonathan Edwards," he said, "was his unwavering belief in the Almighty. He had no doubt," he said. "Absolutely none."

4

When they opened the box, Sterling read, the slave sang a Psalm. He had been sent up from Richmond, Virginia, packaged by the fellow members of the Mount Zion Church of which he had always been a faithful and sustaining member. The box was a crate built from wood bought with his savings. He had left a wife and three children and he had had a fourth child and his wife had gone dumb when the child went on the block and was sold before her eyes. That child had been born in the cotton season, and the other three in the soybean. When they opened the box he had one single five-cent piece in his pocket. The Psalm he sang was *I waited patiently for the Lord, and He heard my prayer.*

His name was Romulus Perkins. From then on they called him Romulus Box Perkins.

Sterling appeared to barely look at the page. His eyes, quite truthfully, might have been shut, or in the half-opened state of prayer. He seemed to have memorized the words he now read.

The wife of Romulus waited with his children for the conductor to return to Virginia. Romulus had taken her cape and told her that the conductor would show her the cape and that this would be the sign to trust him. Before she had gone dumb, when they would speak of freedom, she would say she dreamed of sitting under her own vine and fig tree in a place where none dared to molest her or to make her afraid.

He had traveled in his box on a schooner owned by a law-breaking captain who would carry any kind of freight for a price. He was addressed to James A. Smith, Sudlersville, Maryland, and though his fellow members of the Mount Zion Church had painted "This Side Up" on the box, the law-breaking captain couldn't read a word and so Romulus Box Perkins stood on his head for the journey, nearly thirty-six hours.

His wife belonged to the late Littleton Reeves. Romulus Box Perkins had recently been sold to Joe E. Sadler Esq., a negro trader. The third time on the block, he had been greased and rubbed hard to look shining then lashed to a bench and held by four men while flogged with a broad leather strap. This to show his compliance. He could read and write. He was by all accounts a dark orange color, medium size.

Sterling shifted his gaze to me. It was all a matter of public record, he explained. Just took some digging and the clout he wielded as a judge. He told them he was engaged in a biography of Jonathan Edwards, which, of course, was true, though he spent most of his library time searching for information on Smith. "I don't know why it would matter," he said. "I don't know what I'm afraid of."

We sat in the dining room of the Dew Drop Inn. The notes he had taken were written in his cramped, angry hand in a black-spined notebook, the kind I have always associated with lawyers and judges, and though it was difficult for me to believe Sterling afraid of anything, I imagined him hunched at a long oak library table, one arm guarding the fingers that held the pen that copied the story of Romulus Box Perkins, recorded, apparently, by a freed slave, printed in a limited edition and distributed in Philadelphia. Several years later the edition was printed, again, in a bound collection by a press that brought out the works of Walt Whitman and Ralph Waldo Emerson. The Baltimore public library, free to the white public, had one copy, though Sterling said he suspected he might have been the first to take it from the shelves, given the stiffness of its spine.

"The size of the box and how it was made to fit him most comfortably was of his own ordering. Two feet eight inches deep, two feet wide, and three feet long were the exact dimensions of the box, lined with baize," Sterling continued. "His resources with regard to water and food consisted of the following: one bladder of water and a few small biscuits. His mechanical implement to meet the death-struggle for fresh air, all told, was one large gimlet. Satisfied that it would be far better to peril his life for freedom in this way than to remain under the galling yoke of Slavery, he entered his box, which was safely nailed up and hooped with five hickory hoops, and was then addressed to James A. Smith."

Sterling shut the notebook and looked at me, his eyes watery.

"The previous owner of the house."

"Your house?"

"Mine," he said. "And Randall's. Once. Apparently, Mr. Smith was a station master. That room you and Randall discovered must have been the temporary residence of our Romulus Box."

"A box for Romulus Box," I said. "And family." I was thinking how Randall described the little ones, the girl who sometimes smiled, the one with the plaited hair, the look-alike boys.

"I doubt that," Sterling said. "By all accounts, the law-breaking captain never managed to get back to Virginia; they were ambushed by bounty hunters in King of Prussia. Killed the whole parcel of them. I don't believe she would have had any other means by which to join Romulus."

"But she did," I said. My certainty was uncharacteristic, though I somehow knew she would have tried alone if no one returned with her cape; she would have taken the children, knowing the address the members of the Mount Zion Church had painted on the box that contained her husband. They were eventually there, together; Randall had seen them: a family waiting for a family portrait. Perhaps James A. Smith had opened the door one night to find Eliza square in the doorway, her fingers and toes frostbitten. Perhaps she had tried to speak, her mouth grotesquely contorted, stretched wide as if words might finally come in freedom. She was Eliza, wife of Romulus, she might have said. She loved to sing. The children, behind her, were hungry, barely covered by a stolen horse blanket, chiggers crisscrossing their chests, burrowing beneath their skin in long, raised rows. Ringworms ringed the soles of their feet.

If Eliza could have spoken, she would have said, The Christian wolves pursue me. This is what Randall said. Randall said the ghosts of the family could no longer speak, but if they could have spoken they would have said, The Christian wolves pursue me. It was an expression of the time, he said.

And Randall had been right; the Christian wolves had lain in wait in those woods, the hinges and bolts on their cages oiled as slickly as they would oil the mouths of their fugitive slaves, claiming to have treated them well on the journey back, fed them fresh, greasy meat.

The dining room emptied just after dark, the few other guests farm salesmen who ate alone at the tables along the windows, their newspapers propped on sugar bowls. They seemed mildly curious at Sterling and me; we must have looked peculiar—grandfather and granddaughter they might have guessed; anything else I don't want to imagine.

We ate, at first, in silence. I had washed my face and brushed my hair hard, shaking out the linen suit, changing only my blouse. I wore one, I remember, with a Peter Pan collar, just fashionable at the time, and I had recently had my hair bobbed in the way the girls did who worked on the assembly lines: Daddy called it the Rosie Riveter look, but I didn't care. I felt newly grown-up in the single room Sterling had reserved for me, with a narrow bed covered by a satin spread. A wardrobe stood in one corner and I hung my night-gown on a cedar-smelling wooden hanger and lined my hairbrush and comb along its narrow shelf.

Sterling met me for dinner downstairs, carrying the black-spined notebook as carefully as a tome. But it wasn't until the last salesman stood and stretched to yawn, folding his newspaper under his arm and winking at me as he left, that Sterling cleared his throat and began to read the details of the slaves that had sought refuge in James A. Smith's home. Remember, this was Maryland, 1945. The eastern shore. No one liked to hear about colored people. It was as if everyone pretended they just didn't exist, pretended they were in the midst of a flock of black ghosts, and if they just looked through them and set their expressions, they might wake some morning to find them gone, up and flown on in the middle of the night. Or this is the way your grandfather's best friend, Tate Williams, Dr. Billy, used to put it. He said, that's why they call us crow, you understand.

From Sudlersville, Sterling read, the slaves had gone to Philadel-phia. From Philadelphia, Canada. Apparently many slaves had trav-eled this line of the Railroad, diverted up the eastern shore by the law-breaking captain, known in all records as D.

It was D who had had the change of heart, who had been per-suaded by the fugitive hunters to turn in the station master, James A. Smith. The fugitive hunters ambushed him on a February evening. The details here get sketchy, Sterling said. He had found Smith's obituary in an abolitionist newspaper published out of New York City. He showed me the paper, the sketch of Smith—a man who looked like he might have been a past president, his beard inked in soft lines. James A. Smith alias James Griffin, it read:

Of whom he harbored: Paul Washington alias Thomas Brown, a

tiller of soil under the yoke of Joshua Hitch; Benjamin Ross alias Thomas Stewart, held to the service or labor by D. James Muse; Mary Ennis alias Licia Hemmin, the so-called property of John Ennis. And so on.

James A. Smith, it read, fell in defense of freedom, shot in the groin once and twice through the heart.

"Did they get away?" I asked.

We sat in a center table, away from the dark windows though our reflections were there like silent twins, listening. They blocked the blue moon I had earlier seen from my window. The blue moon, the second moon Randall had taught me, happens one month out of every year. That month the moon rises twice, he said, once at the beginning, once at the end.

"Entirely unclear," Sterling said. "That's the damning thing: this is as far as I got." He took the obituary back and folded it into his black-spined notebook. "You didn't like your fish?" he said.

"I wasn't hungry."

"It's one of the local ones. Shame to waste it." Sterling dabbed his mouth with the linen napkin, looking away, toward the black windows, his face turned to his twin in the glass.

"No trace remains of our friend Mr. Perkins," he said to it. "He may have reached Canada, he may have been killed alongside Mr. Smith. It seems even the abolitionist press didn't see fit to mention one way or the other."

"No, I guess they didn't."

"You guess correctly," he said, turning back to me; it felt a reprimand, for what, I couldn't tell, though it may have been for sitting here as me in my Peter Pan collar, with my bobbed hair. I imagine Randall would have had some better questions; or maybe Randall would have had the answers.

"He might have known."

"Smith?"

"Randall."

Sterling pushed his chair back then, put his napkin on his dinner plate. "We get an early start tomorrow morning," he said.

"He was smart that way; he found clues," I said.

"I'll knock for you punctually, seven A.M."

I looked at him; in remembering I see an old man, his wise eyes fogged by cataracts. He had relearned to walk through sheer force of will, and studied law with the same determination. But old age had begun to defeat him. I see him holding on to that notebook as if it were Randall himself. He had no one left. He had lost his son. I see this now, but at the time I did not. I saw instead someone imperious, someone I wanted to hurt.

"Why didn't you like him?" I said, so cruelly it is difficult to tell you the truth of it.

"I beg your pardon?" he said; he was halfway out of his seat.

"I said, why didn't you like Randall? He never thought you liked him," I added, softer, wanting to shoulder my impudence on a dead Randall.

"What do you mean?" Sterling said. "He was my son." He sat down, again, though his two hands gripped the curtained edge of the table. I could not see but I imagined his bad leg turned out in the way it did when he was tired, a kind of moored rudder: it took great effort, Randall had told me, for Sterling to hold it as if it were an ordinary leg.

"But if Randall hadn't been born, you might have stayed with Ruby," I said.

"He had no idea."

I looked down at the table. "Yes, he did," I said. "He knew."

I felt the dread, the sudden regret, of having spilled this secret, spilled being such an appropriate word to describe my immediate remorse. My feet were wet with it, my head, my heart, dry; I couldn't breathe and instantly wished that I might take the words back, might suck them in as easily as they had spilled out. I would have in a heartbeat.

"I was not aware of that," Sterling said, his voice weakened. I understand now that at that moment he let go of the thin hold he held on his son's life. If I had been brave enough to look up, I would have seen him falling.

5

Sterling quickly excused himself and I followed a few paces behind. He limped out of the dining room and turned the corner to the stairs. The proprietor had shut off the lights in the tiny foyer, and I hesitated there, as if I were contemplating taking one of the magazines from the crowded table up to bed with me, or signing the guest book. I did neither. I stood in the dark of the foyer and thought about what I had said, and what I should do next. I don't need to tell you that I missed Randall terribly.

Somewhere nearby a clock ticked loudly. I saw the ledger still on the check-in desk, imagined the names of the traveling salesmen neatly written in blue ink, the record of their night, their whereabouts, firmly set. My thoughts were jumbled, bumping and lurching, returning to the Japanese fable like a needle skipping over the nicked surface of a record album: *And the rats of Nagasaki met the rats of Satsuma and asked one another how things were and discovered that there was nothing to eat in either Satsuma or Nagasaki. There was no use in going to Nagasaki nor any use in going to Satsuma, so they decided to jump into the sea and drown.*

The first rat began to cry chu chu, *and jumped over with a splash.*
Then another rat cried chu chu, *and jumped over with a splash.*

Why had this made Randall laugh so? What else had he said about the blue moon?

Moths clung to the screen door I closed quietly behind me. I let my eyes adjust to the dark, a dark that would be unfamiliar to you; there were no streetlights, no lights from any city, no highways in the distance, nothing at all, really, except where I stood and what stood before me: a stone path to the road, the road, the plowed fields, the blue moon.

The Dew Drop Inn marked the southeast corner of Sudlersville, where Route 52 crossed Route 34; to get to Randall's house you followed 52 east from town, past the cemetery, the post office, and several farms. That's the direction I headed, walking, no sound but the cicadas, the late-July heat still oppressive though the sun had gone down hours ago. I stopped at the cemetery, thinking I should pay respects to Jeannette's grave, though I couldn't seem to find it. Perhaps it had sunk, as Randall always predicted it would, back to the ground, Randall saying the way the gravestone tilted one day it would no doubt fall flat and before long be grown over with that thick moss. It did seem the graveyard had been forgotten. It housed mostly Civil War soldiers, anyway, a monument to them in the middle of the cemetery ringed with a low wrought-iron fence and a handful of dirty American flags, miniature, the kind once carried by children on Armistice Day.

I can't tell you how long it took me to reach Randall's house. I know I was exhausted by the time I got there, wishing for the ease of the biplane, the way we swooped down to bump along the fields. Still, I never considered turning back. I'm not sure what I expected to find, or whether I even expected to find anything. I know I walked in my good shoes, my mother's linen suit from Bergdorf's. From time to time, when I felt too tired, I tried to picture my mother as a girl my age. She had married at nineteen, my father twenty. They stood in the courthouse—this their description—and got it over with; in those days after the Influenza and the Great War, they would say, people weren't sentimental.

Nearly there, I removed my good shoes and began to run. I had earlier pulled off my stockings, not wanting to ruin them, and so I ran now in bare feet along 52, my stockings in my skirt pocket. If anyone had seen me, what would they have thought? I was nearly sixteen; I had my hair bobbed; I ran in the middle of the night down a dark road, ran, quite truthfully, because I felt if I did I might reach the house in time to find it whole, again: I would run straight through the front door—open for me as doors are open in dreams—and bound up the back stairs, ducking my head to turn the corner, to fit through the passageways, bursting into Randall's room to see him reading as he always was, his head bent low to the page, his back to the bookshelf that lined the window seat. He would look up suddenly—he had been reading, after all—and he would not be a ghost, and he would not be a dead boy. He would simply be Randall, his hair as red as mine. "You're here," he'd say, as if I were the one who had disappeared.

But no dark could resurrect the house. I came upon the same scene I had earlier visited, only now, in the nighttime, the wreckage looked oddly natural, and had you driven by you never would have suspected there had been a Randall's room, a Randall's house. The piles of brick appeared a part of some chaotic landscape, the few remaining oaks casting strange shadows, blue as the moon, across the corpse of the foundation. Whoever had bought the house, bought the land, really, had carted off the beaded glass from the cabinets in the pantry, pried loose the brass hinges and clear crystal doorknobs from the pine doors, striping everything believed to be of value, leaving only the old bones of the place, and the ghosts.

I would like to say I saw them that evening, but I did not. I waited, it's true, wishing them to appear. I sat, leaned against the Gallery of Maps wall, keeping my eyes open though I was terribly tired. I invoked the name, Romulus. It seemed to have a power all its own. But nothing came to me save the dark and the swollen sounds of night. I pulled my knees to my chest and fell asleep despite my best intentions, waking to the first light. You have seen it, haven't you? The sky shot through; a hole right in the center widening as you watch, your breath held, waiting for I don't know what. Someone to step in from the other side; to greet you by name: all you have lost or all you've never known before. It's a feeling you want to spackle into form, to somehow will to life, to give a name: Romulus, Randall, Eliza. And so you wait, breath held, for a wondrous thing to happen, the feeling a scaffold you climb anchored to nothing more than an ordinary morning, and I suppose hope.

I had Randall's diary with me. I had carried it in my suitcase on the ferry crossing, wrapped in my flannel nightgown. I carried it now tucked into the interior pocket of Mother's linen suit jacket. I had thought that I might share it with Sterling at dinner, that I would, at some particularly poignant moment, reach into my jacket as if searching for a tissue, or a mint, and pull out the small record of Randall's life, perhaps still familiar to Sterling as the tiny, empty book his wife had given his son one Christmas. I knew Christmas had become a lonely time for them, that after Jeannette's death the two would try, unsuccessfully, to banish the cold from the living room, lighting a fire in the drafty fireplace, sitting in the wing chairs, or on the rose-covered sofa. This is how Randall explained it. We were too few, he said, for Christmas.

But the Christmas of the diary must have been a warmer one, Randall's thin, pale hands carefully unknotting the ribbon, examining the hard diary cover, the painted gold script words *My Diary* and the blue-lined white paper, each page dated and then not, then blue-lined pages with no dates, with no other commitment than the promise of their own needy blankness.

Anyway, I did not show the diary to Sterling. Instead I chose to puncture his news with my secret, or Randall's really. And then run the mile or so to what had been Randall's house, through the night dark expectant, apprehending nothing more than a jackrabbit perched on the stone step, its long ears flat against its miniature head, listening. Perhaps the emptiness of the place is the reason why I broke my own rule of reading only one entry per day, or perhaps it was for no reason at all, only time, somehow. Soon after I waked I took the diary from my jacket pocket and read what had been Randall's life in its entirety, beginning to end.

6

There is a garden in Kyoto meant to be viewed at night in shadows. An emperor willed it so; he could only tour his gardens after dark, or perhaps it was that he could only tour his gardens with his mistresses after dark. I can't remember. The point is, the entire thing—the pathways, the fountains, the lakes, the cherry trees—is an illusion: colorless shadows without scent cast by large paper cutouts. A scene set from a drama created by the emperor's gardeners specifically to his wishes, changed for the seasons, rearranged— bare trees for trees in full bloom, lakes with frothy waves, lakes still, blossoms far too large to grow in that climate.

I have often imagined the emperor strolling alone, his mistress several paces behind him, her face entirely covered as was the tradition. He is careful, knowing that if he trips, if he stumbles, his foot might come down hard into a shadow pond, his hand might reach for a shadow limb, and then—instantly—the illusion will vanish, replaced by nothing more than shadows.

Imagine how slowly he must walk, one foot so carefully, so deliberately in front of the other, as if he is following a real path.

7

I wish I could say that I learned much about Randall from his diary, that I found something I might have taken back to give to Sterling in the morning, to offer him at breakfast. But there was little, of course; this is the way it always is. He was a boy, after all. Barely seventeen years old. He had reached the volume P in the *Encyclopedia Britannica,* Eleventh Edition, and one of his last entries was on Magellan's discovery of Patagonia, how Magellan had stumbled upon what he called Tierra de Patagones, land of the giants, and how he had captured two of them, a man and a woman, to carry back to Spain for the queen. They died the first day out— they were given last rites by the priest onboard though they did not speak Spanish—and were wrapped in one of the ship's sails and tumbled to the sea. *Chu chu,* Randall had scribbled at the end of it.

Of what I remember: a catalog of important stories to read compiled by Miss Thomas, the librarian, expressly for Randall: James, Henry: "The Beast in the Jungle"; O. Henry: "The Four Million"; Hawthorne: "Rapaccini's Daughter"; and others. And great lists of resolutions: lift weights, make friends, correct Mrs. Statler's grammar, learn Ellen's middle name.

Victoria, I could have told him. After Mother's mother.

I returned to the Dew Drop Inn as I had come, along 52, first attempting to cut through the fields—the land there flat, one farm joining the next in an odd quilting pattern, easy to follow the seams in the right direction toward where you want to go and find yourself, eventually, there. But the grass glistened wet with dew and I felt suddenly cold; remember I had spent the night out of doors, slouched against the one wall still standing of Randall's house.

There had been nothing grand about it. The house, I mean. It was beautiful in the way houses were once intended to suggest beauty, to hold your admiration in the tiniest of details. The beveled moldings—dark wood, perhaps walnut—were like elaborate empty frames to the white-painted walls long since yellowed. The rarely used formal staircase had a carved banister, the grip a griffin's claw in whose talons writhed a copper snake that had at one time served as a lamp, its shade at a perpetual angle of disuse. The only light on the staircase came from the one small stained-glass window, perfectly round, with squares of reds and yellows and blues transforming the round view of Sudlersville's soybean fields to something vaguely European. Perhaps whoever bought Sterling's house cut that stained-glass window from the wall and carted it off to one of those places that specializes in selling such things. But I don't think they valued the griffin's claw, or the serpent's patina, or the dark, river stones that formed the chimney, a wisteria so thickly entwined among them the stones had come loose and when the fires were lit the chimney leaked smoke, Randall even claiming that one spring morning the entire thing erupted in blossoms, the flowers pushing the stones to the ground in a great heap.

Still, it was difficult to leave the property, knowing, as I knew, that I would never return. I imagine that in subsequent years what brick wasn't carted off was worked far down into the soil, and that the shattered glass lost its danger, wore to the smoothness of an old penny. I know the new owners intended to sell the fugitive cage to a museum somewhere. Sterling had told me this at dinner. The land would become a corn or soybean field, Sterling said, and now, I suppose, it is simply the ground beneath several houses, each with a young tree planted next to a smooth blacktop drive.

At this point in my life, I had not yet been to a funeral. Randall was presumed dead; and Sterling had, perhaps for this reason, decided not to memorialize him, though given the solitude of their lives, it may have been enough for Sterling to sit in Randall's room for a while, enough for Sterling to simply say his name. Still, turning away I had the feeling I would later feel at funerals of leaving a grave, of walking from the dead out into the living. This is the best way I know how to say it.

I went straight on 52. The sky had begun to lighten, though plenty of dark remained in it. I must have walked quickly. I seemed to be at the graveyard, the bend in the road, in no time, and once around, I knew, I would be back in view of Sudlersville: the flickering vacancy sign for the Dew Drop Inn, the gas station marked by the winged horse where one huge Ford truck seemed to always be parked. The post office.

The graves were tucked within the maples, out of reach of the sun. Better for the dead, Randall would say. They'll forget what they're missing.

I slowed my pace, thinking I might search again for Jeannette's slanted tombstone in the light, but I was cold, as I have told you, my ankles wet from attempting to cut through the fields. I wonder now, if I had stepped in, what we would have said to one another, whether I might have made amends for my rudeness the night before, or explained myself better, or perhaps given him the whole story. Beyond me Sterling stood within the graveyard, his arms seemingly at his sides. I was at too great a distance to see the tilt of his head, or the exact nature of his expression, but I will say that as I got closer I saw that his hands were clasped in what is universally regarded as prayer, and that his eyes were shut. Perhaps he had seen me; or perhaps he had no idea. I continued on, diary in hand, passing out of the maple overhang, rounding the bend to the scene I've described: the commerce of the intersection and the few homes in town, their kitchen lights already glowing yellow against the rising blue fog.

I passed Sterling's door on my way to my own room at the Dew Drop Inn, and saw that he had left the key in its lock. I put my hand on the cold metal and felt the click of the tumblers, reeling somewhat from the danger. What if he suddenly returned? What if he had never left at all, if he were standing behind the open door, hiding under the bed? What if I had only seen a ghost of Sterling?

But the room was empty, entirely still. Sterling's trousers hung on a hanger hooked to the open door of the armoire, their pockets turned inside out. A soft-bristle brush, a tortoise-shell comb, and a billfold sat on the nightstand between his two narrow beds, each made as neatly as they had been when we first checked in, the white, puckered bedspreads pulled tightly beneath the box springs, pillows flat and hard.

I felt suddenly exhausted, and contemplated lying down on one of Sterling's beds to sleep. They seemed more appealing than the bed in my own room down the hall. Instead, I set Randall's diary on one of the pillows, as if it were the thing that needed the rest. It looked precious there, like one of those rare books you'll see under glass, away from the oil of fingers or bright light, or anything else that might fade the ink. I knew that this was another terrible betrayal of Randall, that he had given me the diary precisely because he did not want his father to see it; still, it was one of the few times in my life when I have done something on impulse that I have never regretted. It almost seemed as if I were bringing Randall back to Sterling, leading Randall in and asking him, as a favor to me, to just sit for a moment in his father's room.

She does not notice him. He takes one of the wooden deck chairs for reading, his glasses low on his face and she stands nearby, against the railing, looking out at a sea that on this morning seems too calm, as if somewhere else a storm has drawn the rougher waves. Her thoughts, understandably, are elsewhere. She has already decided to refuse marriage. Sterling is an honorable man and it will be his first question. Still. Jeannette might agree to keep the baby, or at least keep the baby for some time before they can find someone to adopt him. Him, she thinks. She is entirely sure. A boy. She will write Sterling of it—informally, without panic. She will maintain an even tone: she is an independent woman in Paris. She is a professional, a member of the Cosmopolitan Ladies. She has never intended, not for one minute, to marry. Ludicrous, all of it. How could she have been so stupid?

She startles a bit at his touch. He is next to her now, her friend from the night before, Professor something. She can't remember his name.

"You seem far away," he says.

"Millions of miles."

"It's beautiful." He has turned to face the sea, his profile quite sad, really.

"Yes."

"Last time I was here we were packed in like sardines. I won't even describe for you the stench."

"Please don't."

"Oh, I'm sorry. That's right," he says, facing her again.

"No," she says. "I didn't mean." It is awkward, of course; she has stupidly told him too much. What had she been thinking? "May I see?" she says, pointing to the sketchbook beneath his arm.

"Oh, well," he says. "I'm what they call a minor talent. More of a minor, minor, really. You don't want to bother."

"Please," she says.

He wipes the lead from his fingers and flips back the cover: the lines of her coat, its shoulder seam, the hat the wind has blown to loop around her neck though he has exaggerated the ribbon.

"I don't do figures, generally. But there's nothing green in this blasted sea. Except some of our fellow passengers' faces, I'm afraid."

"I'm flattered," she says, immediately hearing the wrongness of the word, flattered. She is embarrassed by the right word— touched?—and quickly excuses herself.

He watches her go, watches her coat, hat, sink down the metal stairway to the cabins. He would like to take her something, a pot of tea, a whiskey, but he rightly guesses she would rather be alone. He turns to the water, again, squeezing out of his memory that earlier sea, the froth and anger of it, how the boys lay retching, unaware that what awaited them would be far, far worse. He thinks of her instead, the whiteness of her hands, the blush as she held his sketchbook.

*   *   *

She sees him again, here and there on the crossing, at times, even, believing he might be following her. But he is a harmless man. One of the damaged, as Sterling would say. He has clearly been in the war, has mentioned it a few times. He is not a particularly good conversationalist, but that's fine. She's had enough of conversation. And the company of men. She would rather now sit and read. Still, he assuages her loneliness. He has told her of a good hotel in Paris, one little known and thoroughly charming. They will share a taxi and he will help her with her bags. He continues on from there to Amsterdam and then takes the Trans-Siberian railroad east. His journey will end in Japan, he tells her. Europe holds few pleasant memories. America he no longer understands. Best to leave all that is familiar.

Still, he insists upon showing her the hotel. Insists that she will love it: the corner room, the one with the yellow tiles in the bath.

She allows him to accompany her. She is so tired, and he is certainly harmless. Paris has newly awakened, everyone returned from their holidays. The poplars have shed and the children collect their brittle red leaves as they would seashells. They take a taxi together and he points out cathedrals, the names of which she already knows and yet she humors him. The taxi turns, takes a last bridge into a tiny square. Cupid, he says, pointing to a small fountain in the center of it. He's everywhere here in Paris.

She still has her sea legs, she tells him. She needs a rest.

Of course, he says.

They stand under the blue-painted arch of the hotel doorway. Window boxes trail vines to the street. Good-bye, she says. Thank you.

Good-bye, he says. He takes her hand and feels the softness there. Good-bye, he says, again.

He steps back into the taxi and asks the driver to wait until she is safely inside, though it is the middle of a bright day.

*   *   *

She does not unpack her bag until much later. She is terribly tired, and she wishes simply to soak her feet and rest. The yellow tiles are as yellow as he promised, as delicious. She looks out her corner window to the fountain below. What had he said? Cupid? She wishes him back now, though he has already boarded the train for Amsterdam. She might have convinced him otherwise. She might have offered to take him to dinner. She feels suddenly, desperately lonely; she would attempt to telephone Sterling if she knew how. She turns from the window and lies down. This feeling will pass, she knows; it's a feeling that inevitably comes with traveling, and, in this condition, at certain hours of the day. She would like to be home, though she knows that home is not the room she rents month to month in the Gramercy Park Residence for Ladies, it's somewhere in Virginia, somewhere she's never even been—the place on the other side of the woods, the place she and Jeannette were always trying to find. She falls asleep thinking of this, imagining Jeannette and herself as children, hiding from their parents, running away with every intention of going, sitting cross-legged in the woods, imagining everyone looking for them.

When she wakes she feels better. The late afternoon light warms the room. She is certainly glad for the room, glad for Paris, after all; she's in her favorite city and she has days to explore. She will set her attention on work; she will consider the problem on her return, find a solution the next time over the Atlantic.

She steps out of bed and begins to run a bath and while running the bath unstraps the belts that lock her suitcase. There she finds it exactly as he left it, tucked among her clothing. He had meant to surprise her, had found her cabin empty, her suitcase nearly packed. He had placed it there with a note and then, halfway down the hallway to his own cabin, had decided better, had returned to remove the note, to simply leave the book, his name scrawled beneath an inscription he had spent too long composing: *For Ruby and child, with affection.*

The train departs on time, unusual for this season. He sits alone in a compartment, his legs stretched out in front of him. He has tried to keep his eyes focused on his sketchbook, no bigger than his hand. He carries it in his pocket. He draws from memory now: the look of cupid rising out of the dry fountain, the weight of the stone. He would rather not see Belgium and yet, they approach Bruges, the conductor has just called it out, and he remembers this city, remembers the mist rising from the canals, the nunnery, where the nuns wear the habits that look like great, white cones, the men and women on their bicycles. Bicycles! He hasn't ridden one since the war. He would have liked to have suggested they rent a bicycle. He would have liked to have seen her perched on the handlebars as he pedaled the two of them out into the countryside. What was it, September? There would be no more poppies, no more cornflowers. But daisies and lupine, yes. They might have brought a picnic in a basket, taken the cover bedsheet from her hotel room as a blanket. They might have left the bicycle in a ditch, its wheels turned in, its wide leather seat still warm. From the air it might cast a glint as hard as a helmet's spike, but no. This was a bicycle. Perfectly harmless. Perfectly simple. Intended for nothing more than a day in the country, for delivering them to this spot in this sunny pasture, for this picnic.

Picnic, he thinks. Certain words ludicrously innocent. Picnic, he says, allowing himself to turn toward the window. They pass now through a field studded with hay mounds, the mounds the size of dwarfs' homes, all of it out of a fairy tale. Even now, oddly, the war.

Picnic, he says again, the word fanning out to steam the glass.

9

Sterling passed away several years after that last visit, during a particularly fierce January. Mother had received notes from him from time to time, when Rita died, of course, and on certain holidays. In them he would ask after the family, the kind of questions asked in a note, unintended to be answered.

After his death Mother sent me the obituary—I was already at Saint Mary's—that appeared in the *Baltimore Sun,* as well as a longer article published in one of the local newspapers. He had been in the library that evening as was his custom, apparently, though for hours the librarian had been attempting to close the doors and go home. Judge Sterling Jewell was not a man to be kicked out, and so she permitted him to stay, simply giving him the keys. It will be my life's heartache, she was quoted as saying, that I was not there to help that man.

Sterling suffered a stroke, or what was then called a brain attack, as he locked the door. They found him the next morning half-frozen, though they were without a doubt that he had died instantly.

The reporter did not note what books Sterling carried. I don't imagine it would have been of interest to most readers, yet that was what I most wanted to know. I have always pictured him carrying the black-spined notebook under one arm, some local histories under the other. Books that might, on a careful read, reveal more about the skirmish that took place at King of Prussia, mention in a footnote James A. Smith, or the story of Eliza, or the fugitive rogue Captain D, or even Romulus Box Perkins; something he would eventually write to me of. I have told you that he wrote me often. Well, that is not entirely the case. He wrote me only once after that visit. A brief note on a small piece of paper intended, it seemed, for other uses than a letter, a grocery list, perhaps. The note said simply, *Thank you for your company,* and was signed, as was his habit, with his full name.

He never mentioned the diary. He simply knocked on my door that morning at seven o'clock, as we had agreed, and escorted me downstairs, where we ate our breakfast in collective silence, the salesmen all around us obscured by their newspapers. He wore his usual cardigan and, oddly, his brace outside his trousers. The pilot arrived soon after not in his biplane but in Sterling's automobile, and drove us as far as the ferry dock, where my parents collected me, believing we had all made the crossing on the ferry. I never told them we did not. I don't quite know why. Of course, Mother was curious and Betty as well, though she pretended not to be. Still, I felt the transfer of secrets from Randall and me to Sterling and me, or perhaps, to Sterling and Randall and me.

Sterling Jeremiah Jewell requested no mourners, no service, no eulogy, the obituary read. He simply wanted to go into the ground next to his beloved wife, Jeannette Olive Jewell, formerly of Shenandoah, Virginia. This I remember and the business I have already mentioned—that he was a good cook, a master bridge player. That he had somehow been instrumental in influencing the Supreme Court on the state's first desegregation laws, filing a friend-of-the-court brief that was credited in the decision that followed, and that he was considered an expert on Jonathan Edwards, a biography of whom he had been researching up to the day of his untimely death. As you might imagine, Sterling was not the type of scholar to ever believe anything actually finished, though several of his former clerks culled his notes and the first, or perhaps, second draft of his manuscript, publishing it with an introduction explaining that Sterling's devotion to pure truth, to fact, his utter refusal to give up on any sniff of a rumor of inaccuracy, had led to several decades pursuing Edwards's life as a bloodhound would pursue a rabbit. He had even tracked down several of Edwards's ancestors, including a great-great-granddaughter, now in her nineties, who had started a commune in Canada between the wars.

What led this biographer to pursue Edwards so doggedly? the clerks wrote. What leads any biographer to choose a life, any life, over his own? For surely the writing of a life takes precedence over the living of a life, and the biographer must subsume his own self to wear the cloak of his subject.

It was all a bit dramatic, and I'm sure Sterling would have heartily disapproved. Whether he ever intended his study to be published at all remains unclear, though among his papers his clerks had found what they assumed had been intended as an epigram—a scrap of paper that bore Sterling's signature scrawl: *For my son, Randall.*

I understand that at a certain point in his lifetime Jonathan Edwards was as popular as one of our actors today. His sermons drew great crowds and people quoted his comings and goings, his style of dress. A Calvinist, true, yet one of the first men to speak out against slavery, to call into question the hypocrisy of what he called the greatest irony of our country: that our Founding Fathers, our "sons of liberty," were so passionate in their cause for freedom as thousands of slaves were bought and sold every day. This I remember from what Sterling told me. Little else, though Sterling repeatedly mentioned Edwards over the course of that dinner at the Dew Drop Inn as he read from his black-spined notebook and I rearranged the bones of my half-eaten fish against the patterned china. I'm not entirely sure what I took from those Edwards lessons, though I remember at some point wondering whether it in fact was for him, Sterling, that the slave ghosts had returned; whether they stood in the various rooms of the big brick house—the father with his hands reflexively tied, the shoeless children—not for Randall at all but for Sterling to walk in, to see for himself a portrait of great irony.

· Book Four ·

1

What was it you were asking then? About your father? I haven't, quite truthfully, forgotten. The point is, I seem to remember Randall most when I think of him, your father. He was not handsome in the way Randall was handsome—Randall had more delicate looks, the kind of boy with light, long lashes, cheeks that flushed easily, burned red. He put my hand there once, to feel them, but then I already knew. I had the same. It is why I could no more imagine him as a soldier than I could imagine myself. He didn't fit. Literally. When Mother and I met him at the train he stood tall above the other boys in uniform, though he must have been one of the youngest, there in his regulation wool coat, too big, of course, although that seemed to be the style for all of the boys, their shoulders and arms lost within those hideous dark cloaks; coats that belonged on older men.

I woke to find your father gone. Is this what you wanted? He was, as I've said, skittish, skittish in the way some boys were after war.

They pretended to be fine, but if you looked you'd see that they were not fine at all.

We weren't supposed to look. We were supposed to welcome them home, pretending, as they pretended, that they had just been on some great holiday; we were supposed to parade down Main Street in our cheerleading uniforms, twirling our batons, the Veteran band honking along as we jumped up and down as if at a pep rally. And we did; we did as we were supposed to do.

Still. I remember one, Jack Wenzel, who returned in the fall of 1945 when so many of them did. His parents had a house in town, near the corner where we'd turn on our walk to school. Jack had always been a friendly boy; I believe Rita dated him once or twice, then decided he seemed too much of a loosey-goosey for her, too flighty, she said, in the way Rita could say things like this and be completely understood. I have no idea what she didn't like about him; I thought he was dreamy and smart. He had curly black hair and wore thick glasses. He rolled up his shirtsleeves, even in winter, and once, I remember, we were the only two in the lunchroom, studying long after the lunch bell had rung. He asked me what I was doing and when I told him, he smiled and said I seemed more serious than my sisters, but that was fine. Serious girls are a pleasure, he said.

Anyway, Jack had enlisted soon after graduation, leaving in a bus that had been brought into town for recruitment. I have no idea where he ended up, whether he served in Europe, North Africa, or the Pacific front. We never said a word to one another. Well, Jack said not a word to anyone. Everyone in town knew the story: as soon as he returned, stepped off the boat, the train, what have you, he kissed his mother, kissed his father, shook his head, and stopped speaking. Everyone speculated this meant "I'm sorry," but I'm not sure. It might have meant anything. It might have meant he was disgusted with his parents—or baffled—for allowing him to go in the first place. He was, what? Seventeen when he enlisted? Eighteen?

Betty and I would see him on our way to school, sitting on the front porch, staring out toward the street sign as if he'd never seen it before. He grew a beard, or, more accurately, his beard grew. He looked much older than a boy of twenty. He no longer rolled up his shirtsleeves; even if it were warm he wore a heavy sweater and sat with an afghan, the kind knitted by grandmothers for babies, across his knees. Someone dared Trudy Johnson to run up the porch steps and kiss Jack on the mouth, which she did—Trudy Johnson not the type of girl to turn down any dare. Cold as stone, she said. Didn't flinch. Didn't even blink. He's dead, she said. They just propped him up.

I only gradually understood that your father wasn't well. Throughout that October, he would return to my apartment above the Woolworth's in the dead of night—I never locked the door—and I'd wake to the sound of him tapping on the kitchen counter with a spoon, or what sounded like a spoon, and find him waiting for the kettle to boil, impatient. He might be reading a magazine, or some pocketsize paperback, and he would barely look up when I entered the room, wrapping my robe around me.

"Good evening," he would say, as if this were six o'clock on a street corner, and we two neighbors whose paths had just happened to cross.

"Hello," I said.

He set the spoon down and leaned with one elbow on the counter, his eyes so heavy with sleep, or lack of it, that they seemed to belong to a different Henry, one much smaller, and scared, than the Henry I knew or believed I knew.

"I'm glad you've decided to join me," he said.

"Wouldn't miss it for the world."

"Now you're making fun."

"No," I said.

He slouched on one hand, and I had the sudden urge to do a schoolgirl's trick, to press my knees hard against the back of his legs so he would fold to the floor and perhaps laugh. I wanted to see him laugh, again. He hadn't since the night of our dinner.

"I wish you wouldn't shout; I've been up for hours," he said.

"Here?" I said, my voice pitched lower, though I would no more shout than run nude down the center of Main Street. Everything had gone loud on him. A few nights earlier, he had insisted that I close the windows against the sound of the blinking yellow traffic light. Acutely disturbing, he said, the color yellow.

"No. I never come here first."

"Oh," I said.

"I go elsewhere. Everywhere. Everywhere and nowhere specific. Just always here, eventually. Do you mind?"

"No," I said, waiting.

"I'm reading Trollope. You'll be pleased to learn that everyone is quite gay."

"I don't remember."

"No, I wouldn't think you would. You've got other fish to fry."

"I suppose."

"Shakespeare and Shakespeare. Haven't we had enough of him?"

"Shakespeare was the greatest writer who ever lived," I said, feeling immediately ridiculous, as if it needed to be said at all, as if it needed to be said by someone like me, standing in her bathrobe in the middle of the night.

"Yes, and General MacArthur a brilliant strategist."

"I don't know about that."

"He could have taken us all the way to the goddamn moon. The Chinks didn't get there already, did they?"

In some time, I knew, we would come to the end of this conversation, if you could call it that, his words circling and swirling around like leaves in a wind tunnel, funneling up and then drifting down, rising and ebbing, impossibly random though at times wholly purposeful, furious. We would, eventually, find ourselves in my bedroom, in my bed, though at that point we would both stay terribly quiet.

Still, once he said, "You are lovely, aren't you?" I'm not sure whether it was this night or one of the others. They were the same, really. The nights. Beginning out of sleep, in the dead stillness of October, changing, as the season eventually changed, withering then disappearing altogether with the cold.

I lay beside him, waiting for him to leave my bed, as he always would, for the sofa in the other room. "Lovely," he repeated, perhaps because I said nothing in response; I was thinking of the beauty of that word, how lightly it drifted to the floor, how I remembered it from Randall's poet—what had he said? Lovely and durable. *I would think of a thousand things, lovely and durable, and taste them slowly.* I may have repeated those words to your father, I may have simply repeated them to myself. I can't recall; it is simply the word *lovely* that marks that time, and the hollow sound of the coffee spoon waking me from dreams.

2

But I've skipped ahead too suddenly. I should go back to that summer, the summer Sterling sent for me. A few days after my return the bombs were dropped on Hiroshima and Nagasaki, and the Japanese surrendered; the entire world on fire: the conquered and the conquerors.

It was hot as blazes, so Mother said just this once we could go to Jacob's Quarry, polio or no, this a celebration. She and Daddy joined us, everyone on holiday, and I remember how odd it felt to see the two of them in their bathing suits in the middle of the workday—Mother's rounded, freckled shoulders softer than the rest of her, Daddy's pale, thin legs whisped with black hair—dive and swim out past the point, where what seemed like years ago the boys too young for war had competed for Rita's affections, balancing on the rock and repeatedly calling her name.

It was only a few weeks later that Rita wrote to say that Roger would, at last, be on his way home, and that they would visit for Thanksgiving.

He had risen in rank, an honor due in part for his bravery in the

Battle of the Bulge that New Year's, where, he wrote to Rita, he wined and dined on the Siegfried Line, visiting the Club Cologne on the Beautiful Rhine, enjoying the Big 88 band (direct fire artillery) and that famous singer Screaming Mimi (shells). All came, he wrote, the mortar the merrier, though too many of his buddies didn't make it. As the French say, "*C'est la guerre.*"

She had quoted his letter word for word in one of her own to us, and from the way Mother and Daddy talked about it, you would have thought that Roger had singlehandedly wrestled Hitler to the ground.

We'll give Hitler what he wants, he signed off. A CRATER Germany.

I don't remember where else Roger served, exactly, though I do know that after that he spent some months in a hospital near London—Screaming Mimi, as he put it, under his skin—and that during his stay there Rita had a premonition he would fall madly in love with a British chippy, someone with an *accent,* she wrote, and terrible teeth and a tiny, turned-up nose and *moles,* and he would condemn—this her word—her to this godforsaken outback where she would be forced to marry a cowboy with the hideous habit of chewing and spitting tobacco.

We all knew, of course, that she couldn't wait for his return.

They arrived the day before Thanksgiving in their new white Chevy, red with the desert clay Rita had complained she could not clean from her shoes for all the tea in China. We were a frenzy of greeting, so perhaps I might be forgiven for not immediately recognizing the change in her. It was only later that night, as she sat with Betty and me, Mother, Daddy, and Roger at the kitchen table, that I began to feel what I can only call her absence. She stayed unusually quiet, seemed distracted, always. Whenever Roger spoke, she held herself at an odd, unnatural angle, so still I kept thinking of a baby bird I had once found and tried to save in Springfield's orchard—a newborn sparrow, its breast feathers still wet, its black eyes frightened. It had fallen from its nest and lay petrified in the deep thrush beneath a particularly ancient apple, and though I climbed the tree and placed it back there within the tufts of milkweed and whatnot, I knew it wouldn't survive. They never do.

We spent the next day helping Mother prepare the meal, which we devoured, Daddy said, as if we, too, had been at the Battle of the Bulge; after dessert, Roger stood and excused himself. His sister Missy had married and settled down in the next town, and he explained that he had promised to stop by before his nephew was put to bed. It must have been just before sunset when he left. The late afternoon sun lit the windows of the dining room a deep orange, distracting to all of us, so that at first Rita's weeping seemed not a part of our company, though we immediately turned to see it came from her, here, in her usual chair, this desperate sound from Rita with her head bowed.

We watched her for a moment—it seemed deliberate this way, a synchronized motion—then looked to Daddy. He sat stiff in the shirt Rita had sewed for him, his full name, William Theodore, stitched in purple thread along the collar. Who knows what he was thinking? Until that visit Rita had appeared to be fine; her letters filled with the mundane news of the ladies she socialized with wherever she was stationed. They had various clubs and goodwill committees and this one or that one was pregnant, and so all the ladies pitched in to care for the babies, since the husbands were still overseas, though every letter brought one or another back home. With Roger's recent return, she had written about his new job as a salesman for an insurance company, his hope to become division manager. Daddy was the one who read Rita's letters. He read them after dinner before we left the table, against the sound of crickets, the hum of the new refrigerator Daddy had surprised Mother with for their last anniversary, the radio reciting war news or playing organ music, his deep voice giving a grave importance to Rita's words. She was our soldier cast abroad, reporting from towns we'd never heard of: privy, somehow, to the national effort, invaluable to the cause. Had there been a star for the wives of soldiers we would have hung it in our parlor window.

Still, the letters rarely contained a shred of information about her; about her friends, yes. About Roger, of course. But nothing about her. Strange, now, to remember. She had been such a chatterbox when she lived at home, always keeping us up-to-date on whatever crossed her mind at a given moment—whether she might join the flag-twirling squad or agree to go to the farm show with Johnny DeNardio. Mundane details, true, yet Rita had a way of making everything glamorous; she held the throne in our family, sat smack in the center of us. That she was fine must have been our assumption—given Daddy's voice, I suppose, the timbre he gave to her sentences.

Now he didn't say a word. It was Mother who at last leaned over and held Rita's hand.

Tell us, sweetheart, she said.

Rita shook her head and pulled her hand away, her face now buried in one of the linen napkins Mother brought down from the attic for holidays. Roger's lay on his plate at the seat beside her. We had, truth be told, smiled when he excused himself, watching him leave the room with something close to envy. He had traded in his soldier's uniform for the one worn by salesmen at the time, a light gray suit, a thin tie, a fedora. He cut the trim figure of a man out of a cigarette advertisement.

"It's too terrible," Rita said from behind her hands. It was difficult to understand what she said next.

"He's what?" Mother said.

Rita looked up, her eyes blackened by wet mascara. She looked ugly then; this is the only way to put it.

"Mean," she said. "He's turned mean."

Mother stroked Rita's hair and tucked it behind her ears in the way she used to do when we were children. Betty and I looked on from our seats across the table: Mother had moved to Roger's empty chair.

"He's just back," she said. "Give him time to get used to being home."

"It's not that," Rita said. "Anyway, I'm sick of that. Sick of everyone saying exactly that. Jesus Christ, why can't anyone say something new?"

Then she began to cry, again.

Mother looked at Daddy and they passed her between them as one runner might pass a baton to the next.

"I don't want to hear that language at the dinner table," Daddy said.

"I'm sorry," she said. "I'm sorry." She made her weeping sound and rocked and Mother stroked her hair some more and Betty and I sat, unable to think of anything more to say, unable to even ask a question.

"What am I going to do?" she said, but she did not intend to be answered. She rocked and moaned, her face pressed to her hands, and I remember being struck by how different we were from her, Betty and I; how grown-up Rita had become, the square diamond wedding ring on her finger, the newly platinum color of her hair, even the dramatic way in which she cried.

"Rita," Daddy said sternly. "Rita, please. Tell us calmly what's going on."

She wept a bit longer, wept until the hysteria had passed. Then she wiped her eyes and fell silent for a time.

"He hits me," she said. "When he's been drinking. When he's

not been drinking. In the mornings. Sometimes he wakes me up to."

Daddy pressed his fork into a whole pecan.

"Do you make him angry?" Daddy said. "He's got a lot of responsibility at this new job."

"He calls me a stupid bitch. He talks nonsense. He says you've dug your hole now lie in it. I don't understand and when I say I don't understand he calls me a stupid—"

"It's a difficult time."

"Yes."

"I don't think a wife can ever truly appreciate the pressures on a husband."

"No sir."

"Enormous pressures."

Rita started to laugh; she continued as she wiped her eyes again with Mother's linen napkin. It was difficult to look. This I remember: She wore a tiny, gold cross around her neck, a wedding present from her bridesmaids. Her hands went there first, briefly, passed over the cross, touching it as Randall and I had passed over, touched, the horsehead andirons, without special thought, simply as habit to bring us good luck for what we were about to do. She did this and then she began to unbutton her blouse.

As you can imagine, we were a modest family. Even with one another, my sisters and I were private about our bodies. I have been in other households where sisters walk from bathroom to bedroom in brassieres and panties, entirely oblivious to brothers or fathers, where daughters change their underclothes in front of mothers. We were not cut from that cloth. We ducked behind doors. We politely asked one another to leave the room. Even in bathing suits we lay on our stomachs, or quickly got out of the quarry and grabbed our coverup.

To sit at the Thanksgiving table and watch Rita undress should have been all it took to truly understand: who needed the proof of her bruises? She pulled the collar of her blouse over one shoulder, pulled one arm free and then another, shrinking before us in nothing more than a brassiere, the style popular then, stiff, pointy cups, impossibly white and trimmed with lace. I watched her fingers return to the gold cross, finding it too difficult to look at what she intended us to see: the bruises that ringed her elbows, stamped the soft flesh of her upper arms. Some were older than others, faded to yellow; some were still a bright magenta.

"*C'est la guerre,*" she said.

We had just finished our Thanksgiving meal, understand; we were in our good clothes, Mother's holiday linen on the table. And Roger had cut such a handsome figure, standing, as he did, before leaving, bowing, slightly, in a gentlemanly manner, donning his fedora and walking out the front door.

The point is, we were not used to this kind of display, this bare truth. And so we kept quiet, waiting for Daddy to say something more, and when he did not, we waited for Rita to button herself back in, which she did quickly before she left the table.

Her letters after Thanksgiving took on a more cheerful tone. Daddy would read them as before, at the dinner table, down to the Love and Kisses Rita, smiling as he folded the paper back into its envelope, nodding to each one of us as if to say, See? Rita's fine.

I think of this now as I tell you of your father. They were all the damaged, weren't they? Who remained whole? It was that spring that Rita fell down the basement stairs, cracking her skull on the concrete floor.

I don't believe that we ever discussed it; instead we allowed that her fall had been an accident, that she must have tripped on the ties of her robe, it being so early in the morning, as Roger explained, his voice strangely high, excited. He asked to speak to each one of us on the telephone, and when it was my turn, he told me that Rita had always believed I would go far, and that he hoped I wouldn't disappoint her. I thanked him. That's what I said. Thank you, I said, as if I weren't on the telephone to my sister's killer, as if what Rita had said about me to him, the compliment, was far more important than my sister's life.

Not long after Rita's death, Daddy collected all the pictures of her scattered about the house. She had wanted to be a movie star, remember, and so there was no shortage. She always seemed to be tacking some photograph to a wall saying the bright light in the kitchen suited her coloring, or that she looked fine at a distance on the mantel. One in particular we liked the most, a charcoal sketch of Rita's face drawn in a matter of minutes by an artist at one of those stands along the boardwalk in Atlantic City. This had been a rare family vacation, and I can still see the five of us sunburned and exhausted, Daddy walking with his arms around Rita and Betty, flirting with them as if he were one of the teenage boys hawking tickets to the whirling saucers. I believe it was his idea to stop at the artist's stand; or it may have been Rita's after all. Regardless, she sat with her hands in her lap, her head cocked at an awkward angle, instructed to look toward the top rider of the Ferris wheel. Behind her waves broke against the wide beach, the surf lit with the rare pink it takes on at dusk; but the artist didn't sketch this. He simply drew Rita's face and the line of her collar, his hand moving as if drawn by an invisible string.

The portrait hung in the hallway: Rita wearing the expression she reserved for artists and photographers, her gaze strangely heavenward—I couldn't see a gosh darn soul on the Ferris wheel, she said later, and now I've got a crick in my neck. Daddy took this one down, too, and put it with all the others in the trunk of the car. Where he drove them I'm not sure, though we never saw those pictures again. Betty swore he'd burned them, that he couldn't bear to be reminded, but it seems to me that he probably just wanted to take Rita somewhere no one else could find, out of the light, perhaps, her portrait rolled into a scroll, its charcoal lines slightly smeared by the trace of his fingers.

3

Your father left before I waked the last morning. I shouldn't have been surprised. He was looking for Daphne, after all, not me. I have mentioned that he would sleep on my sofa, and that he had more than once noticed *The Gardens of Kyoto*. Indeed, he had held it for a long time that first night I invited him up to my apartment above the Woolworth's, turning from page to page, studying the illustrations. This after I'd attempted to serve the tea, broken the teacup, left to wash my hands and dump the shards of china into the wastebasket.

"What was your cousin's name?" he said. I had walked back into the living room carrying a fresh cup.

"Randall," I said. "He was seventeen years old."

"I'm sorry."

I shrugged; it had become a habit after Rita's death. Whenever people apologized to me, I simply gestured with my shoulders, as if this could deflect the truth of it somehow, or as if the truth of it meant nothing to me. "I didn't know him well," I repeated.

"A terrible battle."

"Yes."

"What division was he in?" he said.

"I have no idea," I said. "It happened after the end of it."

"What do you mean?"

"When it was already over."

"I see," he said, though I'm not sure he understood.

"He wanted to be a writer," I said, "a poet," as if your father had inquired further.

"We had a platoon of psychiatrists," he said. "Everyone wanted to be a shrink. One fellow had already been to school for it. Some goddamn place in Boston. He used to practice on us. Very elemental. Could have used some poets."

"No poets?"

"Not one. I was the minister, for Christ's sake. Great soldiers, let me tell you. Shrinks and a minister and a handful of men who had never left their hometown except for boot camp. And a chemist, that's right. We briefly had a chemist," he said. "He was killed the first day. Everybody kept forgetting he had ever been around. Is that mine?" I had been holding the new teacup, its saucer, in my hand, too nervous to sit down. "Yes," I said, though he did not move to take it.

"Powers," he said.

"What?"

"His name."

I should have noticed then, I suppose; I should have detected something out of place, but he had surprised me, so suddenly appearing, standing before me in the aspen grove in his Eisenhower jacket and trousers—have I told you? There were dead leaves stuck to my coat. Leaves in my hair and smudges of wet dirt, or the smell of it, on my wrists where another girl might have dabbed perfume.

A few days after he left for the last time, I discovered a note folded inside the front cover of *The Gardens of Kyoto*. *I seem to be always writing letters that go unanswered,* he wrote. *To Daphne. Now to you. I don't intend to hear from you. I don't expect to. I am not well. Please accept my apologies. I have enjoyed our conversations, but I am not well. There are certain difficulties. Sleeping. If you do not sleep you are not well and I am not well.*

It was a strange note. But then, I had no idea the symptoms—women rarely did—everything suddenly loud, his fatigue. The night of that last visit, I fell asleep faster than usual. He must have written the note and left so quietly—gathering the quilt, folding it into a neat square and placing it at the foot of the sofa, carrying his teacup into my tiny kitchen, rinsing it and setting it upside down on the counter, a dishrag placed beneath it to catch water. He must have braced the door as it closed behind him, then turned to the rickety stairs, walking down slowly, exhausted, afraid that if he did not hold to the banister he might slip. I would later learn he often slipped in the veteran's hospital, hitting the floor half dreaming, his bruises appearing some hours later, reminders to the nurses to keep him tied, though he pleaded against it: see Lieutenant Rock, they'd say. Here's a new one, sweetheart. We didn't have that yesterday.

They'd tap the pale bruise with their finger and he'd feel a charge of soreness.

Don't, he'd say.

Now, now, they'd say.

They spoke to the difficult ones as they would speak to their difficult children.

They called him sweetheart though he repeatedly requested that they not. He tolerated them as best he could, thinking, instead, of Daphne, what she would say to comfort him, how gently she would roll him on his side, massaging his tightened shoulders and arms, the bruises disappearing like so many violet starlings, flapping up and out the windows.

You don't understand, he'd tell them.

No, sweetheart, they'd say. We don't.

4

Tilsie told me he was breakable. Breakable, Tilsie said. His word. I disliked Tilsie the minute I laid eyes on him. He sucked a mint, or he smelled that way, and he seemed exceptionally nervous, as if he rightly guessed that I knew his story, knew that he was no hero, simply another soldier who had waited in the trenches, entertaining the reporter from *Life* magazine. A little man with close-cropped hair, he looked as if he were still in the Army though he wore civilian clothes.

He worked in his father's luggage store, one of the kind you used to see a lot of in those days on the corners of Main Streets. It sold luggage, true, but also a selection of ties, sport coats, trousers, and various knick-knacks—money clips, fountain pens, key chains—catering to the new traveling breed of businessman.

I had walked in and asked for Tilsie, the store bell tinkling as I shut the door. An older man, most likely his father, sat on a stool behind the counter; he pointed to the back, where Tilsie stood on a footstool measuring the arm of one of his customers. "Five minutes," Tilsie said when I reached him, and so I wandered around, reading the framed articles about Tilsie that lined the store's walls. I had already seen—displayed in the store window in what could only be described as a shrine—the small table covered with black velvet, the plastic rose in the brass vase, the photograph of Bing Crosby shaking Tilsie's hand, the cover of the *Life* magazine in which the article had no doubt appeared, propped on an ornate music stand in front of a sign that said "We Do Alterations."

The store had been easy to track down, everyone wanting to recount the story of Tilsie's heroism, the parade held in his honor by the Mayor of Bayshore: how he might have gone from there to Hollywood, become a big shot, but how he had stayed home to take care of his aging parents.

Tilsie finally came to the front, where I stood, gazing out the window.

"May I help you?" he said.

"Oh," I said. "I'm a friend of Henry's. Henry Rock."

I stuck out my hand, which I am always inclined to do in these situations; I imagine I blushed, as if he knew that I was more than Henry's friend, that at that moment I carried Henry's child and that Henry had no idea.

"Goddamn," he said. He chewed a bit, greased his hair into place. A yellow, cloth measuring tape hung around his neck and a smear of blue chalk marked one cheek. "How's Henry?"

"I don't know. I mean, I do. He's fine. I think. I saw him a few months ago and he seemed fine. But I was hoping you might be able to tell me—"

"Goddamn," he said.

"What?"

"Henry Rock. He's the one. The real McCoy, let me tell you. He don't mince the words. A real philosopher. He used to chew our ears off. Talk, talk, talk, talk. Hey, are you Daphne? Goddamn. You must be Daphne."

I nodded.

"Jesus H. Cranberries. He missed you more than his mother, let me tell you." Someone entered the store and the bell tinkled again; I heard the old man ring the cash register.

"It's nuts around here. Do you want to walk?"

I said yes and so we left the store and went up one side of Main Street and down the other, Tilsie repeatedly stopped by people who still wanted to shake his hand.

"Hard to be a small-town hero," he said, looking at me sideways.

"I can imagine."

"He tell you about that?"

"About what?"

"What I done?"

"I read about it."

He smiled, then, relaxed. He swung his short arms as we walked, and for a moment I thought he might link one in mine.

"So, Daphne herself," he said. "Goddamn. Let me buy you a cup of coffee, Daphne."

We had come to a diner and he opened the door for me, the chatter softening as we entered. We sat in one of the booths and Tilsie insisted I play a song on the jukebox. I chose "Secret Love," I still remember. The Doris Day version.

"So, you saw Henry. How 'bout that. I'd heard he was in the VH out near Oyster Bay. Was thinking of driving up there myself one of these Sundays but you know, they want me to cut ribbons, hold babies. Somebody says I should run for politics. Local. What do you think?"

"I'm sorry?"

"You think I look like a politician?"

He struck a pose, his teeth small and sharp as a ferret's.

"You look like every politician I ever saw," I said. "Truman and Roosevelt combined."

"Poor suckers."

I stirred my coffee, lit a cigarette.

"Listen, Daphne," Tilsie said, leaning in toward me, whispering as if he were telling secrets. "It ain't none of my business, but here you are so I'm going to say it. Henry's a good man. A very good man. He done more for us there than anybody. We couldn't have survived without him, I'm telling you. What I done ain't nothing in comparison."

I nodded.

"Nothing," he said.

I listened to "Secret Love" on the jukebox; it clicked into play, played, and then went silent. That's always the way with your song on a jukebox, isn't it? Just when it's beginning, it's over.

I'm not sure what else Tilsie and I discussed, though discussed is not an accurate word to describe our conversation. He was terribly nervous, and it seemed that only the sound of his own voice could soothe him. He talked and talked, telling me one thing after another, never really stopping to consider why I had sought him out. I realized after some time that I didn't need to concoct any excuse, that he had told me what I needed to know and that I could just sit back and listen, let him wear himself calm. He had several cups of coffee, and cinnamon toast from which he tore the crust. After some time, when I said I had to be on my way, he told me what your father did. Maybe this is what he had been jabbering against—spilling this secret, because I know your father never wanted it mentioned to anyone: how he had tried to save the crucified pilot he had written to me of, how he slid on his belly over 854, how it took hours, the other men watching as best they could though it was a moonless night, before he even reached the man, before he could scale the cross, a bayonet in his mouth, to pry loose the nails. The fog came in around that time, saving your father's life but keeping him trapped, there, with the decomposing pilot.

"Poor son of a bitch," Tilsie said, tearing his crust into smaller pieces, and I wasn't sure whether he meant the pilot or your father. "Ain't no chance he'd be alive, we'd told him, still Henry said he couldn't watch him rot that way, said he'd rather get shot trying.

"He's a good man, Daphne," Tilsie said. "He didn't mean nothing reading them."

I must have looked blank; Tilsie moved in closer.

"Your letters. We swore we wouldn't tell if it ever came to pass. You know. That we was sitting across a table from one another. Don't be mad. They was beautiful; we all said so." Tilsie shrugged. "You wrote the best of all our girls."

The Veterans' Hospital overlooked the Sound, high on a bluff on the North Fork of Long Island, just outside of Port Williams, a town that had once been a fishing village. Most of its residents now worked at the naval munitions factory at the foot of the bluff, its foundries spewing smoke that from the common lounge of the hospital appeared to be a rising, dense fog. The men rarely gathered in the common lounge; they stayed in their own, small rooms, each painted a fleshy tan. I call it a hospital—it called itself a hospital— but the truth is it felt more like a repository. A cluttered toy chest for the damaged.

I sat in the common lounge and watched the smoke, the way the gusts of wind off the Sound broke it into odd clouds, a language from another time. Or at least this is what I was thinking. I remember staring out at the water, its color from that distance nothing more than a flat, December gray, the same gray, no doubt, of the metal the factory employees soldered somewhere below me. I startled when the nurse called my name.

He stood behind me, near one of those sad grand pianos you often see in places like this. No doubt once or twice one of the men had been cajoled into playing "Claire de Lune" or a Strauss waltz or perhaps even "Summertime"—the Gershwin brothers popular in those days—but I imagine that whoever played had lost heart after a while. The piano's black paint had been nicked so often it looked speckled, and the keys were a tobacco-stain yellow.

Your father did an elaborate bow, as if he had just performed a concert. The nurse stood next to him, her hand lightly on his elbow; I wished her gone, and she did, in fact, leave soon after, first explaining that I should probably only stay a half hour, no more.

"You look well," he said, or something to that effect.

"Thank you."

"That color agrees with you."

"It's a new dress."

"I was referring to your hair."

"This?" I touched my head. "I suppose I tried something."

I wanted to break the space between us, to stand and walk straight toward where he stood; but I sensed I should not. There are certain birds of prey, golden eagles, for example, who will attack if you attempt to reach for them: you sit stock still, you wait for their approach. I did this with your father. I waited. I turned back, even, to the ugly view. I tried to breathe.

I don't know how much time passed before he sat down next to me.

He wore pajamas, the standard-issue pajamas of the place, a faded green, and paper slippers torn at the toes. He seemed, in these, practically nude.

"And you've grown a beard," I finally said.

"Have I?"

"Yes."

"They are particular about razors. And mirrors, for that matter. Never let the inmates think their luck has changed."

"It looks nice."

"I had hoped for distinguished."

Strands of red, white, and blue crepe paper fringed the big windows looking out to the Sound. There had been a party of some sort.

"You are not a prisoner," I said.

"But I am," he said. "What did our friend Daphne say? The enemy. That's right. I'm the goddamn enemy."

He lit a cigarette. I heard the scratch of the match, smelled the sulphur, then sweet smoke. I felt terrified to look at him, as if he were, indeed, nude, or as if he might melt or vanish. It had taken me so long to find him.

"I am dangerous," he said. I smelled a different smell then, putrid, and turned to see him rubbing ash on his bare arm, singing the hairs with his cigarette point. He looked up and smiled. "I wouldn't hurt a fly," he said. "That's what the shrink said. He said, I wouldn't hurt a fly. I couldn't. Something about my goddamn mother. The place is crawling with shrinks. They wear these glasses." He stuck his cigarette into the corner of his mouth and held his fingers to his eyes, rounded into glasses. "Worse than Chinks."

"I don't know," I said. I felt I had to say something. His nails were too long, unkempt as his beard, and I had half a mind to find the nurse to ask for nail trimmers and a good pair of scissors. He took the cigarette from his mouth and offered it to me and I accepted only because I wanted to touch him.

"Tilsie sends his regards," I said, trying to change the subject. I took a long puff.

"Ah, you saw Tilsie," he said. "How's our heroic son of a bitch?"

"He works in his father's luggage store."

"A very good time for luggage. The best time ever. Everyone's on the move."

"It's a very successful store," I said.

"Of course it is," he said. "Tilsie's a goddamn movie star." He had lit another cigarette. I stubbed out his first in one of the ashtrays and we sat for a while without speaking. I heard a telephone ringing somewhere; smoothed the lap of my dress—Mother's habit—and drew my breath in.

"Tilsie said you were the heroic one."

"Tilsie doesn't know his ass from his elbow."

"He told me how you risked your life to take that pilot down; how you pried the nails from his—"

"Shut up," he said. "Please," he said. "Shut up." He stood and walked out of the common lounge, or I believed that he did. I sat before the view of the Long Island Sound, the foundry smoke listing then catching the wind. The crepe paper banners rode the blasts of heat from the radiators, a scissored flag. The telephone began to ring, again.

I wish I could tell you what I was thinking, but I can't remember much more outside the look of that room, its scuffed floors and ragged collection of chairs, their arms pocked with cigarette burns and stained by so many hands; the piano and its bench. I suppose this is where he sat. Eventually I heard a few keys, minor, played softly; I thought it best not to turn around.

"She got every one of them, didn't she?" he said, still playing.

"Yes," I said.

"She just never wanted to write back."

"She had the best of intentions."

"Everyone does," he said.

"I suppose."

"I wrote my own after a while. Even signed them for her. An interesting exercise," he said.

He began to play a song, one I did not recognize. I sat and listened, my hands in my lap. Even out of key it was beautiful, and I would have liked to have stood next to him, to have followed the notes, to have turned the music on the stand or to simply have smiled if he looked up, if he noticed me. But I knew if I did, if I even breathed too loudly, let my arms relax at my sides, lit another ciga- rette, that the music would stop, and so I sat, listening, until he closed the lid and left the room.

5

This is none of it how you wanted; none of it right. But I am tired of the old story: your father returning the day after finding me in the aspen grove, dead leaves in my hair, the smell of wet dirt on my wrists where other girls would have smudged perfume. How he drove right up the circular drive to the front door of the school, honking his horn to beat the band, tin cans tied to the bumper of his convertible: Marry me, Ellen, written in shaving cream across the hood and slowly melting, its wintergreen smell strong from the heat of the engine, the heat of the day.

It would have to be a warm day; gloriously warm. In the distance boys play football in shirtsleeves and girls cheerlead in cutoffs, their pyramid perfect. They stand on one another's shoulders; they leap to the field, applauding, bouncing, their ponytails as shiny as their smiles. They are smiling, of course. Everyone is smiling.

I spy him from my third-floor classroom exactly as he'd planned. Now I frantically erase the blackboard, sweep paperclips into my desk drawer, pencil dust into the trash. I grab a few mementos—the drawings that have been addressed to Miss Ellen, the letter from the boy with the crush. There is little that is mine in this classroom. It will stay exactly as it is: its shaded windows, its blackboard, its quotes from Lincoln, Luther, and, for Sterling, Edwards lining the walls. I unpin Edwards from the cork and fold him to a four-cornered square. I won't return, I know. From here my life is with your father.

I take the stairs too quickly, flying around the corners as the students do at last bell, pushing the heavy metal bar on the fire door to charge out, forgetting, setting the alarm: the sound deafening. Your father sits behind the wheel in uniform, his hat shading his handsome face, and I take a fingerful of shaving cream and write a backward Yes across the windshield.

What next? How does the story go?

He steps out of the convertible and we embrace, though hurriedly. The alarm shrills as we round the drive and speed on. He turns to present to me the wildflower stuck in his jacket buttonhole: a violet I tuck behind my ear.

It is nearly five when we run up the steps of the Philadelphia courthouse, the last to be married—they no doubt forget to record it in their books—before they lock the heavy doors.

Then from here, what? What have I told you before? We are Lieutenant and Mrs. Rock; we travel so many places. Then, I can't recall. An automobile? An airplane? The tipping of a kayak on a stormy sea?

He died young, I have said, leaving me no other choice but to lose you. This is the only truth of it: the rest is just another story.

6

It must have been close to the dinner hour at the Veteran's Hospital. I could hear the clang of silverware, the rustle of table setting in the distance. Outside, the weather had cleared, and a trace of weak sunlight, the last of the sunset, slipped through the dusty windows. I must have stayed much longer than a half hour. I believe I dozed. When had I taken off my shoes? When had I found the stiff pillow? I felt dizzy, as if I had climbed too many stairs too quickly; I combed my hair with my fingers. The window was filthy, actually. I hadn't noticed with the gray weather. Now the sky paled to a thin blue, pinkish clouds low over the Sound. A pink dawn, or was it dusk? It felt as if I had been sucked out of my own life into another, a dreamlife. I don't dream often, but when I do my dreams feel this way: with scissored edges, as if the scene in which I stand has been cut from an illustration, or a puzzle, and that if I walk too far to the edge of it, if I turn a corner, I might tumble into nothing. I stood and approached the window, thinking of your father, wondering whether I should attempt to talk to him again that day, or to wait until the following week.

I found myself writing *HELP* on the glass.

The nurse surprised me.

"You're awake," she said.

I turned.

"You seemed so peaceful I didn't have the heart."

"Thank you. That was kind," I said. I began to gather my purse, my cigarettes from the arm of the frayed sofa. "I've stayed too long. I'm sorry." I searched for my cigarette lighter.

"Don't apologize. We don't get many visitors."

I looked up at her. She wore a brown wool skirt and sweater with a nametag too far away to read; if she had been a blonde, she would have reminded me of Rita.

"I've lost my lighter," I said.

She pulled one from her skirt pocket and clicked it open. "Here," she said, approaching me. I saw her name was Julia.

"I didn't mean," I began, then thought better of it and reached for a cigarette.

"It gets lonely around here this time of night," she said. "I'm glad for the company."

I lit my cigarette, letting the smoke out slowly, trying not to cough. The truth is I had given up smoking several weeks earlier, but had found myself purchasing a package on my way to the hospital. The kind they wanted girls to smoke back then; I can't remember the brand. I tapped the cigarette against an ashtray.

"You work nights?" I said, attempting friendliness.

"Nights, days. They blend together here. We lose track of time. Intentionally, that is. They're stung by light so we keep it dark. Part of the therapy," she said, lighting her own cigarette and exhaling. "But then, nights terrify them."

"Oh."

"So we don't like to point out time at all."

"I understand."

"No," she said, smiling. "You don't."

She looked toward the window and continued smoking. I followed her gaze; she must have seen the *HELP*, though she didn't say a word.

"Who did you come for?"

"I'm sorry?"

"Which patient."

Patient. It was the first time that anyone had referred to your father in this way and I understood, quite suddenly, that he was terribly ill.

"Henry," I said. "Henry Rock."

She looked back at me; she was stunningly pretty, and I remember how I felt dowdy in my new dress, my hair dyed the color I believed Rita might have suggested if she were still alive—a rich honey—my eyes rimmed with eyeliner in the style of the time. I had put on my shoes, again, and my newly swollen feet ached, my garter belt pinched my waist. Soon I would no longer be able to hide my condition, and my heart pounded to think of it, to think of what I would possibly do next.

"You must be Daphne," she said. "He talks about you all the time."

"Does he?"

"He's one of my favorites, Henry. You get favorites here; that's the trouble. You get favorites and it breaks your heart to see them leave and it breaks your heart to see them stay and so there's nothing you can do. All day and all night you walk around with your heart breaking."

"I'm sorry."

She dropped her cigarette to the linoleum floor and stubbed it out with her heel. "Terrible habit," she said.

She turned toward the door as if she had forgotten me; the sun had set and the room had gone fairly dark. I wondered if anyone ever bothered to switch on the lamps, or to play the phonograph in the corner, near a stack of what appeared to be old magazines. At some

Kate Walbert

point there must have been great hopes for the Common Lounge, anticipation of game nights and the like, visitations.

"God bless you, Daphne," Julia said; then left me behind.

I should have followed her; she most likely headed toward the main hall of the east wing, which I had passed through to find myself here. One could easily get lost. The hospital had originally been the summer mansion of a robber baron and it sprawled in several directions: its west wing completely boarded up, its widow's walk rotted. On its terraced lawn, the stone walls sprouted moss and fern, wild cherry, the entire landscape fallen into disrepair; the VA, I imagine, barely able to heat the east wing, let alone maintain the grounds. A vast series of straggling box hedges, mazes of former topiaries, defined the once-formal gardens, where stone angels rose from the frozen lily ponds, their wings mottled as cold flesh. Leggy rose bushes overran a tennis court, its torn net sagging under the weight of a honeysuckle; a maple grown to my height sprouted near the half-court line.

On the days preceding my visit, when I had made the approach to the hospital yet could not muster the courage to walk in, I spent my time wandering here. If it weren't too cold, I would settle on a moldy cement bench clearly intended for contemplation. I had brought *The Gardens of Kyoto* along, believing I might show the book to your father, show him Ryoan-ji, the garden with the fifteen rocks—the fifteenth unseen but there for balance—and tell him how Randall would say that on certain days the fifteenth rock was Jeannette, his mother, on other days it was someone else; how I would say mine was someone I had yet to meet, just a feeling of someone I would, eventually. Randall had understood, or pretended to: we were friends like that, I'd tell your father.

*   *   *

246

I did not follow Julia as she left the Common Lounge. I waited until I heard the fading click of her heels and then went in the opposite direction; unclear, suddenly, as to which way I had come in. Before long I got so balled up I couldn't even get back to where I had been. I was lost in the west wing, barely able to see for the narrow hallway windows. Portraits lined the walls—the robber baron's relatives, I presumed—man after man frowning out at me, each ivory painted face a composition of nose, eyes, and mouth, brushstrokes on a canvas within a heavy dark frame. I remembered what Sterling had told me about Roosevelt, how he had died while sitting for his own portrait, the painter having only finished his face. Just a face, Sterling said, and all around it the blank page. Nothing more. Just a perfect face in the middle of nothing.

"What do you think that suggests?" Sterling had said. This as we sat in the backseat of the automobile the pilot drove toward the ferry landing. I wanted to answer, but I had no idea what I thought it suggested.

"I don't know," I said, waiting for Sterling to continue. But that was the end of it.

First I thought I heard a cough and then, strangely, singing.

Was this a dream? They sounded like real voices: men's voices in the rise and fall of a chorus. I walked faster, believing the voices came from behind an ordinary-looking door ahead of me, within a vestibule of sorts. As I approached, the sound of the chorus swelled to an amen. I turned the doorknob and pushed the door open, expecting to find a room packed with hundreds of soldiers in prayer—men leaning on crutches, leaning on canes; handsome, one-armed men, their uniform arms pinned to their elbows; bareheaded men and men wearing hats and men whose heads were wrapped in bandages; a chorus of men holding hymnals, swaying left, swaying right; men spitting and men with rotted teeth; men with their hands in their pockets, unshaven, slouched, and men missing eyes; men with bullet wounds and saber wounds; bumpy, knotted shrapneled flesh; scars that ran the length of their legs and roped their ankles; scars that crisscrossed their backs; mustached men; men with holes blown into their sides; men who dripped or burst or shat or slowly leaked; a room full of soldiers singing, amen.

But the room, of course, was empty.

It appeared to have once been a great ballroom, a chandelier of enormous size—like thousands of crystals sewn to a hoop skirt—hanging from a ceiling painted to resemble a bright blue sky where angels drifted on white clouds, their harps outlined in gold leaf. They eventually spilled into the corners, loafing and preening above the high arched windows. The windows, draped with silk curtains, looked out toward the Sound and it would have been a tremendous view if not for the dozens of chairs, their backs and seats cushioned in a dark, red velvet, circling the perimeter.

The room was a holy place, somehow; a place unaccustomed to visitors. An empty tomb. I wanted to cross it as quickly as possible, to get out. I could see now a door on the other side and in my rush to reach it I might very well not have noticed him. He stood with his back to me, stood at one of those deep windows as if he were still waiting, watching for my arrival. Perhaps I was late. The drive from Chester always so unpredictable. Rita wanting to stop to use the john; or Mother saying she had packed a picnic for Capetown, and couldn't we take a quick detour?

We had promised to be here by noon and now it was nearly one and he had been waiting, hadn't he? How much more time would we take?

"I'm sorry," I said.

I wish I could tell you that he turned around, then; that he shrugged and said, "No matter." But he did not. He simply faded away, blending too quickly into the silk of the drapes, the wavy, milky panes of glass, old as the warrior friezes that lined the walls— all those men I had envisioned, still whole and armored.

7

Tucked within one of the gardens of Kyoto is a shrine to unborn children, to lost children, to children too soon dead; a hidden altar, really, a stone on which women place azalea blossoms, or chrysanthemums; whole oranges, sprigs of cherry, offerings left in groups of seven, or five, or three: harmony, they believe, in odd numbers. The garden is in the northern end of Kyoto, within a heavily wooded area rarely visited by men; its temple, long ago carved from a stone hillside, is reached only by the ascension of a series of small, narrow steps worn into the hillside, according to legend, by the knees of worshipers. Above the temple, Mount Hiei can be seen; the perspective strange, the mountain appearing close enough to touch, its snow so fresh and white as to be mistaken for new snow, though the snow has been frozen there for centuries.

Women come to these woods: the ones who have lost their children, the ones who have never borne them, or borne them and given them away. They climb the steps on their knees, their kimonos hitched above their thighs, obis crooked. They keep their heads down as they climb, one knee up, and then the other, hobbling on bone. Around them azaleas burn against tall dark pines—the all of it a bowl of color: the women's mourning kimonos sea green, or smoke gray, made from the silks dyed in the rivers that run in these same mountains, silks passed to them by their own mothers, grand-mothers.

The women climb in springtime, mostly, though some will come in the winter when the dark pine boughs are weighted by fresh snow and the ground is hard frozen and dirtied by pine drop-pings. When they reach the temple they stand, though remain bow-ing. They know if they look up, toward Mount Hiei, they will be thought imperious, without shame. They are ashamed, of course; it is the reason they have come. There are so many things to ask for-giveness for; so many things. And so they bend low, whispering the names of the unnamed, of the never forgotten, lighting the half-burnt sticks of incense on the porcupined stone altar left by the ones who have come before. The candlewood smell, eucalyptus, seduces them and they straighten a bit, enough to see Mount Hiei, its onyx peaks white-capped, or, if in springtime, lit by mica and bright as rising crystal palace spires. Could they live there, then? Fly away if they wished? Sprout wings from their brittle shoulders? The incense burns to nubbins, flares, then dies. They descend as they came, their kimonos dragging.

8

After Rita's death I wanted to get rid of things: *The Gardens of Kyoto*, Ruby's letter from Paris, and anything else of significance. Betty and I had already packed what remained of Rita's possessions in her attic room, carrying the boxes to the rain cellar, and I had gone from there to my own belongings, folding dresses that no longer fit, matchless socks, whatever I could find that was of no use into a crate, which I carted down to the rain cellar and set next to Rita's. I cleaned with a frenzy just this short of grieving, ending with what remained of Randall's package, which I now kept in the top drawer of my dresser among my underthings and the statement book for my bank account. I had already given up his diary, as I have told you, and other odds and ends would be lost along the way: his broken spectacles with the cracked left lens, the letter opener, the children's primer, the spool of red thread.

No matter.

I took *The Gardens of Kyoto* downstairs and asked Mother for Ruby's address. She did not say a word. She simply recited the address from her recipe box and I printed it on the brown paper shopping bag that wrapped the book. I then folded Ruby's letter from Paris into a clean envelope, dust from the creased, brittle New York something cutout of the swells on the *Mauretania* on my fingers as I addressed it to Ruby in my steady, purposeful hand. Then I licked the stamp.

I should not have to tell you that I could not bring myself to mail the book. Halfway to the post office I tore the paper bag away, as if the illustrations might wilt without air. The letter I sent as intended, addressed to Ruby at the Gramercy Park Residence for Ladies. Had I not been so serious in my determination to send the letter on, I might have stopped and admired the look of that name on the white envelope: the elegance of the words "Residence" and "Ladies." Old-fashioned words, I understand now, as antique as the brass griffin's claw at the base of Randall's stairway.

Mother had once told me of a visit she made there with her Aunt Maude, back, as Mother put it, when The Residence was still a grand place, a hotel for working women. Men came to call and were asked to sit in the parlor downstairs, their polished loafers firm on the oriental rugs that covered the oak floors; beaded sconces lit the walls. A grandfather clock chimed the hour that tea was served, when most of the girls would return from their jobs and prepare for their dates. The girls were buyers for department stores, Mother said, editors at publishing houses; occasionally, models or actresses, ballerinas. They treated one another as sisters would, borrowing jackets to match particular skirts, suggesting drinks after difficult days. Even on gloomy evenings they walked the city, *divine*, they would say, in the fog. They spoke in the way of the popular radio stars and wore dressing gowns on Saturday mornings. They carried silver compacts in their pockets. Their dates took them to The Club Cha Cha and The Escuelita. All illegal, of course; these were the days of Prohibition, though it was like some great game everybody knew they could cheat.

Most of the girls eventually moved on. They married, following husbands to smaller towns. But a few, such as Ruby, stayed, their rooms preserved as they had always been, with a satin bedspread on a single bed and a desk at one angle in the corner where bills, neatly stacked, were paid on Sunday evenings.

I wonder at Ruby opening the envelope, finding her letter from Paris tucked within like a relic from her youth: the hand so assured.

Made a new friend on the crossing, she reads, *who has introduced me to this wonderful little hotel in the Latin quarter.*

And she is suddenly back to that hotel in Paris, to the yellow tiles in the bathroom, to the sound of the bathwater running as she lifts the book from her suitcase, turning to the inscription, expecting something, perhaps, less truthful: *For Ruby and child,* he has written. *With affection.*

She had been right to send it to Randall. It belonged to him as much as it belonged to her. Still, what an impulsive gesture—the book, the note—posted too rashly a few days before his thirteenth birthday. What had she said? You have reached the age of truth, she remembered. All a bit dramatic, but then, she is dramatic. And kind. And alone.

She looks out the window toward the pear trees in the park.

She had not heard a word from him, and now he is dead.

She turns back to the letter and fingers the embossed crest; smells the rainy streets and the sweet Belgian waffles wrapped in white paper sold from wheeled carts. What glory to walk the Seine, to see the world laid out along its banks like so many dishes at a banquet, everything entirely possible.

She had returned in early October, her favorite season, had swung her legs to the side of her bunk and attempted a smile when she saw Sterling at her cabin door. He had bribed a steward or something, he was explaining. Normally they don't let anyone onboard until all of the passengers have debarked.

He held, what? Roses? Some sort of welcoming flower wrapped

in green tissue. She took them and stood, unsure of whether to put them down or to keep them cradled in her arms. They were cold, still cold from the florist's freezer; indeed roses, the peach ones, her favorite. She looked back at him. She had not seen him in over a month and he looked different, somehow, or perhaps he had always looked this way and she had never noticed. He was much older, already in his fifties, and had the stance of a constant thinker, a scholar: hands thrust into the pockets of his trousers, a padded suit-coat ineffective at hiding the stoop of his shoulders. He appeared not to have slept in a while. Was it already exam time?

No, he said, he just—

She put the roses on the bunk, then turned back to him; the word *no*, the saying of it, unnecessary. He had never asked her to explain.

You were a good man, she would have told him were he to appear now, at this moment, in her room in the Gramercy Park Residence for Ladies. He might hang back at the door as he would in the old days, having snuck past the housemother to climb in stocking feet up the long stairway, she leading him, her bracelets in one hand to stop their jangling. Shhh, she'd say, making more noise than he. Where had they been? Dancing, no doubt. They loved dancing. Up to Harlem or to the Snack Shack closer to Columbia, where the graduate students who hunkered over their beers called him Professor Jewell, a name, she told him, she liked the ring of: Sterling Jewell, she'd say. It shines, doesn't it?

They had taken a livery down Fifth, asleep at this time of night, the new Washington Square Arch glistening in what might have been rain, what might have been weak snow. He put his arm around her thin shoulders, the two preferring to sit exposed rather than use the filthy horsehair blanket folded on the seat across from them. He had such long legs; what was called in those days a tall drink of water. But handsome, yes. A good man, a stern teacher, lecturing from a wood pulpit set in the center of the small auditorium, his pupils half-circling him as if he were a philosopher on Mount Olympus. She had come once, surprised him in the way that he liked, sitting in the farthest row back, her hat pulled low to her eyes, legs crossed. Of course the students could barely face him, so curious, as they were, about a grown woman in the back row with seamed stockings and a red hat, gold mesh covering her pretty face.

Sterling pretended not to notice. He simply talked, outlining his points with a yellow chalk on the high blackboard, gesticulating and then reaching, from time to time, for the pipe balanced on the edge of the wood pulpit. Perhaps she fell in love with him that day; she found his lecture oddly arousing. Afterward they walked through Central Park, sitting for a time by one of the larger ponds. He held her hand and said how proud he was to have her in the back row listening. She kissed him deeply. What she had been thinking she is not sure. She only remembers the kiss, that kiss, and the way his big hands went to her thin shoulders, each thumb caressing the bone, as if attempting to mold clay.

Was it that night they first went back to this room? She looks around it now from her place on the rose-covered sofa, still faded as it had been in Jeannette's home; she has been unable to match the fabric, the store on Seventh long closed. The room is not so different, actually: the framed illustrations from *Harper's* on the walls, the mannequin in the corner on which she once pinned all the newspaper photographs from the society columns: her hats worn by various dignitaries and ingenues. Where were those people now? Did they keep her creations on a bolster in the attic? Or was everyone already dead?

He had admired her career, saying he had not realized he was in the presence of such suspected genius.

He kept his hands in his pockets, jingling change.

"Suspected, to be sure," she said.

"That's all we can do with genius," he said, hanging near the door. Behind him a sign stated the rules of the room in blocky, serious letters. The first: "No entertaining men under any circumstance."

He had his hand on the doorknob. "Should I go?" he said.

She pointed to the sign. "You see the rules."

He read them then turned back to her, pulling the chain across the lock. "Under no circumstance will I be entertaining."

"Who was it you said you were, anyway?" she said.

"Just the messenger," he said.

"Ah, the messenger."

"I bring great tidings," he said.

"Hail, thee."

"Absolutely."

He stood so close she could breathe his breath. Earlier, he had taken his pipe from his suit pocket and tapped its bowl against the wood pulpit.

"Sterling Jewell," she said, because something had to be said, the air so thin she felt she might reel backward.

Outside, around Gramercy Park, the pear blossoms fall to the sidewalks, children rushing through to kick the blossoms like dry snow. Ruby has grown to love the sound of the children at this particular time of day. They have a school nearby, and they file into the park in two rows, their teachers in the rear determined to keep their lines straight, the all of them marching beyond the gates and then, what joy! breaking into chaos. She often watches from the window in her room, or from the bench in the park where she likes to eat her lunch. She packs a sandwich in her bag and eats in the sunshine; she slips off her shoes. Perhaps this day she brings the letter, holding it, staring at the name of the Parisian hotel in its modern font, its crest as sophisticated as her rejection of Sterling's proposal, clever as the hat, the pearls, on the rail-thin pretty girl who sits on the park bench smoking, the girl you might have seen before, the one you think you recognize from somewhere but no, she's just one of a hundred girls who look familiar.

9

The singing resumed just as Randall disappeared. The voices faint at first and then full and rich; not the voices of ghosts, but the voices of boys, a chorus of boys I suddenly realized were in fact singing somewhere just beyond the ballroom, their voices exaggerated by its hollowness. I followed them through the far door, finding myself once again in the east wing—the nurses' desk dimly lit ahead.

The voices were coming from a small chapel in front of me, the kind of chapel often found in the homes of rich men. Its doors were propped open and inside, on what appeared to be a makeshift dais, a group of young boys in sweater vests, a glee club of sorts, sang "How Lovely Is Thy Dwelling Place." Odd to think of it. A wonderful hymn. I often heard it as a little girl, when we would go to the Methodist church to hear Dr. Billy preach a Sunday sermon. The boys sang the hymn beautifully, standing on the dais in front of a sign—draped from hand to hand of the crucifix—that read "The University Club." They stood in a deliberate formation, holding music sheets and staring out to the men who lined the pews, an audience who, at first glance, appeared to be listening, though as I got closer it became apparent that they weren't listening at all, that they were in fact mumbling to themselves, their own voices like the rumble of a dirty machine beneath the bright tones of the boys.

The men talked on and on—to their imaginary seatmates, or to the nurses who sat beside them, holding the hands of the few who blocked the center aisle in wheelchairs. One I couldn't see in the front row suddenly began to shout what seemed to be the same unintelligible word again and again, though the boys did their best to pretend they didn't notice. They looked like any boys will, like the boys I had at one time dated. They had bright red cheeks and watered-back hair. Their leader wore a brass whistle around his neck and a hat with reindeer antlers.

I don't know how long it took me to notice your father. He sat in a tiny, circular balcony behind the crucifix, hidden by the elaborately carved wooden beams of the chapel. It was a balcony intended for one—perhaps the robber baron, I don't know, or his mistress—and your father leaned over the scene from there. I believe I waved, thinking he might see me, might sprint down the rounded stairway to join me for the rest of the concert. But he did not; or if he did he pretended he did not. I looked away: to the University Club singers, to the backs of the once-soldiers hunched in their pews. When I could no longer stand it I looked up, again, but your father was gone; the balcony empty. In thinking about it, I suppose the balcony had a secret entrance, intended for viewing services discreetly, or uninterrupted prayer. Still, at the time I wondered whether I hadn't just imagined him, as I had surely imagined Randall waiting for me in the next room.

10

I had every good intention of returning to the Veterans'
Hospital—the following day, the following week. And I did, in
fact. Several times. I would drive up the winding road and park
my rented automobile—an Oldsmobile that reeked of cigarettes—
in the visitors' lot. If it were a nice day, I might get out and walk
the overgrown path into the garden. And if it were a rotten day I
might do the same, a scarf pulled around my head. I would sit on
the cracked cement bench near the tennis court, trying to muster
the courage to again enter the hospital, to ask the nurse if she
might retrieve Henry from his room, to tell him about you, to ask
what he believed I should do. But I never did. Find the courage, I
mean.

Several months passed. I let them. It was early spring, March. Forsythia—a whole grove—had blossomed by my cement bench, and I
had returned to the hospital on that particular day, a glorious one,

with the hope that your father might be well, again. Who could be ill in this weather? Who could be ill in spring? Perhaps I believed that I might forge a new truth from the stories I had already concocted, that I might will the stories real: your father in his red convertible—"Will You Marry Me, Ellen?"—written across its hood in shaving cream. That we would, in fact, somehow marry; that you would be born to the two of us, together.

And so I found my way back to the garden, where I sat for some time. I wore no lipstick, my hair returned to its natural red. You had begun to kick and you were suddenly more important to me than anything else I could think of. I had explained to the school that your father and I had married, that he had been sent away on another military assignment God knows where and that I would have to take the rest of the year off. I had not seen Mother and Daddy in months. Only Betty knew.

I had, truth be told, begun to tell these fictions that have been our history. Your history. Mine. I apologize for this. We are all owed the truth.

There is a garden in Kyoto, Koto-in, built by a warrior in the early seventeenth century, in the years when Shakespeare wrote, that can only be viewed through a window. The window hangs at the end of a long stone walk lined with maples that have been pruned in a way to filter sunlight onto the stones in the shapes of Japanese characters. Words formed at particular times of day, in certain seasons, are read and recited by the visitors to the garden as they walk the stone path, repeated in the way of Japanese poems, their authorship sometimes credited to the Koto-in maples, sometimes to the Koto-in stones. Other Koto-in poems remain unfinished.

The point is the visitor—intent on viewing the garden—follows the stone path to the window frame, hewn from these same maples, and finds a small, bell-shaped window drawn with *shoji,* the window locked and closed.

I tell you this because on that day that I sat on my cement bench on the lower terrace, just beyond a break in the box hedges to the Sound, I held *The Gardens of Kyoto* open to the garden at Koto-in. It has always been my favorite, the woodcut a single window shuttered closed, like one of those children's books, where the reader might lift open the shuttered window to see a lamb in a pasture. But this window is impossible to pry open: the garden as much to the imagination as the endings of the Koto-in poems that are left unfinished, the ones interrupted by a sudden change of weather.

"Daphne?" Julia said. I recognized her voice in an instant and turned. She stood behind me in the same brown ensemble, her hair a blaze of sun.

"Hello," I said. I couldn't think of anything else.

She removed her brown sweater and placed it on the cement bench, then she sat down. "It gives me a chill," she said.

The forsythia's yellow was deafening.

"How long have you been here?" she said.

"I don't know."

She put her hand on my belly in the way that women do.

"It's so terrible about Henry," she said. "I tried to find you but no one knew where you lived."

"Outside Philadelphia," I said. I felt a dull cold against my bare palms; I must have been bracing myself against the bench, though in a deeper place I already understood.

"He was very sick," she said, and I might not have been there at all for the way she said it, as if she were trying to convince herself. "Sometimes they are. Sometimes they're very sick and sometimes they're just sad. We know what to do for the sad ones. How to cheer them up. It's not easy, you know."

"No," I said.

"But Henry. Well. He just couldn't stay in his own skin." She lit a cigarette. "It actually happens quite often. The hospital keeps it quiet. Out of the papers. God knows who would care." She blew smoke out. "I tried to find you but no one knew where you lived."

"Thank you."

"Someone thought you might live in California, but that didn't make sense, and then one of his friends from Korea. Mr. Tilsman?"

"Tilsie—"

"—said you had visited him once and that if you lived in California it would have been too far for you to visit. He thought maybe you lived in Manhattan."

"Outside Philadelphia," I said.

"Right."

She offered me a cigarette and I shook my head, no.

"Of course," she said. "I forgot."

Eventually she placed her own hand over mine.

"No one deserves such a thing," she said. And I didn't know whether she meant me, or Henry, but either way I said, thank you.

We sat on the cement bench for a long while. At one point she stood and took her sweater from beneath her to wrap around my shoulders. "You're shaking," she said.

"Am I?"

"You probably need to rest. The whole thing is shocking, really. We were all shocked."

"Yes," I said.

She helped me up. I carried my handbag, *The Gardens of Kyoto* and the razors I had brought for Henry now tucked inside. We walked along the overgrown path toward the parking lot, passing under a trellis made of stripped branches, heavy now with budding wisteria.

"This must have been a beautiful garden," I said. I wanted to say something.

"Yes," she said. "There's supposed to be a gardener, we heard, but no one ever comes around."

I would like to tell you what else I remember, but that's the most of it, and the rest makes me too sad to recall. Julia walked me to the parking lot, closed the door of my rented Oldsmobile, and leaned into the window. "Are you sure you don't want me to telephone somebody? I could call someone. Or I could drive you where you need to go."

"No, thank you," I said. "I'm fine."

"Yes," she said. "I imagine you've had some time to get used to it."

"A bit," I said.

"I'm glad Tilsie finally found you. It didn't seem right to bury him without his fiancé. We understood your reluctance to attend, of course. Some things can't be faced."

"No," I said. I hesitated a moment. "Tilsie said it was a lovely service."

"Thanks to your letters."

"I'm sorry?"

"Tilsie didn't tell you?"

"Of course," I said. "I asked him to—"

"That's what Tilsie said," she said. "They were beautiful, Daphne."

I sat behind the wheel and Julia leaned in. "You know, Henry told me the story. That time you came to visit. Afterward. He told me how he proposed: the restaurant you loved with those candles on the table in wine bottles, dripping down to nothing but the stubs. The whole thing. He made me promise I wouldn't say a word and I remember I just laughed and said, who would I tell? But he said, please. A lot of men tell me their secrets. It's part of the job." Julia drew back and pulled her sweater more tightly around her. "You would have had a happy life, Daphne," she said. "That's how Henry put it. We're going to have a happy life, he said, and even though I knew he was one of the sick ones I said I believed you would, because I did believe it." Then she smiled in that way that women will to erase whatever terrible thing they have just said, and told me she had to get back inside. I pulled on my gloves, turned the ignition key, and drew the clutch into reverse.

"God bless you, Daphne," I believe she said before I left. I don't know. I know that my hands shook so hard I had to grip the wheel, and that you kicked and kicked, kicked in the way I should have kicked, should have lashed at the stupidity of them, of all of them who put him here. I should have torn my hair from its roots, howling. But I said nothing. I simply drove away.

11

Iago says, I am not what I am, and for this he is called deceit-
ful, a villain. Odd, isn't it? I have always found him to be the most
truthful of Shakespeare's creations. We are none of us who we are.

After I learned of your father's death, I drove that rental car to the
Sound, or to where the Sound met the shore, a park not far from
the munitions factory. I sat for a time watching the seagulls,
imagining what life we might have had if I had had the courage to
tell him the truth of you, the truth of me, or Daphne. I called
Tilsie and he met me in the park. I can still remember him hurrying over, wearing a tan raincoat, ringing his hands like some,
God knows, guilty man. I told him I was Ellen, and that Daphne
was for all I knew still in Europe or perhaps at Radcliffe after all.
He told me how when the squad saw the article in *Life* magazine
they held a mock ceremony for him, how someone fashioned a
Silver Star out of a K-ration tin, looped it on a piece of leather

bootstrap and how your father delivered an honorary address.

"It was so goddamn funny," Tilsie said. "So goddamn serious and funny." He laughed then, remembering. He had given me his raincoat; I couldn't stop shivering. "But the thing was, I believed it," Tilsie said. "I mean, I somehow believed it, believed that goddamn K-ration Silver Star was straight from Eisenhower, believed all those goddamn heroic things the writer said I'd done were true, and all those nice things Henry was saying."

"I know," I said, because I somehow did, though Tilsie didn't seem to hear me. He stared straight ahead, addressing no one, the yellow measuring tape still draped around his neck.

I had every intention of carrying out my original plans—returning to the school with you in tow; reciting the story of Henry's accident; raising you to believe these fictions as our real life.

But your father's death drained me of all courage. And so I resigned myself to go along with what Betty insisted, what Mother and Daddy surely would have if they were told the truth. Tilsie knew of a place: a convent not so great a distance from his hometown and far enough away from mine. Soon after that day in the garden he drove me there, carrying my suitcase across the lawn and into the Mother Superior's office.

I remember little of it: nuns hovered in the corners; the hallways were long and bleak.

The Mother Superior, a woman who reminded me of Sister Pat, looked from Tilsie to me and lifted her eyebrows. Tilsie told her we had several children at home, that he had recently lost his job as a machine operator and that his wife felt incapacitated, I remember that word, by the thought of another child. Incapacitated, he said, and it suddenly struck me that Tilsie was a very good liar.

The Mother Superior placed her two figgy hands on her desktop papers; the loose skin of her neck draped in many folds. She believed none of it.

"I'll pray for your sorrow," she said, words that, at the time, meant little to me, though I've thought of them almost daily since.

Tilsie walked with my suitcase to the small room where the Mother Superior directed us. I imagine women such as myself came and stayed here often, though I was the only one at that time, my room a single cot, a washing basin, a small crucifix over a chest of drawers. I remember a stained piece of lace draped across the wooden chest top, strangely decadent within that chaste place.

Tilsie set my suitcase next to the cot and promised he would return in the morning. I understood that he would not: I was too close to the lie of his own life; and he was too close to the lie of mine.

No one knew where I was, not even Betty. My suitcase stayed next to the cot, where Tilsie had deposited it; I wore the same, simple shift every day and ate my meals in silence with the nuns. After vespers, Sister Charlotte, my favorite, would bring me a glass of warmed milk and two slices of buttered bread fresh from the kitchen ovens, one for the mother, she would say, and one for the little one. Sister Charlotte must have been close to sixty, and though I never saw her without her habit, I imagine she had curly gray hair cut short. Her hands were the softest hands I ever held.

*   *   *

My labor began on a sweltering July day. I had been sitting in the courtyard, thinking, when I felt the first contraction, a pain so sharp I cried out, a little, though there was no one around to hear me. I had been told by the Mother Superior that when the time came I was to walk to her office and ring the brass bell she kept on her desk for emergencies. I did this, steadying myself against the cool, dark wall of that long hallway, my eyes still blinded by the bright outdoor sunshine.

The doctor was immediately called; the Mother Superior, familiar with labor pains, understood even though I did not that you would be born quickly, violently. Sister Charlotte was also called, and she helped me to walk to the larger room where births and deaths were staged, to undress, guiding me into the heavy mahogany bed, turning down the white sheets that smelled vaguely of antiseptic. She held my hand, then, though I wanted to walk, I told her; I wanted to remain in the courtyard garden, where geraniums in large clay pots surrounded a dry fountain, its basin cracked. I wanted to stay there, I told her. Please.

But it was against the rules and besides, there was no time; the doctor said as much. You would be born within the hour, he said. And you were; you tore your way out.

I was not allowed to see you: there was a system in those days, and this was part of the system. The doctor followed the rules. He immediately handed you—I could hear your cries— to the Mother Superior, and she whisked you away to God knows where, a hidden room for such things, where you would be washed and wrapped in a bunting, where papers would be signed before you were given away. The point is, Sister Charlotte did not follow the protocol. She returned soon after the others had left the room, returned with you in her arms, saying if a rule was cruel it deserved to be broken, damn the torpedoes.

I lay propped on hard pillows, a smaller pillow filled with ice between my legs to staunch the swelling. She gave you to me so I could see for myself that you were, as she had promised, perfect—ten fingers, ten toes—and that you were indeed a girl as I had imagined. I don't know how long Sister Charlotte let me hold you. It seemed like no time and an eternity at once. In those days, you must understand, this was a terrible breach. I imagine they believed that if I saw you I might change my mind, might keep you for my own.

No matter.

I only know that I did. Hold you, I mean, and that you were beautiful, and that before Sister Charlotte took you away I named you Rita.

· *Book Five* ·

There was only one thing Randall insisted I remember about the art of dramatic presentation. It was the first rule of thumb, what I would have to understand if I were going to understand anything at all. You speak, he told me, to an audience of one —a solitary listener to whom you direct your presentation, to whom you project your voice in the telling; a person whom you picture as you confide.

You have been mine since the day you were born.

Randall's was the poet whose name I've forgotten. The famous one who fought in the First World War. A man no older than a boy; a poet known to all of England and to anyone versed, Randall said, in the glories of Verdun, Ypres, Passchendaele, the Somme.

He told me he pictured his poet not as a dead soldier, but as a soldier in the trenches, writing the poem that would be read in Saint Paul's Cathedral, Easter Day, 1915, writing despite his frostbitten

fingers, his blackened feet, the stench of those fallen around him—
the men, Randall said, who had already crossed the river Styx.

This again the day my family reluctantly arrived at Randall's
house, Rita saying, for the love of Pete, the place looks so gloomy
and haunted, why are we here at all? Don't we have better things to
do than meet old, dusty relatives who aren't even nice? Mother saying, shhh. . . . Who told her Sterling wasn't nice?

You! Rita said, getting Mother to laugh as she would only laugh
at Rita, Betty saying, that's right, Mother, you did say such a thing,
and Mother laughing in the front seat, refusing to look at Daddy,
shaking her head and saying, John Brown, when did her girls turn to
magpies?

While all the time Randall waited behind that heavy front door,
not wanting to open it—what were they doing idling there for so
long?—though breathless with the thought of three cousins. And
then, unable to refrain, he did. He opened the door before we were
even out of Daddy's Ford, just a crack, enough to see from where he
hid: the tallest, prettiest one; the one who looked a bit like him.

We sat in the diner near the train station—this after Randall said
the business about Hog Phelps, the boy he had met from
Louisville—in silence. We were particularly good at silence as readers tend to be. There were certain Easter visits when a whole silent
hour might go by as the two of us read in his room, entirely still, not
a word spoken. I had learned early on never to interrupt Randall to
ask a question, or to puzzle something out that I didn't understand.
Not understanding was part of it, he had told me.

Around us soldiers scraped back their chairs, quickly leaving
the other tables, an entire regiment on their way west. They exited
the diner with great purpose—laughing loudly, voices pitched high,
cheeks still ruddy with the wind of the outdoors and the heat of the

steamy restaurant and the anticipation of what they were too soon
to do.

"Well," I said, smoothing the lap of my skirt.

"Well," Randall said.

The last soldier closed the door. The waiters disappeared into
the kitchen. Mother was elsewhere, lingering in the bathroom. She
knew enough to know that we were both terribly shy, and that if we
were going to speak at all we needed time and, in truth, a quiet
place empty of patrons and the waiters' constant attentions. It did
seem as if a thundering hurricane had spun on. We sat in the wake
of its destruction: forks and spoons and dirty plates strewn across
every table, chairs knocked to the floor and a single red, lost mitten.

Randall drummed the tabletop with his pale fingers. I believe I
had asked him about training.

"Instruction," he corrected me. "Everything is instruction.
When you fasten your bayonet and lunge at a scarecrow, that's
instruction in close combat. When you miss the shooting target and
they wave Maggie's drawers at you, that's instruction in humiliation.
There's a lot of instruction in that. Humiliation. They might as well
give you a college degree. A doctor of philosophy in humiliation."

He drummed the table.

"Maggie's drawers?"

"A red flag, that's all it is. I don't know where Maggie came
from."

A waiter appeared to offer us coffee. I pushed my cup closer
toward him and watched him pour. He walked away and the silence
descended, again. I sipped my coffee. Randall resumed his drumming. I felt his duffel bag beneath the table, a reminder that soon he
would be on his way.

"And marching," Randall said. "There's a boatload of instruction in marching. Left, right. Left, right. Drop. Left, right, left, right.
Drop. And never run straight across a field. Nothing more lonesome
than a corpse in a field."

I looked at him. I had never heard anyone use that word.

Randall shrugged. "They want to frighten you into staying alive."

"I guess," I said.

He stopped his drumming. "I don't know the meaning of lonesome. We're alike that way, aren't we?" It seemed a question tinged with something else.

"What way?" I said.

"Oh, I don't know. The way that matters."

There was an unused fork near my coffee cup, and scatterings of our lunch on our uncleared plates: Mother's bacon, lettuce, and tomato; my tunafish, only partially eaten. Randall had ordered soup, though he had hardly tasted it. Now he pushed the spoon around the bowl.

"The funny thing is, I missed home," he said. "All that time thinking that as soon as I left I'd just keep going, and then what I thought about at night, lights out, I mean, was how good it would be to pass back through on my way here. To sit in my room and read, again. And then, when I got there, I couldn't concentrate on a single word. It was as if I didn't even know *how* to do it. Every time I opened a book all the words went gray and it just seemed like a colossal waste of time."

I listened, my hands in my lap.

"I took a walk. I had a thousand things to do, but I went for a walk. I asked him but he didn't want to go. It was raining, he said."

Randall stared at his soup and pushed his spoon around.

"I walked toward the McCleans' and then turned around because he was right, it was raining, and then I was almost home and the rain let up a bit. I could see the house and the one light on in his study and it didn't even look like anyone's house. It looked like a painting of a house. I went in the side way so that I'd pass his door. He was at his desk so I stopped. I thought maybe he planned to talk to me before I left, but he didn't seem to want to say anything. Just, good night. I don't know what I expected. Not some great good-bye or to thine own self be true. I don't want that from anybody—" here he looked up—"except you, of course."

"Of course," I said. I might have kicked him underneath the table, or that might have been the duffel bag. I know I felt a sudden charge between us. I looked away; it seemed too unbearable to watch: Randall in his dull Army clothes—entirely wool, the kind that looks scratchy—a pair of olive green trousers and a khaki shirt and an olive green tie, of all things.

"But a conversation," Randall said. "Anything to get the mind off. I was sick with thinking. At camp they kept you running and then you fell asleep in your proverbial boots. That was their plan. They'd already told you it's hell. You'll see your best buddies, the ones you're training with, blown to smithereens. You might lose your mind. I kept hearing the rats of Nagasaki jumping into the sea, you know, *chu chu, chu chu,* until I thought I'd already been to Japan, or wherever the hell they're going to send us. I'd already been there and I'd already lost my mind—"

"No," I said. I wanted him to stop because he was frightening me, because I couldn't think of anything else to say. I wished us back to the dark of the slaves' hiding place, counting heartbeats, or to the dinner table, biding our time before we could ask to be excused.

"I started packing, but that didn't take long. Then it began to rain, again. I don't know if you've ever heard it in our house. The whole place leaks like a sieve, and when it rains hard you'd think the roof might cave in and you sit there listening, holding your breath because at any minute you might be washed away. Mother used to say we should hitch a lifeboat to the side of the house so we wouldn't drown."

Randall let his soup spoon drop to the bowl, waking me from my trance. He had never been much of a talker, and listening to his voice for so long had felt like hearing a story that carried me out of my own life and into another, where I stood in Randall's room in the rain near the window, watching the water slosh down those old windows, the oak limbs shivering with the stormy wind, their last dead leaves blown to smithereens. I could see how the rain pummeled the glass, how the wind blew twigs and whatnot against it, the sound a *ping, ping, ping* sound, staccato as gunfire. Soon, I knew, the storm would lift, abating as quickly as it descended, and if it were morning the mocking birds would resume their catcalls, and if it were evening the clouds would break and out of them slip the yellow moon.

Randall continued. He told me how he had gathered what he would miss, mostly books from his bookshelves, and tried again through the night to read, it against regulations to take books—something about censures—and he wanted to have those poets in his ears.

"The funny thing is," Randall said, "I could only stand *The Gardens of Kyoto*. Remember?"

I looked at him. Of course I did.

"I may soon be like him," he said.

"Who?"

"Our damaged professor. Professor X. Madly and tragically in love with the girl."

"He was in love with her?"

Randall looked at me and smiled.

"You had to read between the lines," he said.

Have I told you his was a beautiful smile? Not the smile of a cynic, nor the easy, hungry smile of boys his age, those smiles that aim to get them somewhere, are a commodity in exchange for God knows what. No. His was completely without intent; an accident of a smile. The kind of smile that would have surprised him if he could have seen it for himself. But he was too young to know his own extraordinariness.

*   *   *

"Anyway, I left it to you," he said.

"What?"

"Our professor, birdbrain. The book. Given the likelihood of the inevitable *chu chu*, you will be the owner of the property in question."

"Nonsense," I said, or, "Don't be foolish."

Randall looked away and I understood too late that I had broken something too delicate to repair.

"You'll be fine, I promise," I said, smoothing my lap, again, as Mother walked up, fiddling with her handbag. She did not like the role of chaperon, and though she certainly cared for Randall, Randall had a way of standing apart from adults, as if he knew that he would never cross the line into their territory.

"Ready?" she said, a bit too cheerfully.

Randall nodded and pushed back his chair. I did the same, reaching for my coat, which I had folded over its back, when Randall intervened, taking my coat to hold out for me as if we were closing a date. He no longer appeared scared, or nervous. Certainly not talkative. He seemed more resigned, somehow, and oddly purposeful, as if for me to put on my coat, for him to hold it steady as I did so, was perhaps the most important thing in the world. And so I slipped my arms through, me in my pink sweater and skirt, my hands trembling; him in that tie that earlier he had looped upside down, crossing his eyes and sticking out his tongue as if the tie were a noose, as if he were a boy hanged.

We followed Mother out of the diner, crossing the street to the train platform, the train already crowded, a raucous group of boys dangling from the windows, shouting messages to a similar group of boys who dangled from the windows at the farthest end. The air smelled of popcorn and there was music—a few members from the local high school band there to cheer the soldiers off or maybe a soldier himself had brought along his brass trumpet. I don't know. I know the whole thing felt a circus, frenzied and dangerous. I climbed the steps to the platform with Randall near enough to touch, one gloved hand in a pocket, one out to grip the steprail. Then we stood, the three of us, as if awaiting instruction. I wiped my nose with my perfumed handkerchief, wishing, again, that I had remembered my compact. Around me women who may have been mothers, who may have been wives, wore the anxious looks of women traveling, though they were staying behind, their sons and husbands suddenly animated, hurrying as the station master called, All aboard.

Randall turned to Mother and said something that made her laugh. She patted his shoulder and reached around to hug him. Then she let go and Randall turned to me. I smelled tobacco smoke in his red scarf and then the sharp, cold air as he pulled away and left to join the soldiers crowding into the narrow open spaces between the train compartments. Mother said she was freezing and that she would meet me in the station. I watched her part the thinning crowd, then turned back to the train. We were only women on the platform now: the mute women who had jostled out of Mother's way, who now stood dumbly watching as the wheels of the train began to turn, as the whistle blew, because it did, in those days, blow, releasing a great scream of steam.

It was then—just as the whistle blew—that Randall got off; then that he turned to wave to us and finding only me stepped down— the whistle blowing, the train slowly moving—to push his way to where I stood, my hands deep in my pockets. Perhaps his uniform made him brave, perhaps he understood more than I did what he was about to do: he pressed his hands on either side of my face as if to warm them and looked directly at me.

"I'm switching allegiances," he said.

"I'm sorry?"

"You're it. My new audience. To hell with dead poets."

"Thank you," I said. I didn't know what else.

He rolled his eyes.

"In this my last confession, you'll have to do better than that, sweetheart."

Where had this Randall come from? This young man in drab woolen pants, a tie, and a soldier's coat—his knobby wrists, his long fingers, near enough to kiss?

"*Merci*," I said. It was a word I had been saving for my first letter to him.

He laughed, I believe, though I could barely hear a thing, the sound of his *sweetheart* ringing loudly in my ears. "Good-bye, Ellen," he said, staring at me as if he might be counting my bones. I looked down, then up, again, though he was already gone, already running for the train, the ending so predictable: the boy leaves for war; the boy dies.

And I let him go. I might have pulled out my hands. I might have brought them up around him. I might have kept them that way until the train left the station. I could have easily done it. I could have simply held on, wrapping my arms so tightly no one would have dared pry him loose.

epilogue

I did, in fact, see Daphne again. Once, accidentally. It must have been ten or eleven years ago. She was sitting in a restaurant, at a table near the front plate-glass window, and I passed by, in the city for an education symposium or one of the endless teacher training sessions they required of us in those days. I'm sure I looked to her as I look to any stranger—a middle-aged woman, stern in carriage. Or this is how she would have seen me; how my students do, I'm afraid, though I have on more than one occasion led them in to the aspen grove, asking them to please, for a moment, take off their coats, their burdensome shoes, remove the gum from their mouths.

I recognized her immediately. She sat at a table with a boy who looked to be about the age we were when we first met, a bit older. She did not see me. I was on the street and she was sitting inside, engaged in conversation with the boy. I'm not sure why I felt so determined to speak to her. Perhaps I should have simply passed by, glad for the chance to know she survived.

Still, I entered the restaurant and walked toward her table. She must have felt my determination because she looked up before I was even halfway across the room. I wish I could say she seemed happy to see me, but it would be more accurate to say she looked at me as if I were an apparition from a past she wanted no part of.

"Ellen?" she said. I had reached her table.

"Daphne. You're here. Daphne."

The boy looked from her to me and I could see now their extraordinary resemblance. He had his mother's intensity, her full, gray eyes, and for an instant we both stared at him, as if he would somehow tell us what to do next.

"This is my son," Daphne said. "Alex."

"Oh," I said. I believe we shook hands.

"This is Ellen, an old friend," Daphne said. "Alex is a graduate student at Penn."

The boy smiled and I saw he did not entirely resemble her; he had too great a calm about him.

"I haven't seen your mother in years," I said. I felt I had to explain.

"And she hasn't aged a bit, right?"

I looked at Daphne.

"She's a much better dresser," I said. Daphne wore a dark blue cashmere suit with a silk blouse, and she had let her hair, cropped short, gray to a stark white, the beautiful white of an older intellectual. Her face looked even thinner than I remembered, more finely featured; she had on tiny copper-framed glasses that were just beginning to be popular.

"You've changed your glasses," I said.

She smiled at me.

"Sit down, Ellen. Join us, please. I would love to hear your news."

It seemed so formal, all of it: the way Daphne spoke and her cashmere suit, the restaurant with its silver bowls of breadsticks and large, full wineglasses and tuxedoed waiters, even her son, so composed for a boy, a student, as if he had nothing left to learn.

I looked at my watch, or pretended to do so. "I really can't," I said. "I'm expected at an education panel."

"You teach?" she said.

I nodded. "High school. Literature."

"Mother's the chairman of the history department at Wellesley," Alex said.

"That must be gratifying," I said.

"No, not really. Mostly committee work. I have very little time for my own research."

"Oh," I said.

It seemed to be all we were.

"Well," I said. "It was wonderful to see you."

"And you," Daphne said. They both stood up

"Good-bye," I said.

"Good-bye," they said.

I was close to Liberty Park when I heard her call my name. I turned and saw her walking briskly toward me, her coat unbuttoned; she waved.

"I'm so sorry," she said when she reached me. "Really."

"For what?" I said.

She shrugged and looked around her. "Let's sit," she said, and so we sat on one of the cold metal benches that outline the park, barren after the lunch hour. Before us stood the Liberty Bell, surrounded by a fence covered in graffiti. Daphne shivered and reached into her coat pocket for a package of cigarettes. I declined and she lit hers.

"This is exactly what I have wanted to do," she said. She took a long drag on her cigarette and let the smoke out. "Sit in this ugly little park and smoke cigarette after cigarette and talk about, what? God knows where to begin. Nothing. Let's just sit and talk about absolutely nothing. Can we do that? Can we talk about absolutely nothing? Would you mind, terribly, missing your engagement so you could sit here with me?"

"No," I said.

People passing by may have thought us sisters, or old, old friends. We sat for a good long while. It began to snow, the snow that looks like rain at first, then takes on weight and drift; the snow soon covered the Liberty Bell and the graffitied rails of the fence and the ground and our own bench.

"He's a beautiful boy, Daphne," I said after a time.

"Yes," she said. "Isn't he?"

acknowledgments

Two books were invaluable to me in my research: *A Guide to the Gardens of Kyoto* by Marc Treib and Ron Herman; and *The Underground Railroad: A Record of Facts, Authentic Narratives, Letters, etc. Narrating the Hardships Hair-breadth Escapes and Death Struggles of the Slaves in their efforts for Freedom as related By Themselves and Others or Witnessed by the Author* by William Still. I have quoted directly from Still's book: the list of names in book three, chapter 4, as well as many of the details from the harrowing escape of William Box Peel Jones for the character of Romulus Box Perkins

I'm thankful for the use of the collection of slave narratives at the Beinecke Rare Book and Manuscript Library at Yale University, and to the exhibit organized by Elisabeth Fairman at the Yale Center for British Art entitled *Doomed Youth: The Poetry and Pity of the First World War*. Sara Bader at the History Channel generously shared with me a selection of letters written by men stationed in the Pacific and Europe. Certain lines from the letter of Frank J. Conwell, sent from the Western Front February 6, 1945, are quoted as Roger's in book four, chapter 2.

I would also like to thank the National Endowment for the Arts for their support during the writing of this book, and Maria Massie, Gillian Blake, and Nan Graham for their guidance.

A special thanks to Rafael, to Delia, to Polly, and to my family, especially my mother and father.

Turn the page for a preview of
Kate Walbert's novel

THE

SUNKEN

CATHEDRAL

Available June 2015 from Scribner

III

The mothers, dressed for exercise, gather on the steps of Progressive K–8—Stephanie G. at the center, forty-five, give or take, her hair in short braids, dandelions woven into the bands—Elizabeth sees her and sidesteps but too late.

"Elizabeth!" Stephanie G. calls. "Elizabeth!"

How had she agreed to the idea at all? Now Stephanie G. blocks her path, clearly determined to see the vision fulfilled: Who We Are stories line the hallways of Progressive K–8 like so many snowflake cutouts in winter, each sincere and beautiful and excruciatingly heartbreaking for reasons Elizabeth cannot name and does not want to examine. The idea had grown out of the school's pledge for better communication by way of stronger community, dialoguing through dialogue, something like that, one of those tautologically challenged declarations beloved by their new interim head of school—Dr. Constantine—an elderly woman whose early advocacy of sexual education in pre-K put her on the academic map. If everyone could share their roots, or dig down to their roots, or expose their roots the school might come together in a grand way, or at least in a way that would increase the parent participation in the annual fund drive.

It had all been outlined in an e-mail: IMPORTANT ANNOUNCE-
MENT FROM DR. CONSTANTINE, which Elizabeth opened expecting to
read of another outbreak of nits on a fifth grader's scalp or an
additional plea for vigilance when patrolling the City blocks
after pickup. This, Elizabeth's favorite parental responsibility:
mothers and the occasional bemused father wandering Bleecker
Street in pairs regardless the weather, dressed in bright orange
vests and carrying heavy walkie-talkies, a bit over-the-top, yet
still: vigilance must be maintained, Dr. Constantine stressed,
especially in the event of a What If.*

Last month Elizabeth had patrol duty with a woman
whose son was in first grade, a woman tall and thin with dark,
New York hair and glasses suggesting a love of books or at
least a graduate degree in the humanities. The two had wandered the block greeting other mothers they knew, nodding to
clusters of students and telling them to get along, eyeing any
stray man who seemed not to have a destination in mind, their
hands gripping the walkie-talkies just in case they needed to
call back in to, whom? Dr. Constantine? Central control? The
crackle of static had felt comforting, as was the idea of a direct
link to someone who might allay her more general fears. Dirty
bomb a hoax, the voice would whisper; organic beef as good
as grass-fed.

But this e-mail had a different message:

What's Your Story? it read. We're asking the Progressive

---

*What Ifs were favorites of Dr. Constantine's, who often opened her monthly
Cappuccinos with Constantine by tossing What Ifs to the crowd: What If an
earthquake were to knock out the power grid? What If an outbreak of avian flu
occurred during a blizzard? What If I never do my homework? Elizabeth's son,
Ben, newly thirteen, now liked to throw back at her, What If I refuse to get out
of bed?

K–8 Community to participate in a 3-E endeavor to Enliven, Engage, and Enlighten with Who We Are stories. Everyone has one: Great-Uncle Vic worked as a tailor for Chiang Kai-shek; Grandmother Sanchez escaped from Castro's Cuba. Whatever it is, we want to know! And please, include pictures!

"So, who are we?" Ben asked that night at the dinner table.

"What?" Elizabeth said, distracted by the amount of cheese he had stuffed in his taco.

"Dr. Constantine said we were supposed to remind you," Ben said, negotiating a bite. "I'm reminding you."

"Oh, that," she said, turning to her husband, who scooped the meat with a spoon and whose pale, delicate fingers, long and tapered, looked as if he should be playing a musical instrument. "What?" Pete said. "What are we talking about?"

"We're supposed to write a Who We Are story," Elizabeth said. "You know, where we come from, how we ended up here. They're asking everyone to do it. One of those community things."

Pete looked at her as if not comprehending. She had noticed this more and more about him, these brief synapses—hamster trances, Ben called them—and wondered if it had to do with his not sleeping, or maybe the hours he spent sitting at a desk staring at small numbers moving across a computer screen or on the device held in his palm. Perhaps he was waiting for his wife and son to morph into something else, for the trading feed to begin its loop across the bottom of the page: information, statistics, the rise and fall of the stock exchange; or possibly he hoped the text might offer links to other sites, sites that would explicate his family's deeper, troubling mysteries—his wife's increasing restlessness, his son's unpredictable moods.

"My ancestors were Welsh," Pete said. "You could write about that. The Welsh are interesting."

"I thought Holland," Elizabeth says.

Pete shrugs. "Somebody sailed from Rotterdam before the Revolution, but then there was also something about Wales. Nobody really knows."

"If you were a girl you could be a member of the DAR," Elizabeth says to Ben. "That's kinda cool."

Ben looks from one to the other then takes a tremendous bite of his taco, tomatoes and cheese and lettuce shreds raining down on his plate, and to the side of the plate onto the good tablecloth.

"Promise me you won't take your first date out for tacos," Elizabeth says.

"I promise I won't take my first date out for tacos," Ben says, his mouth full. When did he get so large, so ungainly, so hairy? He is all arms and legs, as if he can't even fit into his chair. They sit on the chairs she and Pete bought in Mexico, right after their wedding. The chairs have rattan seats the cat has destroyed and are grease-stained and worn but when she looks at them she thinks of Pete speaking broken Spanish, attempting to bribe someone at the post office in Oaxaca to mail them freight.

"We could write how we had tacos on our first date," Elizabeth says to Pete, feeling suddenly expansive, young; she might be twenty-eight; she might be walking on that beach in Mexico, the one where they stayed before leaving for Oaxaca, where the chickens and seagulls followed them for crumbs. They were eating galletas; they were leaving a trail in case they got lost. "We could write that when I took the first bite he wondered if he could have a second date, much less spend the rest of his life with me."

"I did wonder that," Pete says.

"First date?" Elizabeth says.

"What did we do?" Pete says.

"Chinese," Elizabeth says.

"Right," Pete says. "I was thinking egg roll."

"Chinatown," Elizabeth says.

"Right, right. You had the spicy braised fish," he says, though she didn't—at the time she refused to eat anything with scales.

"And then we went to hear music," she says.

"Muddy Waters," Pete says.

"Willie Dixon," Elizabeth says. "And ate those little balls with the toothpicks for dessert. They were too sweet. They're always too sweet."

"I moved into your mother's apartment. It was above Sherm's—" Pete says to Ben.

"Sherman's was an upscale diner and all day Sunday you smelled all the delicious—" says Elizabeth.

"Sausage."

"Your father didn't have a dime. We never ate out again," Elizabeth says.

"One time your mother found this stray dog and asked the waiters if they had any leftover sausage—"

"Oh God!"

"For the dog," Pete says. He smiles, remembering.

Ben has his eyes covered, head on the table, or the pretty tablecloth. "Should I be writing this down?" he says.

Two fathers sprint past Stephanie G., their jacket tails flying as if they can't wait to get the hell to their jobs. Certain days the fathers turn out in impressive numbers, walking their young children to school, looking handsome and freshly showered, many in well-cut suits and a few in jeans and bomber jackets, good shoes, and one or two in grungy clothes. The fathers must exercise at different times, maybe earlier in the morning before they have showered, or possibly at night or possibly not at all, though in general the fathers look more physically fit than the mothers and, truth be told, Elizabeth thinks, younger. How could you account for this? How can you possibly reconcile the great inequities of gender—coupled with the perversions of age and the general randomness of everything? Who could you call to complain? Or is it *whom*?

"Elizabeth?" Stephanie G. is saying. "Are you with me?"

"Oh, sorry," Elizabeth says, too quickly. "Yes, of course. Absolutely. What?"

"I was saying we're trying to get one hundred percent participation. It's part of the General Mandate. I saw you signed up for the Environmental Committee, too," she says. "Of course there's no saying you can't do both." Stephanie G. cocks her head to one side. She actually looks cute in braids, Elizabeth thinks. Maybe how she looked as a child, eager, happy, always ready to include the third girl or stand up to the bully. She clerked for a Supreme Court justice until she had her second son—now there are four—worked as the editor of the law review, supported her alcoholic mother, et cetera, et cetera. When she had started putting dandelions in her hair Elizabeth can't quite remember, though it may have been right around the time Stephanie G. cochaired the third-grade flower drive. Those days you would never see her without a potted plant in her hands or a sprig of something behind her ear.

"I mean unless you want to," Stephanie G. says. "If you want to, that would be terrific."

"No, I'm good," Elizabeth says. "That sounds great," she adds, not quite understanding what she's agreed or not agreed to. She had joined the Environmental Committee after the e-mail went out that every parent was expected to serve on a volunteer committee or two, given the lackluster response to the all-volunteer volunteer committees. She had a vision of herself with the rest of the committee in gloves and comfortable boots, the sun streaming down as they tended to the delicate morning glories entwining the chain-link fence that guarded the children from running off the roof playground, or clipped a potted hedgerow or two, possibly, or watered a copse of birch, birch mostly foreign to the City, especially downtown, but for a while she could picture it: the kindergartners tricycling through the birch, their little legs turning the wheels as fast as they could, careering around the roof playground as if they had suddenly found themselves in a magic forest. The birch might even mute the sounds of traffic and attract the wildlife from farther north, near Central Park, the families of squirrel and raccoon and even otter.

"Anyway, there's no rush," Stephanie G. is saying, "though we do hope to get everything in by the end of the year."

"All right," Elizabeth says. "We'll think of something," she says.

"Wonderful!" Stephanie G. says, striding down the steps and disappearing into the band of suitably stretched women. They will run from here a few blocks north, across Fourteenth Street, then up the West Side Highway bike path as far as they can go, some of them, even, sprinting the GW Bridge to the Palisades, these the most determined, the marathoners, the ones who, heads down, feet sneakered, push and push their tired hearts, as that runner once did to warn the Athenians of the Spartans, or maybe it was the other way around.

Turn the page for a preview of
Kate Walbert's novel

A SHORT
HISTORY
OF WOMEN

Available from Scribner

Wardsbury, Grayshead-on-Heath, England,
1914–1918

Mum starved herself for suffrage, Grandmother claiming it was just like Mum to take a cause too far. Mum said she had no choice. Besides, she said, starving made the world brighter, took away the dull edges, the disappointment. She said this in hospital, the place not entirely unpleasant—a private room, windows ammonia-washed looking out to a tree branch on windless days, an ivy-covered wall.

For instance, those, she said. Someone had sent greenhouse lilies, suffrage white, to their favorite cause célèbre, lilies now stuffed in a hospital pot intended for urine or bile. She said she had never known them to have that smell. She'd been blessed by this, she said, the smell of lilies. She said this when she was still speaking, or when she still could be heard, before she twisted into a shape reserved for cracked sticks and hard as that, before they gave her the drip intended for the dying soldiers and here, said the attendant, wasted on a woman by her own hand. Then I was afraid I might break Mum if I breathed, or spoke a word. Before I had tried and tried. Then I gave up like Mum did and went quiet.

Grandmother said to her, "You're too smart." She sat in the

chair knitting, like Madame Lafarge waiting for heads to drop. She talked and she talked. She didn't know whom to blame, she said. She had the attendant bring in the blue-veined china soup tureen she'd carried to hospital from her wedding collection, unwrapped from its velvet sack, and a spoon from the silverware she would later promise me, six place settings of a certain filigree. "You're too smart to be so stupid," she said to Mum as the attendant looked on, ladling broth on the ancient blue Chinaman in the matching bowl. "Nobody is paying a damn bit of attention."

But Mum simply turned away.

William wore his barrister's wig to the viewing; the papers reporting he had temporarily lost his mind. I never believed any of it. Besides, this was already December. Everyone had temporarily lost his mind—the war not yet won and miserably proceeding, the trenches entrenched. Wily, Mum had called William. A sparkling prig, she said, as if he were in the room and she were still flirting, arguing in the way they did. That she loved him desperately I understood, though she never fully said it—William still married to an important person's daughter, Mum a widow or worse, an educated woman, and left long ago by my father, lost or dead in Ceylon. What she said was, "William's an old, old friend," or, "Sometimes we misbehave."

Before she died he would come around, or he would not, but at the viewing he stayed a long, long time, wigged and ready. Beside him Mum lay like a dead offering in her simple box, a lavender Votes for Women sash across her small, unquivering bosom, her button-up kid gloves buttoned up to her stiff elbows, her hair à la pompadour.

To my godmother Alexandra's suggestion that I play the

piano, I flat out said, No. I was newly thirteen and could do as I pleased. Besides, Thomas would play. Thomas would always play. And so beautifully, who could know whether the mourners were weeping at the sight of Mum dead or the talents of her crippled son? The promise of him drove me mad—the way Mum had always listened, the way Nurse and Penny applauded from the kitchen. Even the bird in its cage, a canary kept to sound the alarm, sat all still and silent when my brother, Thomas, played. So it was around the beautiful Thomas that the mourners gathered, touching him—the top of his head, patting his arm, his shoulder—as if he were holy water. He paid little attention, slouched over the keys performing one of her favorites, his elbows akimbo, slicing the air. Soon, he knows, he will be shipped across the ocean to America. Grandmother said she could afford to keep one of us but two would be a handful. A new family has been found for him, old friends in San Francisco.

Good riddance, I thought, listening with the others—Grandmother and Alexandra and the few neighbors and the ladies Mum called compatriots and William before he bowed and closed the parlor door on his way out. The ladies rustled back to their dance chairs, folding their hands over the printed verse Grandmother said Mum would have preferred. Everyone sat and closed their eyes as if to dream of elsewhere.

I ducked into the kitchen to keep Nurse and Penny company. And what of them? Nurse will marry the milkman, Michael, and settle with him in Wales to live a perfectly miserable life. Children and children. Chores. Michael will drink in the way men do and one thing will lead to the other. Penny will pack her cardboard box and take a train east. She'll disappear like our father did, long before we can even remember him. He fancied himself Lord Byron, Mum said, though he was only a sir and that sir a result of money changing hands. Why she had married him at all she could not say. He vanished in Ceylon, or perhaps the natives devoured him. For my sixth birthday, I received a box containing some of his possessions—cuff links and a blanket woven from hemp; a dictionary of lost words called *The Dictionary of Lost Words* that I, predictably, misplaced, everything and everyone dropping through my hands, even Grandmother, eventually, a few years after Mum died.

She said she thought it best I leave Wardsbury and move to Madame Lane's, an educational establishment out of harm's way. She said she had enjoyed my company, but in light of the endless war and the bloated zeppelins overhead, I should be farther north. There I would learn what I should in the relative peace of distance, peace such as it is, she said. There, she promised, I would find other girls my age and teachers of a kinder disposition and she had last heard that the facilities were still quite respectable: a home that once served as an inn to travelers, near enough to York, in a place called Grayshead-on-Heath. She said all this at the dining table, she and I at opposite ends, where we would meet for meals before returning to our rooms. It had become our custom to live together alone: me in my books and Grandmother engaged with cards or needlepoint or the conversation she called her lifeblood, her friends, the elderly women who lived within visiting distance and arrived in a regular stream to place their small white cards in the silver bowl reserved for guests.

Out the windows I watched a streak of sunset fading.

Besides, she said, you need softening. You are as hard as rock, she said, and for a young woman your age this is not attractive, and, although she did not say it, what she thought was, look what happened to your mother.

"I no longer have the strength to be in loco parentis," she said, slicing the meat off the chicken bone, scraping one of her silver knives across the china. She planned, she said, chewing, to debunk for Newquay, her rheumatism acute. "I'd like a regular week, a Monday or Tuesday on my own," Grandmother said.